BURIED SECRETS

L. H. STACEY

*Best Wishes
Lynda Stacey
x*

B
Boldwood

First published in 2019 as Keeper of Secrets. This edition published in Great Britain in 2024 by Boldwood Books Ltd.

Copyright © L. H. Stacey, 2019

Cover Design by Head Design Ltd.

Cover Photography: iStock

The moral right of L. H. Stacey to be identified as the author of this work has been asserted in accordance with the Copyright, Designs and Patents Act 1988.

All rights reserved. No part of this book may be reproduced in any form or by any electronic or mechanical means, including information storage and retrieval systems, without written permission from the author, except for the use of brief quotations in a book review.

This book is a work of fiction and, except in the case of historical fact, any resemblance to actual persons, living or dead, is purely coincidental.

Every effort has been made to obtain the necessary permissions with reference to copyright material, both illustrative and quoted. We apologise for any omissions in this respect and will be pleased to make the appropriate acknowledgements in any future edition.

A CIP catalogue record for this book is available from the British Library.

Paperback ISBN 978-1-83533-086-9

Hardback ISBN 978-1-83533-088-3

Large Print ISBN 978-1-83533-087-6

Ebook ISBN 978-1-83533-085-2

Kindle ISBN 978-1-83533-084-5

Audio CD ISBN 978-1-83533-093-7

MP3 CD ISBN 978-1-83533-092-0

Digital audio download ISBN 978-1-83533-089-0

Boldwood Books Ltd
23 Bowerdean Street
London SW6 3TN
www.boldwoodbooks.com

For Jayne and Alan

You were two of the first people to ever read one of my manuscripts. You told me that I could do it, that I could become an author and you encouraged me to keep going, even on days when I found it difficult.

Thank you so much for your constant support; it's a pleasure to call you family xx

PROLOGUE
JUNE 2005

Cassie was determined not to cry. She closed her eyes, bit down on her lip and then spun around to stare at the crowd of bullies, who all seemed to push, poke and prod at her eleven-year-old body.

'Please, please, leave me alone,' she begged, trying to hold back the tears.

She was scared, bruised and needed to do something to make the nightmare stop. Launching a swift kick at the bully who stood closest to her, she caught her square in the shin and a loud high-pitched scream erupted from the girl's mouth.

'Ouch, the bitch kicked me!' she yelled as she hopped up and down on the spot. 'You're gonna pay for that.'

'Go on, Carol. Give her a slap.' The voice came from within the crowd. A hand flashed before Cassie's eyes and a sharp pain struck her across the cheek. Ducking, she raised her school bag in front of her face in a vain attempt to protect herself from the blows that were now raining down upon her.

'You think that'll protect you, do you?' Carol grabbed at the bag, threw it to the floor and Cassie saw it land in a puddle. She gasped, turned to the wall and closed her eyes. She couldn't look, knowing that the water was undoubtedly spoiling all of her precious books.

'Your dad, he's a dirty tea leaf, he is!' a ginger-haired girl shouted, her voice ringing out like a high-pitched siren, making Cassie cringe. 'Go on, say it.' She grabbed at Cassie's shirt collar, turned her around and stood nose to nose. 'I said, say it,' she growled, looking over her shoulder and pulling a face at the crowd, making the other girls laugh and jeer. 'Steals from the villagers, he does.'

Cassie shook her head. 'He doesn't. Honest, he doesn't. He does tattoos, that's all.' She pleaded her father's innocence and crossed her heart with a finger. Her father was a tattoo artist. He was one of the best in Yorkshire and she'd often watched and admired his artistry and creativity, especially when the tattoo had covered the whole of a man's back, arm or leg.

Carol stepped forward and poked Cassie hard in the ribs making her squeal out loud, much to the delight of those standing close. A smirk crossed her face and a hand shot out, delivering another painful prod to Cassie's ribs. 'Oh yes he does. Gets information out of his customers, he does. Knows exactly when their houses are gonna be empty and then him and his mates, they break in and take all the jewellery and anything else they can carry. So, in my book, that makes him a dirty tea leaf thief and you need to say it.'

Cassie's whole body was trembling. 'He doesn't, honest. He just does the tattoos, that's all,' she repeated.

The accusations made her feel sick, her stomach turned, and she began taking short sharp breaths as bile rose up her throat. She felt trapped. Her mind spun. She needed to escape, to run and most of all she wanted to go home to her mum, but the girls stood all around her, blocking her route.

'Cassie...' Her sister Lisa suddenly pushed her way through the crowd towards her. 'That's where you are. Come on, we're going home.' She held out a hand as her eyes connected with Cassie's, all the time scanning the playground, looking for an escape. But the ginger-haired girl now grabbed at Lisa's long dark hair, pulling it hard.

'Sticking your nose in, are you?' she questioned, twisting Lisa's hair around and forcing her to drop down onto her knees. 'You'll wish you hadn't bothered.'

'Go on, Deborah, give it them both, after all, he's her dad too,' Carol shouted, taking over the hair pulling as Deborah nodded, smirked and delved into her bag to pull out a small box of eggs.

'Do it... do it... do it...' the crowd of girls chanted.

A sadistic but nervous smile crossed Deborah's face as she passed two eggs to Carol, two to another girl and kept hold of the last two eggs for herself.

Cassie took in a sharp breath and dropped down next to Lisa, giving her a look of apology before closing her eyes. She knew what was coming, she'd seen it many times before and a sob caught in her throat as she felt the first egg crash down on the top of her head. She yelped as sharp pieces of shell were pressed down and rubbed into her scalp. She tried to push herself further into the corner and held onto Lisa's arm, just as a flash of white powder filled the air. The smell of flour filled her nostrils, making her cough, as hands began rubbing the flour into the egg that now ran in globules down her face and all over her clothes.

'Tomorrow, you'll do as you're told and tell us all what a dirty tea leaf your dad is, won't you?' Deborah shouted. 'Now, go on, bugger off.' She laughed as the sisters stood up, then she pushed them both violently from behind, making them both stumble. Cassie fell, her knees scraping the floor and she felt her only pair of black school tights tear.

She wanted to go home. She wanted to ask her mum if it was true about Dad, but wasn't sure that she dared and for a while she just sat staring at her reflection in one of the playground puddles. She could see what they'd done to her and knew that the bullying was getting worse. The daily pushing and shoving had gone on for almost a week. And even though every part of her hurt from the constant attacks, she hadn't said a word about it at home, hoping that if she didn't make a fuss the girls would soon become bored and move onto someone else. But the eggs and flour had been a new and more vicious attack and she apologetically stared at her sister's dirty tear-stained face, wishing that their life was different. She wished that it would change, that something would happen to alter their destiny and that she could be anyone else in the whole world... so long as it wasn't Cassandra Hunt.

'If I could just be someone different so that I never have to go to that school or face those girls ever again,' Cassie sobbed, looking up at the cloud-filled sky. 'Please God. I don't care where else you send me and our Lisa, just please, keep us together and let it be anywhere else in the world but here.'

Lisa's arms encircled her as she pulled Cassie up, picked up her sodden school bag and walked her away from the jeering group of girls and towards home. 'Oh, Cass. Please don't wish to be someone else. I mean... it isn't right, who else would you be?'

'Mum's going to be really cross, isn't she?' Cassie whispered as she looked at her once navy-blue school skirt and the second-hand grey blazer that Lisa wore. Their school clothes were ruined and she knew their mum would be furious. But that would be nothing compared to her temper once she found out what the bullies had said about their dad. 'Is it true, Lisa, you know, about our dad?' she asked cautiously. 'Is that what people are saying?' She felt Lisa's hand grip tightly onto hers as they walked silently down the ginnel, past the six blocks of houses and across the road. Then she turned and looked up at her sister whose tears now fell unreservedly down her face. Lisa's lips were pursed, but she didn't answer. She didn't need to. Her eyes said it all.

'I know. Let's hide in here for a minute,' Lisa whispered and Cassie felt herself being dragged behind a wheelie bin and into one of the gate holes that lined the ginnel. 'We'll sit down and think of what to say to Mum when we get home.'

Another huge sob left Cassie's throat and a look of understanding passed between the sisters. But then the sound of screaming and shouting thundered towards them. There was a sudden crash, followed by another scream. The yelling and swearing got louder. There was a sound of heavy footsteps and Lisa's face contorted with fear, making Cassie lean forward to sneak a look at a man who was now running towards them. He stopped right next to the wheelie bin behind which they hid; his eyes scanning the ginnel, searching for an escape. He was young, and obviously terrified, with eyes as wide as saucers. His torn white vest was splattered in blood. But it was the tattoo Cassie felt drawn to.

Instinctively she knew she should be scared, knew the man was dangerous. But still she stared at the snake tattoo that seemed to coil itself around the man's shoulder, its two piercing bright yellow eyes staring right at her. Cassie felt mesmerised. But she didn't know why. The tattoo was all wrong. The scales were all lined up down the middle, with the ones down the side all pointing in different directions. It was red, seeping and its edges were blurred, and Cassie realised that it had only just been done. But what she couldn't understand was why a tattoo that looked so wrong could look so right? She was sure she'd seen it before and thought back to her dad's sketchbook. Holding her breath, she and Lisa shrank further and further back behind the wheelie bin and closer to the wall.

Suddenly the man turned and ran, disappearing into the distance. It was only then that a blood-curdling scream filled the ginnel. Their neighbours began yelling, shouting and crying all at once.

'An ambulance, someone... call a bloody ambulance!' they heard their mother scream in a high-pitched and unnatural tone. 'He's... he's been stabbed... That man... he just stabbed my Dave.' One neighbour ran down the ginnel as fast as they could go, and Cassie clung to her sister. She was too terrified to move, knowing that back there, back in that playground, she'd wished for change... she'd prayed to God that he would change their life.

And now... now he had.

1

HERCULANEUM, AUGUST 2018

Cassie sat back, moved her pointed trowel and bristle brush to one side, and took a moment to study the pair of partially exposed skeletons that lay in the excavation before her.

'Over two thousand years,' she whispered to the bones. 'Two thousand years since Vesuvius erupted and you ran for your lives.' She paused and sighed. 'But instead, you ran to your deaths, didn't you?' She blinked away tears of emotion, took a wooden chopstick from her tool bag, and began to use it to scratch at the dirt. It wasn't really a tool, but still, it was useful. It was less likely to damage the bones than a trowel and by using it she could create a clear and defined edge to the remains. The skeletons lay side by side, with what looked like one hand from each of the bodies clasped tightly together, high above their heads. Their faces were turned towards one another in what appeared to be a final look of desperation or prayer, before their bodies had been covered in the hot volcanic ash, buried and hidden from the world from that day to this. Unlike the many skeletons of Pompeii, that during their own excavation had been encased in plaster many years before, a huge proportion of the

Herculaneum bones were still intact and being excavated on a daily basis.

Cassie crossed herself, and momentarily closed her eyes in prayer. As with all remains, she felt that the bodies deserved a moment's respect, a moment of recognition for lives lost and she whispered a few words that came from deep within her. 'Amen,' she mumbled as she sat back, pulled off her latex gloves and looked around her.

The site was busy, with whole teams of archaeologists working on their own grid of land, all uncovering new and exciting artefacts. With each new find a buzz of excitement would travel through the air and a series of whoops and pats on the back would follow. Working on the Herculaneum site had fast become number one on every archaeologist's wish list, which meant that everyone who actually got to be here, without exception, felt privileged. Being offered a year-long contract had amounted to Cassie's lifetime ambition, all wrapped up in one job and, although she knew that here she'd still be learning and had had no choice but to take a step backwards in the pecking order, she'd taken the position without hesitation. Every day had brought her new knowledge, a new understanding of her trade and with another six months still left on her contract, she was in the centre of her own archaeologist's dream.

Cassie sighed and once again spoke to the bones. 'You were running away, hoping to escape, just like me.' Her eyes searched the ground that surrounded the bodies, looking for clues. 'Did you ever wish for a new life, for something to happen that would change the way you lived forever?' she asked, remembering the day when she'd wished for just that.

She'd been just eleven years old when her whole world had collapsed around her. Her father had been murdered and the life she knew had turned into a huge and unexplainable nightmare.

She'd always felt guilty that she'd prayed to God, wishing that she could escape the life that she had. But, at such a young age, she hadn't realised the enormity of what she'd wished for or how much her life was about to change. In her eyes, her dad had been perfect and certainly hadn't deserved to die. With her he'd always been loving, kind and she could picture him now with the biggest smile on his face and not a worry in the world. But in a single violent act he'd been taken from them and overnight, along with her mother and Lisa, they as a family had lost everything, leaving them with no choice but to move away and live with her mother's oldest sister, Aunt Aggie, in a tiny terraced house on the other side of town.

In one week, they'd moved, changed schools and had had to get used to a new way of living. But if Cassie was totally honest, she'd been just a little bit more than relieved that she didn't have to go back to that awful school or face the bullies ever again. And at first, they'd been happy, the house had been small, cosy, but they'd all muddled along together. Until, three years after they'd moved to Aunt Aggie's, their lives changed again. Their mum had taken ill and died, leaving Aggie to pick up the pieces. Overnight she'd become mother, father and aunt to both Cassie and Lisa and had done her best to bring them up the only way she knew how.

Cassie brought herself back to the present. Back to Herculaneum and back to her skeletons.

'What were your lives like and where did you live?' she whispered to the bones, but then looked up at the rows of ruined houses, the simple structures and the alleys that ran between them. The terraced houses of Herculaneum were similar to the terrace where she, Lisa and Aggie had lived. And here, like there, she suspected that life had been challenging, that the people had struggled, just as Aggie had. Money had always been tight. The décor had left a lot to the imagination, with holes in the floorboards and threadbare rugs, and lino in the kitchen that had seen better days. They'd had hot water, but to heat it up meant feeding the meter, so the water had often stayed cold. Besides, the bathroom had been upstairs and with no central heating, more often than not they'd preferred to boil pans of water on the open fire and get washed in the warmth of the kitchen.

Again, Cassie studied the partially uncovered skeletons and noticed that one looked to be distinctively smaller than the other. 'Is that what you are? Are you siblings like Lisa and me? Were you hoping to escape like we did?' She'd often wondered what would have happened if Lisa hadn't met her from school that day; if they hadn't both been delayed from going home at the usual time. And although the bullying had terrified them, the thought that they could have been in the house at the time their dad had been murdered was far worse. But the reverse thought had often plagued her. What if they had got home on time? Would the murder have happened at all?

She wiped the wooden chopstick on an old rag and placed it back in her tool roll, before pulling on a pair of latex gloves and once again picking up the bristle brush. She began using it to create soft sweeping motions over the bones in the hope that she'd find an undiscovered clue as to what had happened.

Being almost at the end of the stratum, she glanced over to where her notebook, camera and laptop bag stood propped up against a wall. She picked them up and, with compass in place, she began taking photographs from every angle, showing as much detail as possible of where and how the bodies lay. There was still so much she needed to do and she had just a few more hours in which to do it.

'Are you going to reveal your secrets for me?' she whispered. 'I'd love to know more about you.' Cassie's eyes traced the parts of the body she could clearly see; the hands, the shape of the skull, and the top of the spinal column. She took more photographs and then put the camera back in its bag and picked up her notebook with a sigh. She knew she should continue cataloguing the find, but for some reason she felt the need to carry on with the excavation, to expose more of the bones. Putting the notebook aside, she once again pulled the chopstick from the tool roll and began poking the dirt away from around one of the shoulders. Stopping, she gave a half smile as her favourite bone, the scapula, began to emerge from beneath the dirt. She just loved the way it joined the humerus to the clavicle and how the left was almost always a perfect mirror image of the right. She sat back, thoughtful and wondered if it was wrong to have a favourite bone? Was it odd to admire its shape, or curvature? She smiled and nodded her head, knowing that it was the shape of the scapula that made it her favourite. The bone's shape was similar to that of her favourite tool: the trowel.

It had been Aunt Aggie's avid interest in archaeology that had inspired her. Her aunt was always reading about it, looking at how, why and when digs would happen. She'd had such a passion for the subject and when she realised that Cassie shared her interest, she'd bought more and more books. In fact, it had been Aggie that had bought Cassie her first trowel and bristle brush one Christmas, along with the second-hand metal detector that they'd both gone out with to scour the local fields on a daily basis. In fact, Cassie couldn't remember a single day when Aggie hadn't been there, giving her time and love generously. She'd taken good care of both her and Lisa, even when at sixteen Lisa had become pregnant, and Becky had been born. Nothing had been too much trouble and the tiny living room had immediately been filled with every piece of baby equipment that Aggie could afford; some had been new, some second-hand, but all had been clean. It was just Aggie's way. There might not have been much money, but her home had always been full of love and people. Aggie's sister, Nelly, had lived next door, her cousin Ida over the road and if it was not them then any one of their neighbours seemed to walk in without knocking. They all sat down without invitation, and when the chairs and settee were full, people had simply sat around on the floor and without exception, as every visitor arrived, coffee had always been made.

But once the evening had turned to night, the house had emptied and Becky had been safely tucked up in her cot, Aggie's attention had always reverted back to archaeology. She'd often sat by the light of the fire, while speaking of 'the sand pit', an old sandstone quarry that used to lie right beneath where a tower block now stood. The quarry had been there for years, yet it was the Sand House that people still spoke of. A whole house that had stood within the quarry. It had been carved from the sandstone by its owner Henry Senior back in the mid-1850s and from its modest beginnings as a two-up-two-down dwelling, it had grown to become a ten-roomed mansion, complete with stable and ballroom. Dances and other major social events had taken place in that very house and its 'sunken garden'; and guests were allowed to explore the property's extensive tunnels and admire the abundance of carvings hewn from the sandstone within. The tunnels had gone on and on, right under what was now a bypass, and had ended somewhere beneath the cemetery. But it had been Aggie's description of the unique carvings in the catacombs that had gained Cassie's attention the most and she'd often wished that she might have seen the famous 'Elephant and his Mahout', amongst the other impressive carvings. All were still there, now buried deep beneath the pavement, deep beneath the streets and in the shadow of a seventeen-storey block of flats, where hundreds of people walked every single day, most not knowing what lay right beneath their feet.

Cassie pulled off her hat, and gloves, untied her long dark hair and allowed it to fall loosely over her shoulders. It was damp with the warmth and she could feel the rivulets of sweat that now ran freely down the centre of her back as the Italian heat soared high into the thirties. She pulled at the shoestring straps of her vest top in an attempt to stop it from clinging, then picked up her hat and used it to fan her face. She longed for a cold shower, but instead she looked around for her shirt, which she'd carelessly thrown over a rock earlier but now needed to put on or, with her pale skin, her shoulders and back would soon burn and become painful.

Using her hand to shield her eyes, Cassie looked up. The sun was high overhead and she guessed that the day was already half over. At this time of year, the afternoons were hotter than mornings, and the evenings would become close with barely any air at all, but she didn't care, and she took a moment to stare at the beauty that surrounded her. But the moment was spoiled, and her skin began to prickle when her gaze landed on Declan. He was one of the labourers who never seemed to do any work and, as usual, he was stood with his arms folded, watching her from a distance. She looked about her, hoping to see something or someone else that he might be looking at, but for once, no one was around and she purposely looked away, pretending to take great interest in the gravel that lay by her feet. She didn't want to encourage him, nor did she want him to walk across and speak to her as he had on many occasions. Each time, he'd hovered around like a lovesick puppy and had acted awkwardly. Then one minute he'd be bouncing on the spot, chatting with the excitement of a child, and the next he'd become withdrawn, with slouched shoulders and an averted gaze. His whole persona had made her feel uncomfortable and, unless she had to, socialising with him was an experience she'd rather avoid.

'So, have you begun to melt yet?' Sasha asked as she walked towards Cassie, her slender arms full of bottles. 'Here, you need to drink some water. They're still cold from the fridge.'

Cassie smiled. 'Just what I need.' She took the bottle from her friend, stepped away from the dig, unscrewed the cap and quickly poured the liquid over her face and then took a long drink. 'Does he ever do anything other than stare?' She wiped her mouth on the back of her hand and pointed to where Declan still stood watching her, as she reached for her shirt and pulled it on. 'He gives me the creeps.'

'Who? Declan? Oh, I know he's a bit, well... peculiar, but I'm sure he's harmless.' Sasha sat down on the gravel and crossed her legs. 'Besides, you're gorgeous, why wouldn't he look at you?' She laughed and pointed to the bones. 'Anyhow, what have we got?' She held her hand out for Cassie's notes, while her eyes scanned the skeletons.

Thankful that she had something else to concentrate on, Cassie looked at the bones. 'Well, we have two skeletons, one possibly mid-twenties, the other looks a little younger and I'd say, without doubt, they're definitely both very dead.' The corners of her mouth turned up slightly as she stated the obvious while stretching her arms up high over her head. 'Unlike me, who really needs some food before I collapse and end up in the grave alongside them.'

Sasha glanced up at Cassie, smiled and then returned her gaze to the skeletons. 'Ohhh, Cassie, look... they were holding hands.' She let out a deep sigh, picked up the soft bristle brush and with careful but deliberate sweeping movements, she began dusting over the bones to move the odd particles of earth that still congregated around the area where the fingers were clasped together. 'They were in love, right?' Sasha asked. It was a simple question, one that didn't really need answering, but Cassie, who'd just taken a large gulp of water, began to choke and took a moment to catch her breath.

'Oh, I don't know. Right now, I have no idea of the age, the sex or the relationship. I just hope they didn't suffer too much.' She knelt back down beside Sasha. 'All we really know is that Vesuvius erupted, and they tried to make it to the sea, and to the boats. Such a shame they didn't make it. If they had, they might just have survived.'

Sasha pointed to the bridge. It was quite visible from most places in Herculaneum and was right at the start of the commercial area, where all the tourists crossed to gain entry to the site. 'They wouldn't have had too far to go. That's where the sea and the boats would have been.'

Cassie glanced back to where Declan had been standing. Spinning around on the spot, she turned left and then right. He'd disappeared and she didn't know whether to feel relieved that he'd gone or anxious because she didn't know where he'd show up next. She took in a deep breath as her whole body began to bristle with a ripple of nerves that began to spread upwards from her toes and didn't stop.

'We've all seen the skeletons that are piled up in the boat sheds,' Sasha continued. 'The poisonous gases would have killed them all, they simply died where they dropped, all huddled together, or like these two, still running, still holding hands. I don't think any of them could have escaped.' Sasha's eyes filled with tears, she paused and then turned and rested her hand lightly on Cassie's shoulder. 'They didn't stand a chance, did they? The only consolation is that they had each other.' Again, Sasha paused. 'Cass, can you imagine loving someone that much?'

Cassie was only half listening. She continued to scan the rows of visitors, labourers and other archaeologists. Another crowd of tourists had arrived. They were all stood, staring over the bridge with mouths open wide. But then something flashed, something caught her eye and once again she spotted Declan. He stood to the side of the bridge, a cloth and a chisel in his hand, which he rubbed as though cleaning it. He looked up and smiled awkwardly. It was an unnatural, sly curve of his lips that made her catch her breath and look away. The sheer sight of him made her nervous and every time she glanced at him, he seemed to be dragging the cloth across the tool in a suggestive, almost threatening action. Cassie mentally kicked herself, shaking her head; in reality he was doing nothing wrong. To the rest of the site, he was cleaning one of his tools. So why did she feel so threatened? And why did his behaviour make her ask herself a whole list of questions. Was she being paranoid? Was she imagining his actions? Was he really looking at her? Should she report him? And if she did, what would she say apart from the fact that she didn't like the way he looked at her and that he made her feel uneasy?

'Cassie, did you hear me?'

'No, sorry, what?' Cassie turned back to both Sasha and the bones.

'I was asking if you could imagine loving someone that much?' Sasha sighed and pointed to the skeletons. 'Whatever their relationship, they really, really loved each other, didn't they?'

Cassie leaned back against the ruined stone wall that had once been a house and drew shapes in the dirt with the toe of her boot as she pondered the question. She thought of the people she loved. The people who'd been the bedrock of her life: of her father and mother who she'd lost far too young; of Aggie; and of

Lisa, Marcus and the children; and then, then there had been Noah...

'I'm sure they loved each other, but whether they were "in love" we will never know,' she answered eventually.

Sasha pulled her bleach blonde hair back, tied it up in a topknot bobble and then sat for a moment in thought. 'Oh, Cassie. I do hope there's a love like that. I mean, it would be lovely, wouldn't it, and it'd be quite sad to grow old alone, don't you think?'

With that, Sasha quickly jumped up and pulled at her tiny denim shorts. 'Anyhow, what did the boss say? Will they be excavated on-site, or block lifted?' She turned to where Cassie still sat. 'Because if they're being excavated in situ, I'm guessing you'll be needing the tarpaulin?' She danced on the spot and looked up at the sun with her hand half covering her eyes. 'Don't want the bones in this heat for too long, do you?'

Cassie immediately leapt to her feet, berating herself. The bones, they needed to be dried, but not like this, not this quickly and she should have known better than to leave them exposed for so long. She looked around for the oversized tent that she'd normally have erected as soon as she'd unearthed the very first bone. So why hadn't she?

'Cassie... here *velocemente*...' a voice shouted from a Portakabin that was being used as the site office. '*Telephono*. England.' The Italian voice sang out the broken English and Cassie felt her heart skip a beat.

No one ever contacted her, not at work, not during the day and the fact that someone had made her anxious. 'Why didn't they phone direct...?' She patted down her pockets, felt for her mobile, pulled it out and stared at the screen. 'Flat battery, great.'

Looking between the Portakabin and Sasha she spoke as she ran. 'Hun, would you mind putting the tarpaulin up for me, and then,' she screwed up her face in apology, 'could you take a soil sample before it's spoiled? Sorry.'

'*Carlo, il telefono, per me? Veramente? Chi è?*' she questioned as she entered the office, but Carlo shrugged, stamped out a cigarette and pulled at his dust-covered string vest, before heading out towards the Portaloo with a newspaper under his arm.

'Hello.' She waited for the response. 'Hello, it's Cassie here.' She paused and listened, but the phone crackled. 'Hello, who is it?' She walked around, hoping for a better signal and glanced across to where Sasha had begun constructing a tall, tent-like frame over the trench. Two labourers were helping her, and Cassie noticed how Sasha was doing her normal trick of getting them to do all the hard work, while she stood directing them with her hands on her hips, smiling. But the smile disappeared, as Declan approached, asked a question and Cassie noticed how Sasha's shoulders dropped as she pointed in the direction of the Portakabin.

'Cassie? It's... it's Lisa... I... I tried your mobile, but...'

Cassie froze on the spot at the sound of her sister's voice. She sounded upset, distant. The vibrancy and strength in her voice was gone and, instead, all Cassie could hear was a shaking undertone as she spoke.

'Lisa, I'm here. What's wrong? Are... are you okay? Becky? The boys? Marcus?' The names stuck in her throat. 'Aggie?' The phone went silent and Cassie held it away from her ear, while staring at the handset. A sob could be heard, followed by a deep inward breath. 'Lisa, please, tell me?' she questioned, but the silence at the other end of the phone spoke volumes. It seemed to go on forever and Cassie physically felt the floor move beneath her as the air expelled itself from her lungs. She could barely breathe, her mind spun, and she tried to pull in deep breaths while all the time turning in circles as though looking for a way to escape. A random chair stood to the side of the room and she felt herself moving towards it in slow motion. 'Lisa, please... are... are you okay?'

'No.' The word was simple. But said everything. 'Cass... it's Aggie... she's sick... really sick.'

Cassie gasped. Tears filled her eyes and her hand moved to her mouth. The bile rose and fell again, and she looked around for a waste bin but found nothing.

'She's in hospital but there's nothing more they can do for her. They're talking about end-of-life management and they... they want her to go...' again Cassie could hear the difficulty in Lisa's breathing '...go into a... a hospice. They're trying to... get... her a bed.'

'Hospice?' Cassie was shocked. 'But... Aggie isn't old. And... and a hospice... that's where...' She immediately knew that Aggie would be moved there to die. 'But... what do you mean by end-of-life management... what happened? She was fine. I phoned her just a few days ago. What the hell happened since then?' Cassie clung to the phone. Her eyes searched the ceiling and then the floor. She could feel herself physically holding her breath as she waited for Lisa to answer.

'A lot has happened... she's still in the hospital at the moment and will stay there until they can find her a place.' Again, a breath was taken. 'Aggie's been a good actress and, well, I was sworn to secrecy. I wasn't allowed to tell you how ill she was, and she's always made sure it was a good day when she contacted you.' Again, Lisa paused. 'It's cervical cancer, Cass. Terminal. Stage four. Just like Mum.' Lisa's voice broke, and the mere mention of their mother caused her to sob. 'She... she's known for quite a while.'

Cassie stared at the wall. 'Why didn't you tell me? Lisa, I

mean, Jesus Christ, why didn't *she* tell me?' Leaning forward, the threatened bile once again rose up her throat and she ran to the door, stretching the phone cable behind her, and heaved.

'She wanted to wait, Cass. She knew how much Herculaneum meant to you. She desperately wanted you to complete your contract. But then... then the excavation began.'

'What excavation?' Cassie questioned.

'They have permission to excavate the Sand House, the tunnels that Aggie always spoke of... they're going down there, Cass. There's been talk about it for months, loads of council meetings, residents' meetings and all that. But now the diggers are here, they arrived just a few days ago and Aggie, she seemed okay until then, but the minute the workmen started digging, she seemed to give up. It was as though someone had pulled her plug out. She was sobbing uncontrollably over the phone and when I got there, I found her curled up on the floor, holding onto her stomach and staring at the wall. She was horrified, kept mumbling about the catacombs... about them being opened. She kept saying something about danger, that it might collapse... that she couldn't bear it to happen, not again... oh, I don't know. None of it made sense.' Lisa paused and, for a moment, Cassie thought she'd put the phone down and gone. 'Why, Cass? Why is this happening now?' She had spoken sporadically between sobs. 'What would Aggie suddenly be so afraid of? She goes on and on about the Elephant and Mahout, and then about a secret. She won't tell me what it is, says it has to be you. She says that only you can help her.' Lisa paused, breathless.

'How is she now?' Cassie was concerned. She'd always known that Aggie could talk, some days she never stopped, but to lay on the floor and ramble? She pondered the thought, knowing that that wasn't the Aggie they knew and loved and that something was seriously wrong.

Eventually, Lisa spoke. 'She's okay, I guess. They gave her some medication and that seems to have settled her. But... she won't talk to me, keeps asking for you and, well, it's simple, I... I need you to come home,' her sister's voice insisted. Gone were the tears and in their place was a strong and determined voice. 'I can't cope, not with this, you know I don't like hospitals, not after Mum.' She paused. 'So... you have to come back, you see? I... I need you. Aggie needs you.'

Cassie closed her eyes, sighed and then looked out of the door to where Sasha now sat on a rock rolling her eyes, with Declan sat by her side constantly talking. She looked up, smiled and waved. But Cassie felt numb, she didn't wave back and instead she looked down. She had to come up with a plan. 'Yes, of course. I'll... I'll look into flights. I'll come as soon as I can. Lisa, look after her till I get there. Love you.' Cassie put the phone down and took in deep, measured breaths. She couldn't remember Aggie ever being sick. She'd always been the one to look after everyone else. She'd been the strong one. The one who coped, and Cassie slumped into the chair as every ounce of energy suddenly left her body.

After what seemed like an age Cassie used the counter to pull herself up. She stood for a moment and then walked back to the door and looked out at the Herculaneum she loved, the place she had no choice but to leave. Sasha was now sat alone, cross-legged on the ground, under the shade of the newly erected tarpaulin and, with bristle brush in hand, was excavating the skeletons. No one knew death like they did, no one understood more about what was left once the soul had gone. And the thought of losing Aggie terrified her but she had no choice, she couldn't and wouldn't allow Aggie to die alone.

2

'Hey there, Tabitha. How are you doing?' Cassie smiled at the stray black kitten as she jumped up onto their first-floor balcony, weaving her way around the side of the tomato plant, and brushing herself against Cassie's legs with a meow. 'I take it you're hungry?'

Cassie opened the cupboard, reached up and pulled out a small tin of cat food. The cat didn't belong to them, but she and Sasha had taken to feeding her on a daily basis. Both loved having her as a visitor and coppered up each week to ensure that, as well as feeding themselves, they could also afford kitten food and litter. They'd even bought her a blanket to lie on when she visited, although she always seemed to prefer to sit on one of their laps.

'You want some of this?' She shook the tin in the air, opened it and began forking some food out onto a saucer. 'There you go.' She placed the saucer on the floor, opened the fridge and placed the remainder of the tin inside, while looking for the milk.

'Sasha... did you drink the last of the milk?' she shouted, but only a grunt came from the bedroom, which probably meant that

Sasha was still sulking, sleeping, or like most nights, laid out on her bed, iPad on her knee, FaceTiming her boyfriend. 'Sasha...' Cassie tapped on her bedroom door and pushed it open. 'We're out of milk.'

Sasha turned over and sighed. 'Sorry, Cass. I drank it earlier. I really don't feel too well,' she whined. 'I meant to get some more. Honest.' She pulled a face and stuck out her tongue. 'I think I've spent too long in the heat.'

Cassie looked at her friend's tear-filled eyes and the red rings around them. She knew that the sun had had nothing to do with Sasha's sudden illness. The news that Cassie had to go back to England immediately hadn't gone down too well and to say that Sasha had been upset was an understatement. After all, they'd been together since that very first day when they'd arrived in Italy. They'd both stood in the arrivals lounge looking lost while waiting for transfers. They'd gravitated towards one another and after just one conversation it had felt as though they'd known each other for years. They'd quickly decided that, if they'd be working together, it would make sense to live together and before long they were sharing a flat, clothes, a tomato plant called Bill and the stray cat called Tabitha.

'I am sorry. You know... about leaving. I wouldn't, not unless I had to.' Cassie stumbled over the words and watched as Sasha pulled the duvet up and under her chin. She stared at where Cassie stood, while her bottom lip began to wobble. Cassie felt uncomfortable. The last thing she wanted was to set Sasha off crying again, something she'd done all afternoon since Cassie had booked her flight home.

Sasha reached out and grabbed hold of her hand. 'I know... but...' Tears once again filled her eyes. 'I'm going to really miss you.'

Cassie nodded. She'd miss Sasha too, but leaving Italy wasn't a choice. And knowing that time was of the essence; she had to go home now. She thought back to when her mum took ill, how one minute she'd seemed to be fine, then just a couple of weeks later they'd all been in Rose Hill Crematorium saying goodbye.

'It won't be for long,' Cassie whispered. She knew it was a lie and, in truth, she had no idea how long she'd be away.

'But you're going tomorrow... I hardly have time to get used to the idea and... and... we're at the end of the stratum. How do I look after the skeletons without you?' She shuffled up against her pillows, her face pale, and Cassie sat down beside her, lifted a hand, and placed it against Sasha's forehead, checking her temperature.

'Look, we have time to sort everything out. I don't leave till six o'clock tomorrow night and, in the morning, we'll go to the site and we'll make a plan. We'll excavate as much as we can before I go.' She stared into Sasha's eyes. 'Deal?'

Sasha nodded.

'Right, I'm going to the shop. We need milk, seeing as one of us drank the last of it,' she teased, 'and Tabitha is giving me the eye... you know the one where she thinks we don't love her any more.' Cassie winked, stood up and walked to the door. 'You get some rest. I won't be long.' She watched as Sasha snuggled down into her quilt. 'Shall I bring some wine back? We could sit on the balcony and cheer ourselves up?'

Sasha nodded with a cheeky grin, which made Cassie smile before she made her way to the door, down the concrete steps and into the alley below.

The small village where they lived was just a few kilometres outside Naples, and was a mishmash of alleyways that led off in every direction between hundreds of stone-built houses of two or three storeys. Most had bright pink and purple bougainvillea flower baskets either hanging over the balconies or sitting neatly up the side of the steps. Some were family homes, but others were flats, shared houses or student accommodation, and a good majority of them were taken up by the other archaeologists, apprentices or lecturers working at either Herculaneum or Pompeii.

Cassie strolled through the maze of alleyways, each one a duplicate of the next. It hadn't been that long ago that she'd got lost each and every time she'd left the house and had spent many frustrating hours wandering up and down the cobbled walkways trying to find her way home. 'I'll never get used to it,' she remembered saying to Sasha. 'Every house looks the same.'

'Well, at least I can get to the shop and to the bus depot now. I guess that's an improvement, isn't it?' she whispered to herself as her hand went up to touch the flowers. She pulled one from its stalk and lifted it to her nose. Taking in the aroma she smiled, then placed it in her hair.

'Just along here and to the right,' she said to herself as she turned. The shop was on the corner ahead. But she frowned as she got closer and saw the signage on the front door. Staring at it, it took her a moment to decipher the words.

Chiuso a causa di un lutto familiare...!

'Closed... family... lutto?' She pulled her phone from her pocket and searched for the meaning of *lutto familiare*. 'Family mourning... Damn... a funeral. Why tonight of all nights.' She leaned against the wall, wondering what she should do. 'Tonight, I just wanted to buy some bloody milk for a cat that I don't even own... and then... then all I wanted was to drink some wine with Sasha, have a hot bath, climb into my pj's, crawl into bed and read a book. Not too much to ask, is it?'

'You alright there, Cass? Hot bath and pj's, now that sounds like fun. You need some company?' Declan appeared from nowhere. She hadn't realised that she'd spoken out loud and felt a little vulnerable knowing he'd overheard her. Her initial reaction was to turn and leave, but Declan seemed to circle where she stood, like an over-enthusiastic puppy. He was tall, broad and, for a man in his late thirties, he acted a little more than awkward and looked almost animated in his actions, making Cassie's imagination run wild. She could see him taking part in *Scooby Doo* as the perfect villain or becoming a long-lost cousin in an episode of *The Addams Family*.

'Declan. What are you doing here?' Cassie stepped backwards. She looked over her shoulder and inched towards the alley as she slowly began to retrace her steps. 'Do you live around here?' Cassie searched the gardens, the windows and the alleys, wishing that someone, anyone would notice her or walk past. She began to tremble. Her heart began to race. She didn't like him being near her. There was no real reason for this but just something about him put her on edge. She needed to leave. But Declan had walked ahead and now stood right in front of her, in the alley she wanted to walk down. He'd gone quiet. He stepped from foot to foot, pursed his lips, looked uneasy and then he stared down at his boots, but didn't reply. Cassie stood still. She didn't know what to do or how to react. His behaviour wasn't normal. It made her uneasy and she stepped around him to walk down an uncharacteristically quiet alley. The shop being closed had kept people away and, in an area that was normally busy at all times, today the streets were now empty. There was no one to be seen.

'Cass, are you going home?' he questioned, dropping into step with her and walking closely by her side. But Cassie spun around on the spot, turned and took a different route. She was worried he'd follow her. She didn't want him to know where she lived.

'Declan, look, I'm not going home, the shop was closed, and I'm going for milk.' She pointed down the long alley that led through the centre of the houses and turned her back. 'Then, I'm off to see some friends. So...' she lied and continued walking but could still hear his footsteps behind her, and oddly, she could hear his breathing which seemed to get louder and louder. Frantically she began looking around, searching the houses she passed, hoping that a door would open and that someone she knew would come out or lean over a balcony. Cassie swallowed hard. She could feel her own heartbeat pounding like a bass drum in her ears. Stopping, she looked left and then right, but suddenly nothing looked familiar, she didn't recognise any of the houses. She was lost. 'Stop, think, retrace.' Isn't that what Aunt Aggie had always told her, but she'd taken too many turns and she knew that retracing her steps was no longer an option.

Sensing her indecision, Declan stepped closer. His hand shot out and landed on her shoulder. He spun her around to face him and suddenly his mouth was pressing down upon hers. An overwhelming taste of garlic, tomato and fish hit the back of her throat. Her hands went up to push him away, but he was strong. She couldn't breathe. Her whole body crashed against the wall and he pinned her to it. Then, she felt his tongue invade her mouth and she gagged. Twisting, she managed to get a small space between them, her hand moved upwards catching him under the chin, and as he moved, she bit down on his lip as hard as she could.

Then, as soon as it had begun, it stopped. Stepping back, Declan looked uncertain. He grabbed at his mouth. 'Bitch, you... you bit me,' he shouted and without warning she felt the back of his hand crash into one side of her face as the other side collided with the wall. Pain shot through her, and she held back a scream. She was shaking inside and out. Every part of her wanted to sit down and sob. She was back in that playground. Once again, she wanted to run but couldn't. His hand pushed her again and she saw the anger in his eyes. But she stood firm, she was no longer an eleven-year-old child and she held her chin up high. She was terrified but determined that he wouldn't see the fear that coursed through her.

'Get away from me,' she growled. She felt as though she might collapse, and her hand held onto the wall. 'You get away right now.' She began to slowly inch along the alley, her back to the wall, her hands feeling the way, her eyes constantly watching every move he made. But her retreat was halted as she came to the end of the wall. She quickly looked over her shoulder and knew that to turn the corner she'd have to turn her back on where Declan now stood, something she really didn't want to do.

'I'm sorry.' His words were spat out as he took another step towards her. 'I thought you liked me. I saw you watching me, looking out for me, staring.'

'I swear to God, if you take one step closer, I will scream and I'll... I'll have you locked up for assault. Is that clear?' Her voice shook as she spoke, and she saw the hesitation in his stance.

'I said I was sorry. I heard you were leaving... and I...' He took another step towards her and Cassie jumped to one side. 'I'm gonna be here for months, so—'

'So you thought you'd assault me in a bloody alley, did you?' Her mind did a somersault, knowing that even if she screamed, there was a chance that no one would hear. He'd easily be able to run and without a doubt he'd become lost in the maze of alleys before anyone came.

'It... it wasn't supposed to be like that... we're alike you and me and I saw you watching me earlier. I thought you liked me, and... you can't blame a bloke for trying, can you, so...'

Cassie was furious, the adrenaline had kicked in, and she wanted him gone. Her hand lifted to wipe her mouth and when she looked down, she saw tiny droplets of blood covering her fingers.

'Watching you? I have no idea what the hell made you think that! If anything, your damn staring at me gave me the creeps. You give me the creeps. I was only looking to see where you'd bloody well gone or to see where you were likely to pop up next.' She glared in his direction, held her hand out to show him the blood, almost pushing it in his face and screamed. 'And this... this is not something you do to a woman that you like. Not ever. Have you got that?'

Again, he moved towards her but seeing the fury in her eyes, changed his mind and stepped back. She breathed in slow and deep, feeling the wall behind her. She felt alone, trapped and vulnerable. The memory of the school playground remained in the back of her mind, and she knew she had to get away. Once again, he stepped forward. Fear coursed through her and without warning, she screamed as loud as she could and lashed out, catching him square in the face, and had the satisfaction of seeing blood spurt from his nose. Cassie saw the shock, followed by the anger in his eyes and for a moment she waited for the punch to come back at her. But then he turned and ran back in the direction in which they'd come, quickly disappearing out of sight.

A sudden sense of relief hit her, and Cassie slipped down the wall until she was sat on the ground, where she finally allowed herself to sob. Questions began to fly through her mind. Had she given him any reason to do this? Had she overreacted? Would he report her to the police for hitting him? She shook her head. Surely, he wouldn't. Surely it would be classed as self-defence, wouldn't it?

Her scream had attracted an older Italian woman who came running from one of the houses, with a tea towel in her hands.

'He attacked me,' she said as her body was wracked with sobs. Then there were more women. They suddenly appeared from nowhere. One of the women dabbed at Cassie's lip with a hanky, another stroked her hair, while a third ran down the alley with a broom in her hand in search of Declan. It was at times like this that Cassie realised just how far away from home she was. She thought of Lisa, of Becky, of the twins, Oliver and Thomas, and finally, she thought of Aggie and of how much she missed them all.

She began to shake, knowing that her encounter with Declan could have been much worse. She tried not to think of what could have happened, how bad it could have been and with tears running down her face she pulled a tissue from her bag, dried her eyes, dabbed at her lip and then with the help of the women she slowly stood up.

'*Scusa. Grazie. Devo andare.*' She thanked the women and excused herself in her stuttered, broken Italian, and then made her way down one alley and then another, until she found her way back to the street where it had all begun. The street where the shop stood. A shop that was ironically now open.

3

Cassie walked through the darkness and across the tarmac, dragging her small wheelie case behind her. She stared up at the rear doors of Doncaster Sheffield Airport, her eyes fixed on the long queue of people waiting to go in. They were all huddled together like penguins on a snowy cliff edge, all facing forwards, all shivering and trying to move.

'And this is what happens when you land at the same time as two other airplanes,' she growled at the aircraft that she'd just disembarked from as she made her way towards the crowd that all stood in what was best described as some industrial cattle run; a metal barrier that forced the queues of people to move round and round in rows until they finally reached the back door of the tiny room they called passport control. Her feet were cold, and she gave an involuntary shiver. Looking down she tutted at her flip-flops, knowing that she should have changed into trainers the moment she'd left the Italian sunshine. Being the end of August, the temperature in Doncaster wasn't freezing, but no match for what she'd left behind.

Cassie pulled her scarf up and around her face. She was quite aware that her cheekbone was bruised, that her lip was swollen and split, and that people were looking at her battered face, which she'd unsuccessfully tried to cover with make-up. She shivered, shuffled forwards and watched the luggage carts and catering trucks as they sped back and forth between the planes and the terminal, emptying and refilling the aircraft.

Cassie was tired and closed her eyes, but then quickly opened them again as she was nudged from behind and her feet began to move forward. The crowd controlled the speed and she felt as though she and her small wheelie case were being slowly pushed along, without a choice – much as she felt about returning home. At the sound of raindrops hitting the plastic roofing under which they stood, her heart sank and she wished herself back in Herculaneum. She wished she were back in the warmth, sat on her balcony with a glass of cheap local wine, chatting to Sasha about the most stupid things, as they shared sweets, cake or pizza.

It had only been a few hours since she'd left a hot, sunny Naples Airport where Sasha had stood before her, fidgeting with her hair and then twisting her hands together, before finally reaching out and clinging to Cassie as they hugged until they cried. Both had made a whole list of promises that neither knew if they would or could keep.

Cassie had promised that she'd be back within days and in return Sasha would look after their flat, water Bill the tomato plant and feed Tabitha. But, most importantly, she'd made Sasha promise to keep well away from Declan. Of course, men had made passes at her before, and if it had been just that she wouldn't have thought more about it, but he'd been strong and the brutal attack had been uncalled for, which had left Cassie with no choice but to report him to her supervisor before going back to the flat, to sit in the bath and sob, while Sasha had sat on the bathroom floor feeding her glasses from the cheap bottle of wine that Cassie had bought in the shop, alongside the milk.

Cassie took a deep breath. In truth she had no idea how long she would be staying in England. The fact that Aggie was sick had changed everything. The words terminal and cancer had been used in the same sentence, but Cassie didn't know what that meant. Would Aggie have weeks, months or years to live? Or, like her mother, would she die quickly, within days? 'Please, God, let her have years,' Cassie thought as she pictured Aggie's face, her smile, the way her lips curled up slightly to one side and how her eyes sparkled as she spoke. 'You can't leave me, Aggie. You just can't,' she whispered as once again, the crowd surged forward.

Cassie wondered how much Aggie had been told. Did she know how poorly she was? Did she know she was nearing the end? Was she hoping for a cure or, after seeing her sister die of the same thing, had she given up hope?

Once again, the queue moved forward and Cassie thought of her skeletons and how on that fateful day they'd have been just going about their everyday routine; working, doing chores, or simply walking to one of the many vendors that had food to sell along the streets. They certainly hadn't known that when the volcano erupted, that that day would be their last.

'Look after our skeletons,' Cassie had said to Sasha just before check in. 'Keep them in the shade, take daily soil samples and excavate just enough so that we can identify them when I get back.' Cassie had scribbled a phone number on a piece of paper. 'If you can't get hold of me on my mobile and you have any problems, this is my sister's number. Phone me and don't you dare sex them. Not without me.' Cassie remembered the look on Sasha's face, and the blush that covered her cheeks as people turned and stared.

'Yeah, yeah, yeah,' Sasha mouthed.

'You will wait for me to help with the identification, won't you?' Cassie had repeated, but she already knew that Sasha would wait. The identification was something they'd always done together. Finding out who your skeletons were just had to be the most interesting part of the dig and it had been a kind of ritual they'd shared with every find since arriving in Herculaneum. A ritual she didn't want to change.

But what if she didn't get to go back? She sighed and resigned herself to the fact that Sasha might just have to finish the dig by herself. She made a mental note to message her later, let her know she'd arrived at Aggie's house safely and, once she knew more about Aggie's condition, perhaps give her permission to carry on with the dig alone.

Moving through the back doors of the airport and into passport control, Cassie finally handed her passport to the controller and smiled. The woman looked down at the photograph and then up to where Cassie stood and then she stared back at the picture. A swift nod of her head followed, she returned the passport and Cassie walked through the double sliding doors to where the luggage carousel rotated in a slow and monotonous motion. She stood, patiently waiting. Finally, she pulled her phone from her pocket, pressed the button on the top and waited for it to kick into action. She looked down her names list, tapped on Aggie's name, but then looked up at the clock. It was late, after ten, and she wondered whether Aggie would be sleeping or not.

'It wouldn't hurt to text, would it? At least then, when she wakes she'll know I'm here,' Cassie thought as she began to tap the screen.

I've landed. Waiting for luggage. Be home within the hour. Hope you're okay, I'll come and see you tomorrow. x

Cassie then repeated a similar message to Lisa, watched her phone for a few moments but when no response came from either of them, she began to concentrate on the carousel. Nothing seemed to be happening, except for the constant movement of children who used the conveyor belt as a ride on toy and parents who screamed at them to stop.

Finally, after what seemed like an age, the bags began to appear. Cassie spotted her case as it flew upwards and landed in a position where it literally hung onto the edge of the rubber matting, making her run to collect it. She then turned towards the exit doors, dragging the heavy suitcase behind her, with the small wheelie case carefully balanced on top, and her rucksack on her back. 'I should have put on warmer clothes,' she said as the full force of the Yorkshire weather blew through the doors and continued to seep into her soul. The rain was now coming down in force, and she hesitated just inside the doors, watching the queue of taxis as they filled up in turn. Cassie glanced over her shoulder, desperate to find somewhere she could sit, drink coffee and delay her exit. But it was late and the coffee shop had long since closed. She dreaded going home and knew that Aggie's house would be cold, empty and lacking the woman she wished could be there.

Cassie could still hear the panic in Lisa's voice. 'Why, Cass? Why is this happening now? Aggie's always been so positive about the catacombs, but now it's as though she's afraid. I don't understand, what is Aggie suddenly so afraid of? She keeps mumbling about the tunnels, about the carvings she's always talked about, especially the Elephant and Mahout, and then she goes on about a secret. She won't tell me what it is, says it has to be you she tells. Says that only you can help her.'

Cassie still had no idea what Lisa had been talking about or what Aggie had been so afraid of. What secret did the Elephant and Mahout hold? What secret was Aggie hiding after all the years of talking about the catacombs with a wistful look in her eye? Of course, she'd mentioned the dangers, threatened Cass and Lisa that even if they did find a way in, they should never go into the tunnels, and that they shouldn't play near the old cemetery entrance. But, on the other hand, she'd continually said how amazing the tunnels had been, of how they'd been her childhood playground and the main reason behind her love of archaeology. Which once again raised the question as to why it would upset her so much that the tunnels were now being opened?

And now... now Aggie was sick. Cassie mentally kicked herself. What had she been thinking? How could she not have known? How could she have left her at a time when she'd needed her the most?

Cassie dug in her suitcase and pulled out a sports jacket and a pair of pumps, slipped off the flip-flops and slid them into the case. 'You should have stayed here, worked here,' she chastised herself, knowing that the only offers of work she'd had in England had either been in Cornwall or Scotland, both of which would have still meant her leaving home, leaving Aggie and sleeping in dormitories or tents. 'There would have been other jobs. Other careers.' She stared at the floor and at the pumps she now wore. 'But other careers wouldn't have taken me to Herculaneum, that's why. And other careers certainly wouldn't have given me my skeletons.' She thought back to the day before, to when she'd first uncovered the bones, to a moment when she'd had no idea that Aggie was so sick, or that by this time today she'd be stood looking through the sliding doors of Doncaster Airport, watching the taxis pull up, load and leave, as the rain poured, and the queue finally got shorter and shorter.

The sound of her ringtone came from her bag and Cassie

pulled it open, grabbed the phone and answered. 'Lisa. Hi, how you doing? Are you coming for me, or—'

'Honey, I wish I could. Honestly. But I can't. Becky went AWOL, Marcus is out looking for her and I have no one else to watch the boys... and you... you have no idea how hard it is to look after three-year-old twins. I've had a two-and-a-half-hour struggle to get them to sleep, and if I disturb them now, they'll be up all night.' She paused. 'Sorry, hun.'

Cassie pulled the phone from her ear. 'Welcome home,' she whispered before taking a determined breath in and lifting it back to her ear. 'Fine, I'll get a cab. I'll go to Aggie's and I'll try and get over to see you tomorrow, right?'

'That'd be great. I'd have asked you to come here tonight, but... as I say, they've only just got to sleep.' Lisa sounded defeated. 'And if they hear your voice, that'd be it. None of us would get any sleep.'

Cassie once again looked out of the terminal doors. The rain hadn't slowed, but the taxis had diminished. 'How is Aggie? Did you go and see her today?'

'Yes. I went this morning. She's really not good. You need to prepare yourself. She... well, she's lost a lot of weight since the hysterectomy and...' Lisa paused, her voice thoughtful. 'The radiation therapy alongside the chemo, well... it hasn't done her any good and she's lost a lot of her hair. Try not to look shocked when you see her.'

Cassie held onto her suitcase for support. Hysterectomy? Radiation therapy? Chemotherapy? She'd had no idea that Aggie had gone through all of that in the past six months and she could feel the anger rise up within her. 'Lisa, why the hell didn't anyone tell me that all of this was happening? How come I'm the last to know?'

Lisa sighed. 'We've gone over this. She forbade us to tell you.'

Cassie said her goodbyes after promising to phone Lisa the next day as soon as she'd been to see Aggie. 'Yes, definitely, get something good in for lunch,' she remembered saying, while her mind had been exploding with fear of the unknown and the trepidation of what was to come. 'How could all of this have happened without me knowing?' she whispered, pulling her scarf around her face and her hoody up and over her head as she stepped out of the building into the night air and straight into a waiting taxi.

4

Cassie's eyes shot open. The sound of banging pulled her out of a deep sleep. Her heart immediately began to pound and she sat up with a jolt, listening.

The noise echoed around the room and for a few moments she felt confused. But the sight of the pretty pink curtains of her childhood bedroom brought back the memory of the previous day and of the taxi that had brought her home from the airport the night before. It had pulled up over a hundred metres from Aggie's house and Cassie had been shocked by the amount of construction that was crowding the street. Barriers had been erected, and what had been the road and car park behind her house was now full of diggers, drilling equipment, Portakabins and heaps of spoils that had already been excavated, making Cassie wonder where the residents of the high-rise flats were parking and if getting in and out of their homes was now a major problem.

'No wonder Aggie was so upset,' she'd thought as she'd paid the taxi driver and climbed out from the back seat. She'd stood for a moment, taking in what was happening before negotiating a route to Aggie's house and dragging her cases behind her past the maisonettes, the other terraced houses and between the caged compounds where the excavation equipment stood.

Cassie had stopped in her tracks as a security guard stepped out of his Portakabin and flashed his torch in her direction. He'd stood on his tiptoes, paid far more attention to her than she'd have expected and glared as she'd made her way towards the back gate of her aunt's terraced house that stood on Stirling Street. Putting her hand through the opening, she unlatched the gate, walked to the back door and placed her key in the lock. Cassie looked over her shoulder, squinting to look through the spaces in the fencing, and wondered if the man had gone. Declan had made her nervous of all men who stared and even though she knew he was now miles away and that the security man was there to protect the site, she still didn't like how closely he watched her.

Cassie now threw the duvet back as another bang was followed by the sound of drilling. She poked a toe out of bed and shivered. For an August morning, it was cold. Or at least it felt cold to Cassie after being in Italy, where the daily temperature had easily been in the thirties and, on most days, she'd foolishly moaned about the heat.

Looking around the room, she spied her old pink towelling dressing gown hanging on the back of the bedroom door and she jumped out of bed, reached for it, and pulled it around her shoulders. Snuggling into the soft familiar material she took in a deep breath and smelt the familiar soap powder that Aggie had always used, before padding across to the window, dragging open the curtains and staring out at the circus that surrounded the streets behind.

Their terraced house was in the middle of the row. A narrow ginnel ran behind the property, another row of houses stood beyond, and to the right and directly in front of those houses stood a road that could clearly be seen from the back windows of Aggie's house. It was on this road that the site had been set up, in the shadow of a seventeen-storey block of flats that loomed high above them. Each flat had a balcony and rather than the bougainvillea of Italy, here each balcony was adorned with a mixture of England flags, sandcastle windmills, garden chairs, satellite dishes and washing lines full of laundry that barely had any space in which to dry.

'For God's sake,' Cassie growled as more men with hammers, jigger picks and hard hats climbed out of a van. 'How many men does it take?' She thought back to Herculaneum, to how she and Sasha had worked on their own grid, by themselves. Each find was of such huge significance that it had its own pair of archaeologists and even though most finds on the site had been buried for thousands of years, each grain of sand was removed with the utmost care and control.

She turned her nose up at the equipment. It was nothing like she'd been used to in Italy, but then again everything in Italy was different to here. Here it looked as though they were going in like bulls in china shops, all guns-a-blazing and a huge pile of spoil was already visible.

The sight of an old man walking out and onto his balcony caught her eye. He was scantily dressed in just a white vest and tight boxer shorts. He looked as though he'd literally just climbed out of bed and he hung over the balcony so far that Cassie wondered if he might topple over. 'Be quiet, I'm sleeping,' he bellowed.

The words made Cassie giggle. He was obviously not sleeping because he was stood on the balcony. 'Maybe you should have said you'd just been woken,' she said with a sigh at the irony that she'd been woken too but would never have lowered herself into opening the door and screaming out like a banshee.

She looked back at her bed that stood in one corner, right next to the one that had been Lisa's, with just a small space for a cupboard between. They both looked warm, and welcoming, with matching quilts. It had been too long since she'd been at home, and she'd missed curling up on the mattress that had moulded to her body shape. It had been university that had dragged her away first, then Lisa had married Marcus and staying at their house on a weekend had been fun, and different, especially while Becky had been a toddler. Lisa's dislike of hospitals meant that much to the midwife's disapproval, the twins had been born at home. It was her second pregnancy and she'd seen no reason to go to the hospital as she'd had to with Becky, which meant that Cassie had been there the night that Lisa had given birth to two boys: Oliver and Thomas. Identical twins. Both had cried, and both had needed feeding and changing at almost exactly the same time. Marcus worked full-time and Lisa had suffered terribly with sleep deprivation, which meant that she'd needed help from Cassie on a daily basis, and, of course, Aggie, who'd eagerly been on hand. But now Aggie was sick, and Cassie wondered if she should have made more of an effort to be here, at her house, with her. She'd missed all those weekends when she hadn't come home, all those bank holidays when she'd gone to stay with friends and all of those Christmases where they'd all chosen to eat at Lisa's. But now, now she felt guilty. She should have wanted to be here, in Aggie's house, where she'd always felt safe, loved and cared for.

Her attention returned to the Portakabin that she could clearly see from her upstairs window. The security guard from the night before was nowhere to be seen, but in the distance, a familiar-looking man marched up and down wearing a high-vis vest and looking as though he might be in charge. He had a hard hat loosely perched on top of his head that masked his face and Cassie found herself twisting and turning in order to see. He had a clipboard that he constantly looked up and down from, occasionally tapping at it with a pen. 'Well, aren't you just a little easy on the eye,' she whispered as she stood and stared. He was tall, well proportioned, with dark hair and a square jawline. He seemed to smile at everyone, while all the time giving them more and more work to do, which meant that as well as being good-looking, he was probably just a little more than annoying to go with it.

'Come on, take off the hat. Let me get a look at you.' Cassie pulled the net curtain back and looked a little closer and, as though her wish had been granted, the man pulled his hard hat from his head and ran a hand through his overgrown dark hair. 'Noah?' She'd thought the man had looked familiar, and that was because he was. 'Oh, my word, Noah Flanagan, is that really you?'

She watched him replace his hat, walk to the shaft, peer downwards and then he seemed to look across to where she stood. 'Well, haven't you grown up?' Noah was broader, more solid looking than she remembered. His face had matured, and his jawline seemed much squarer than it had before. She tipped her head to one side, as though by doing so she'd get a different perspective. 'Maybe it's the beard, maybe it's that that makes you look more mature.' It was well trimmed, more like stubble than a real beard, and seemed to perfectly frame his face. 'Very sexy,' Cassie whispered under her breath just as Noah turned, and looked again in her direction, making her drop the net curtain and hide from his view.

Noah had been her friend. He'd been at the same university as her and they'd met on the very first day. They'd spent a lot of time together; studied together, gone for lunches and had spent their evenings getting drunk. Yet, no matter how much Cassie had liked him, he'd never made her more than a friend. He'd always played the 'big brother' card, acted like a mate and Cassie had often felt hurt that he hadn't wanted it to be more. Eventually, she'd made new friends and so had Noah.

Turning away from the window, she took in a deep breath and screwed up her nose. There was a strange, musty smell in the house, a smell that hadn't been there before and she decided to turn her attention to cleaning and so set to work with the vacuum, furniture polish and bleach.

'When I bring Aggie home, it just has to be clean,' she whispered as she moved systematically from room to room, checking for anything that might be out of place. The house was small, compact, but homely. There were two rooms downstairs, a living room and a kitchen, and three rooms upstairs, which were two bedrooms and a bathroom. The only other room to the house was the cellar, where Aggie kept the coal, the fire sticks and the Christmas tree. It was dark, damp and a place Cassie didn't like to go, not unless she had to.

Pushing a vacuum cleaner across the carpet, Cassie kept one eye focused on the kitchen window. She'd forgotten to close the gate the night before, but now felt pleased with herself as she had a clear view of Noah and what he was doing. She felt a massive urge to bounce outside, say hello and hug him. But what would be the point? He'd obviously had no interest in her back then, so why would he care now? Besides, after just one look at her battered and bruised face, he'd run a mile.

'You're certainly not looking your best right now, are you?' she asked herself as she caught sight of her reflection in the china cabinet glass and winced. The bruising had come out; her whole cheekbone was a mixture of blues, greens and reds and her lip was split and dry. She walked into the kitchen, grabbed at the tea towel and ran the corner of it under the tap, before dabbing it on her lip in an attempt to reduce the swelling and get rid of the dried blood that seemed to continually scab the moment she wiped it off.

With tea towel in hand, she glanced across at the site. There he was, standing with three other men, laughing, nodding. They were all looking down the shaft that was obviously becoming more extensive by the minute.

'This excavation has upset my lovely Aggie so much,' she snarled, but then thought over what Lisa had said about Aggie and the tunnels. None of it had really made sense and Cassie checked her watch. Two hours. That was how much time she had left before she could visit Aggie. Which meant she had time for breakfast and a much-needed shower, something she should have done the previous evening but it had been almost midnight when she'd arrived home and an immediate deep and overwhelming sadness had overcome her. The house had been empty, and she'd simply dropped her cases in the doorway, walked through the kitchen and into the lounge where she stood for what seemed like forever just staring at the cold, empty grate. Without Aggie in it, the room had looked so very different even though nothing had really changed. The woodchip wallpaper had been up as long as Cassie could remember, a new colour of paint had been put over the top every couple of years along with new curtains which had always made the room look fresh and clean, even though most of the furniture had remained the same. There were photographs of her mum, of her and Lisa as teenagers, one of Lisa and Marcus on their wedding day, and various pictures of Becky and the twins. They were all framed, all standing in pride of place along both the mantelpiece and on the small table that stood beside Aggie's chair. It was a chair that should have long since been replaced, but Aggie wouldn't hear of it. 'I love this chair, it's moulded itself to my bones,' she'd always said, and Cassie smiled at the memory as her hand reached out and stroked the old, faded, threadbare material.

The thought that Aggie might never sit in that chair again had brought tears to Cassie's eyes and she'd sat for a while, simply staring at the chair with a million memories flying through her mind. Eventually, she'd felt her eyes closing, exhaustion had overtaken her and she'd made her way up the stairs and into the familiarity of her teenage bedroom, where the tears had dripped down her cheeks as she'd taken in the sight of her bed. It looked as though she'd just climbed out – the range of teddy bears, bedside lamps and a picture of her mother still stood on the dresser. She'd allowed her finger to stroke the silver frame, before she'd pulled open a drawer, grabbed at a pair of pyjamas and sniffed at them for freshness. They'd smelled as though they'd just been laundered, which probably meant that they had. 'Thanks, Aggie,' she'd mouthed as she'd thrown off her travelling clothes, changed as quickly as she could and climbed into the old familiar bed.

Cassie brought herself back to the present, filled the kettle and switched it on. 'Right, let's get some breakfast. Then I'll lay the fire ready for later.' She knew it was still only August, but after how cold she'd felt the night before she couldn't wait to see the room looking all warm and homely again, just as it always had once the fire was lit, with the flames licking the back of the fireplace and a log or two crackling on top of the coal.

Pulling open the fridge, she turned her nose up at the contents. 'What do we have in here?' There was a jar of jam, a Cadbury's Flake, one egg and a small piece of cheese that had clearly seen better days. Nodding, she pulled some of the items out and turned to the cooker. 'Looks like it's a cheese omelette then,' she announced to the walls as she opened a cupboard in search of other food. She found a tin of beans, along with a small tin of spaghetti hoops and, in comparison, the largest tin of peaches she'd ever seen. 'And... I think I need to go shopping.' Looking at her watch, she weighed up how much time she had. 'Now then, do I go on the way to the hospital, or on the way home?' She decided on the latter, pulled her purse from her handbag, opened it and sighed. The only currency she had was euros. Her only English ten-pound note had been used for the taxi home and her bank account was running just a little closer to empty than she'd have liked. She hurriedly broke the egg into the pan, swirled it around and turned to the cheese. 'You really don't look that appetising, do you?' she said, and threw it in the bin. 'Maybe I'll just have the egg and beans,' Cassie thought as she began opening and closing cupboards, making a list of things she needed to buy.

After finishing her breakfast, Cassie sent a text to Lisa.

Hey, sis. Hope you got something in for lunch, 'cos the cupboards are bare here and I'm a bit skint till payday xx

Cassie then went into the living room and built the fire by curling rolls of newspaper into tight twists, just as Aggie had taught her. 'As good as any firelighter or stick,' Cassie remembered her once saying as she added lumps of coal in a circle and a log on the top. 'There, that'll do it...' she said as she thought of getting home that night and for the second night in a row being all alone in Aggie's house. She pondered the thought. 'Had she ever been alone here before?' She shook her head and her eyes once again drifted to Aggie's chair. 'She'd always been there, sat right there, in that chair.'

The thought made her sigh. It suddenly occurred to her that

Aggie really hadn't had much of a life outside of her, Lisa and Becky. She'd always stayed at home. She'd always been the one to babysit and had always been there when needed.

After laying the fire, Cassie made her way up the stairs to take a shower as a response from Lisa came.

Sure, call me after visiting. I'll try and make something edible. Xx

Cassie smiled at the 'edible' comment. Lisa's culinary attempts in the past had been known to be somewhat dubious and Cassie remembered the dinner party she'd once hosted. Potatoes had been tipped out of a packet and into a bowl and Cassie had bounced them with her knife, much to Lisa's horror. 'But it said ready to eat on the packet,' she'd announced to the room, while pulling the packet out of the bin and everyone had laughed as they'd all read out in unison, 'Ready to eat... in five minutes.'

But at least lunch was sorted and whatever it was, it simply had to be better than the big tin of peaches. Cassie threw her pyjamas off and onto the bed. 'Right, shower, then visiting.'

She padded across the landing, entered the bathroom, turned on the taps, pulled the shower curtain across the bath and stepped under the hot, steaming water. She closed her eyes with the water hitting her straight in the face and just stood, allowing the heat to warm her. She was in heaven. The shower gel that Aggie had bought smelled of lemons making Cassie lather the gel up and breathe it in. She was momentarily back in Italy. The warmth, the smell and then... then without warning the water stopped, mid-flow, mid-shower and Cassie was still covered in soap.

'What the hell... seriously?' Cassie chuntered, opening her eyes, and turning the taps back on and off repeatedly. 'This isn't happening,' she shouted at the tiles. 'Not today, it can't happen today. Come on...' Again, she turned the taps, on, off, on, off.

She could hear voices outside. Raised voices. Holding her hands up in front of her, she stood and stared at the showerhead willing the water to come back on. 'Damn it, come on!' she screamed, just as a loud knocking could be heard at the back door. 'Okay, okay, wait a minute,' she shouted as she rubbed the worst of the soap off, and then wrapped a bath towel around her body, before stomping down the stairs. 'What?' She flung open the door to see Noah, complete with his clipboard, standing right in front of her.

'I... oh, I mean, sorry.' He blushed as he spoke, lowered his eyes and then suddenly looked up, realising who she was. 'Cassie? Oh my God, is that you?' His look of astonishment was replaced with a huge and cheeky smile. 'What... what are you doing here?' He stepped forward as though he were about to hug her, took note of her state of undress and quickly changed his mind.

'It's my aunt's house, I kind of live here, well... sometimes, I actually live in Italy too. I've been working in Herculaneum for the past six months.' She smiled, proudly, knowing he'd be impressed but then waved a hand around in the air as though brushing the words to one side. 'But that's another story.' She rolled her eyes and pulled the edge of the towel up in an attempt to hide the bruising on her face. But Noah had already seen it.

'What the hell happened to your face? Are you okay?' He looked concerned, his hand lifted towards her making her think he would touch her bruises, but then he retreated, looking as though he didn't know what to do next and finally, he gripped the clipboard tightly in front of him.

'It's nothing. I'm fine. Honestly.' She looked beyond him to where water gushed out of the shaft. 'Look, I'd invite you in, but as you can see, I was in the shower. So, unless this is a uni reunion, I really need to get the soap rinsed off me.' She paused. 'That's if I can get the water to come back on.'

He gave a nervous laugh. 'Well... that's the problem. I just wanted to let you and the other residents know that, well... the water, it's off, and it could be off for a while...' His soft Irish accent rang out as he turned his head in an attempt to avoid staring at her scantily clad body. 'But I'm kind of guessing that you're already knowing that.'

Cassie sighed. 'Not at all. I normally answer the door to strange men, covered in soap suds and wrapped up in a bloody beach towel.'

'Hey, less of the strange. I thought I was a friend.' Again he blushed as his eyes caught hers. 'And a good friend at that.'

Cassie looked down and pulled at the towel. She suddenly felt extremely relieved that even though her hair was wet, she hadn't yet covered it in shampoo and the thought crossed her mind that the situation could be a whole lot worse. She began to laugh. She mentally added bottled water to her shopping list, at least if she had some in the house, she could have warmed it on the stove.

'So... when will the water be back on, because I'm on a deadline to get to the hospital to visit my aunt and I really need to wash my hair.' She lifted a hand to her sodden hair and pulled at its length. 'See, still really dirty. In fact, it's probably still full of Italian sand, gravel and volcanic ash.' She hopped from foot to foot with nerves. 'Only got back last night and you have no idea how much I needed that shower.' Her hand grabbed at the towel, which suddenly felt as though it were about to slip off and hit the floor. 'So...' She raised her eyebrows and tapped her bare foot on the concrete doorstep. 'Come on, Noah. How long? An answer of "in two minutes" would be really good.'

Again, Noah made an obvious attempt to turn his gaze away. He looked in every single direction except directly at her. 'Well... you see, as I said already, that's the problem. We've hit a water main, as you can see. Luckily, it was only a bore hole and the water shouldn't impede the shaft.' He pointed to the water that flew up in the air. 'So, it could be off for a while.' He looked down at his clipboard that was still clasped tightly to him.

'Tremendous... and... how the hell did you do that? Didn't you or your men learn anything at uni? Don't they have a utilities map? Or do you just have a whole group of Neanderthals digging away without any thought of what pipes or cables lie beneath the surface?' She stood on her tiptoes to look over his shoulder and towards a group of men who were all stood beyond her gate, all staring, giggling like schoolboys and making it more than obvious that work was the last thing on their mind, especially while they had a partially naked woman in their sights. 'Jesus, Noah. Haven't they ever seen a woman before?'

Taking in a deep breath, she pulled the towel tightly around her body and used the door as a shield.

'Look, give me ten minutes, let me see what I can do.'

'Great,' she said, 'that makes me feel so much better.' She made an attempt at a smile. 'But, in the meantime, I'd love for you to magic up some really hot water. Seriously, it'd go down really, really well.' Cassie watched as Noah turned and started to walk away. He looked over his shoulder and then stopped.

'Okay, I'll tell you what. I'll make you a deal.' He grinned. 'If I get you some hot water... you'll come down the pub tonight, you know, keep me company?' He gave her one of his grins and pointed towards the railway. 'Do you know the pub near the railway?' he questioned, and Cassie noticed the sparkle that suddenly came from deep within his eyes. 'Six thirty?'

'But...' She was a little unsure; it had been years since she'd been in his company. Yet, she'd missed him and, what's more, she really did want to see him and find out what had happened to him over the past few years, but her fingers lifted to the bruising on her face. 'Look, I'm not at my best right now, and—'

'Oh, no you don't.' Noah shook his head. 'I'm not taking no for an answer. It's a pub quiz, Cass. No need to dress up, there's no one to impress but me and the lads, and trust me, I've seen you look so much worse than that.' He laughed. 'So, it doesn't matter if you don't feel at your best, does it?' He stood back. 'So... what is it? Hot water delivered to your door and pub quiz with yours truly, or am I going to be leaving you all covered in soap?' His Irish accent sang out like a melody and Cassie began to laugh.

'Okay, okay. But you have to provide the water, or the deal is off!' she shouted as he walked away.

5

'Aggie, hey... how are you doing?' Cassie whispered as she finally sat down by her aunt's bedside. It had taken her a good ten minutes to let her presence be known. She'd stood in the doorway, gripping the door frame and gasping for breath. The sight of a sleeping Aggie lying in a hospital bed attached to drips had shocked her and Cassie felt tears drop down her face as images and memories of her mum tormented her mind. She'd managed to stifle her sobs as she took in what she saw. Several bags of fluids hung from an IV stand and she could only guess at what they were pumping into her beloved aunt, the woman who had lost so much weight and hair that she no longer looked like the Aggie she knew and loved.

Cassie had crept onto the ward on her tiptoes in an attempt not to disturb her aunt. She'd made her way between the beds where three other ladies lay, two of them sleeping. But one woman was propped up against her pillows. She was weak, too weak to eat, and a lady who Cassie presumed to be a relation was spoon-feeding her from a bowl. She felt her chest heave with sorrow at the thought that without doubt it wouldn't be too long before her Aggie could be that poorly too.

'Cassie, you're here.' Aggie's unmistakable Yorkshire accent could only just be heard, and her mouth moved into a brief smile, but her eyes stayed half closed.

Cassie leaned in. Her hand touched Aggie's face and she gently placed a kiss on her aunt's cheek. 'I'm here, Aggie. I came.' Her eyes searched Aggie's face. 'How are you?'

Aggie sighed. 'I'm fine, my girl.' She opened her eyes and looked closely at Cassie. 'Especially now you are here. Tell me about Italy. I want every detail.'

Cassie was more than aware that her face was still bruised. She'd used as much make-up as she could to hide it but even so, she sat with her face slightly turned. 'Italy was lovely,' she whispered, but her words dried on her lips as she stared at her aunt.

There was so much she wanted to know, so many questions she wanted to ask, all of which had answers she knew she didn't want to hear. She could feel the heat rise up within her and she got hotter and hotter until she quickly pulled off her jacket and hung it on the chair behind her. She desperately needed to cool down and took in deep breaths in the hope that it would control her nausea. Her mind began to whizz around in circles and she looked down at the floor, praying that the feeling would pass.

Turning back to Aggie, she took her hand in hers. The paper-thin skin felt smooth, silk-like, but delicate, and she worried that if she held the hand too tightly, the skin would tear or bruise.

'Italy was lovely,' she repeated and for Aggie's sake she tried to sound cheerful. 'You'd really like it there.' She momentarily forgot about the bruising and looked up into Aggie's face, and into the eyes that used to sparkle back at her. 'When you're better, I'll take you to see my flat... you can come and meet Sasha, she's lovely and... and Tabitha, our stray cat, she'd love to curl up on your knee.' She paused. 'Would you like that, Aggie?'

Aggie nodded tentatively and gave Cassie a distant look. 'Oh, my darling girl. You know I'd love to see it, don't you?' She stared into the corner of the room. Her eyes glazed over, and Cassie knew she had thoughts of Italy, of excavations and of archaeology on her mind.

Aggie reached across and picked up a glass. She sipped at the water but struggled to swallow. She then went to lie back against the pillows, but as she did, she turned, caught sight of Cassie's face and then with every ounce of her energy, she grabbed at the sheets, pushed herself up in the hospital bed and glared at the damage. 'What... the hell happened?' She flopped back against the pillows, but the anger in her eyes was clear to see.

Cassie tried to laugh, lessen Aggie's distress. 'It was just this guy...' She paused and tried to think of the words. How did you tell someone that you went for milk and were attacked less than half a mile from where you lived? 'He kind of thought I liked him, and, well, he got a bit... you know, overexcited.'

Aggie's hands were twisting the bed sheet as though she were ringing out cloths. 'He hurt you?' The words were both a statement and a question.

Cassie moved uncomfortably in the chair. 'No. Not really. He just tried it on. You know what it's like. But I stopped him.' She could still remember the look of anger, fury and embarrassment that had passed through Declan's eyes. Then suddenly she saw Aggie's hand lift up. It slowly went to Cassie's face and, in the gentlest of movements, her fingers touched the bruise and a tear fell down her face.

'He hurt you?' she said again.

Cassie shook her head and sighed. 'Anyhow, let's think about you, we need to get you all better so that you can come and see

Italy.' She picked up her handbag and began digging around for her phone. 'I took some pictures of Tabitha before I left,' she said, but as she looked up, Aggie was silent. She'd lain back against the pillows, her eyes were closed, and for a moment, Cassie presumed she'd drifted off into a restless sleep. Her hands were clasped together, and once again she looked as though she was wringing out an imaginary cloth, while her head went from side to side.

Moving her chair closer, Cassie once again took hold of Aggie's hand and leaned forward to rest her head against the white cotton pillow beside her aunt's. Her breathing soon fell into a rhythm, and she felt herself drifting in and out of sleep, with dreams of Italy, of running down alleys, of trying to escape Declan's clutches, but she couldn't. Her whole body felt as though it were moving at speed, rushing, searching, looking for a way home. A way that was blocked, leaving her trapped, afraid and unable to move.

Aggie's hand stirred. Cassie heard her mumble and suddenly it was as though someone was dragging her out of a deep, dense fog. Her whole body felt weak, lethargic, as though every muscle had suddenly become fatigued. Her hand automatically went up to her neck. Her head felt like lead and she moved into a position where she could look up and into Aggie's eyes. 'Aggie, are you okay?' She watched as Aggie gave a half smile.

A metal trolley could be heard somewhere in the distance, rattling towards them. It seemed to be making its way down the corridor, the voice of whoever was pushing it singing out as she went.

Cassie watched with interest as an elderly, jolly-looking care assistant rounded the corner. She pushed a tea trolley onto the ward and smiled. Her rotund body made hard work of the few steps that she took. 'Now then, Agatha, would you like a fresh cup of tea, my darling?'

Aggie blinked, her head made a slight nod and the assistant carried on regardless. 'White with one sugar, isn't that right?' she said as she made the tea and poured it into a plastic beaker, with a straw attachment. 'If I put it in this, you won't go burning yourself, my lovely, will you?' She walked across to the side of Aggie's bed. 'I'll put it on your bedside table for a minute. It's a bit hot, so you let it cool down, won't you.'

She gave Cassie a warm smile, but her eyes were sad as her hand reached out to pat Aggie on the shoulder. It was more than obvious that the woman had seen this before, she'd most probably made friends with many of the patients on this ward, only to wheel her trolley down the same corridor the very next day and for half of the beds to be either empty or to have new and just as poorly occupants in them.

Cassie smiled. 'Thank you... er... I'm sure she'll appreciate it,' she said as she touched the beaker to test the temperature.

'Patty. I'm Patty my lovely.' She pulled her cap down over her grey hair and looked over her shoulder. 'And what about you, you look as though some coffee wouldn't go amiss?' Again, she turned and began filling a cup without waiting for an answer.

Cassie had to agree, there had been a distinct lack of coffee, milk or any other item that resembled appetizing food in Aggie's house that morning, which reminded her that she needed to go shopping. She'd managed to blag her lunch out of Lisa, but without the shopping she'd genuinely have to starve the day after. She gratefully accepted the drink.

'Thank you, Patty. That's really kind of you.' She blew on the coffee, and watched as Patty moved onto the next bed, to the next patient and the next set of relations.

'Are they still digging?' Aggie suddenly asked, her eyes now open wide, making Cassie place her cup on the side.

'Yes, they're there. They are opening a shaft, an entrance to the tunnels.' She didn't want to lie, but from what Lisa had said, the opening of the tunnels had upset Aggie and the last thing she wanted was to distress her further.

Aggie grabbed hold of her hand and squeezed tight. 'I... I need you to help me. It's important.'

Cassie saw the terror in Aggie's eyes and felt the breath suddenly leave her lungs. 'Help? Help you with what?' Cassie moved to the edge of her chair.

'I never thought the tunnels would be opened. Not ever. Not after the last time.' Aggie stared at her feet that moved restlessly around under the bed sheet. 'They'll arrest me. They'll send me to prison.' Her hand now held tightly onto Cassie's. Her whole body shook in fear and Cassie moved to sit beside Aggie on the side of the bed.

'Aggie, what on earth did you do?' She stared into the old woman's eyes while her mind did somersaults.

'Prison...' It was all she managed to say. Her eyes were wide like saucers and her breathing became laboured with an obvious fear.

'Aggie. What did you do?' Cassie repeated. 'Was it anything to do with my dad, with those rumours of the robberies?' It was all she could think to ask. After all, if that was the truth, then if anyone should have gone to prison, it should have been him.

Aggie's head moved from side to side, her distress more than obvious. 'There is so much you need to know.' She pulled the blanket up around her chest. 'I had no choice, you see, they were going to send me away and I couldn't go there, I'd heard what happened to the girls like me.' Again, her hand reached out to touch Cassie's face and traced the bruising in a gentle and loving way.

Cassie looked over her shoulder, before turning back to Aggie. 'What do you mean, girls like you?' She watched the tears roll down her aunt's face. She couldn't bear to see Aggie so upset and quickly pulled the curtain around them. Nervously, she moved around the bed, kicking off her shoes as she went. Cassie then climbed up and onto the bed where she immediately put her arms around her aunt and cuddled up behind her.

She heard Aggie take in a deep breath. 'Do you remember when we all used to do this? Me, you and our Lisa? All in one single bed, all cuddled up together,' Cassie asked, fully expecting a nurse to turn up, poke her head around the curtain and order her to get off the bed. But right now, she didn't care.

Aggie nodded. 'You... smell of... my shower gel.' Her words came between the sobs and Cassie vowed to hold her until the tears had stopped. She thought about telling Aggie the tale of how the shower had stopped while she'd been covered in the gel and then how miraculously three brand new orange buckets of hot water had turned up on the back doorstep, courtesy of Noah. She wondered what Aggie would think to her meeting up with Noah again and to her agreeing to a night at the pub. She shook her head, it was all too odd to be true and she pushed herself up on one arm, while her other hand stroked what was left of Aggie's hair.

'Aggie. What do you need me to do?' The trembling continued. Aggie's whole body shook with nerves and Cassie hugged her closer. 'Aggie, you're frightening me.'

'Cassie. I'm dying.' Her finger pointed up and into the air and Cassie felt the tears catch in her throat. 'The tunnels...' Her voice became weak, her hands clutching her stomach. 'They're the reason I've always been interested... in archaeology,' she whispered. Her hand rested on Cassie's, but the trembling continued. 'I'm a stupid old woman who always thought that somehow she'd get down there herself.'

Aggie gripped the bed sheets; her pain was obvious as she clutched at her stomach and buried her face in her pillow as she tried to muffle the yell that came from within her.

'Aggie.' Cassie moved off the bed, inched the curtain back and looked around for a nurse. 'Shall I get someone?' She turned back to her aunt.

But Aggie just glared at her. 'I need a promise. A big promise...' She paused, her hand once again went to her stomach and Cassie could see the pain travel through her face. 'It's something I know you'll not want to do.'

'Aggie,' Cassie's voice broke, 'you... you know I'll do anything for you... if I can. But... this, well this sounds either dangerous or illegal.' Her eyes searched her aunt's. 'Which is it?'

For a few moments, Aggie was silent. It was as though she was trying to magic the words. But Cassie was frightened. Aggie had never spoken in this way before and she had no idea what she could or would ask of her and her mind scrambled as she tried to work out what it could be.

Aggie tapped the bed with her hand. 'Lie down again with me...' She waited for Cassie to get comfortable, before taking a deep breath. She took her time. A sob left her throat and she sat up, reached for her tea and took a sip before she began.

'You have to realise that I was so very young at the time. Just fifteen years old and John... John was sixteen.' She paused and stared into the air somewhere far in the distance. 'Oh, I know that some would say he took advantage of me. But he didn't. It was the most wonderful and most loving time of my life.'

Cassie emulated her aunt and grabbed at the edge of the

sheet. She began twisting it around and around in her hand. 'You mean, he... you... but, Aggie... fifteen... Wasn't that illegal?'

Aggie shook her head. 'Can you ever call love illegal?' She wiped the tears from her eyes. 'Oh, my darling girl, if it were illegal then I'm as guilty as charged,' she whispered, patting Cassie's arm. She laughed and continued in whispered tones, 'I won't give you the gory details. It's not something you need to hear from your aunt.' Tears now fell relentlessly down Aggie's face and Cassie pulled a tissue from the box and passed it to her. 'I had a baby.'

Cassie could feel her heart beating wildly in her chest. Aggie's words had been clear but heartbreaking. Her aunt had 'had' a baby and Cassie was already thinking ahead and putting two and two together. 'Aunt Aggie, is... was... was my mum your daughter?'

The sound of coughing came from one of the other beds, and a nurse could be heard comforting her. Aggie held a finger to her lips until she was sure that the nurse had gone. 'Oh no, my girl, your mother was not mine, though I wish she had been, my life might have been so much easier.' A deep and heart-wrenching sob left Aggie's throat and again, she reached for the tea. Sipping it carefully, she stared into space, a way of giving herself time and Cassie knew she was thinking carefully about the next words she'd say.

'But you were pregnant, at fifteen,' Cassie confirmed and without waiting for an answer continued, 'which is why you were so understanding when Lisa got pregnant so young?'

Aggie nodded. 'I could see it happening, I could see the love grow between her and Marcus and I knew it had gone further than she'd said. It was no surprise when I found her crying in her bed.' She straightened the bedding that covered her legs. 'She needed our love, our support and that baby, Becky, she needed us too. It wasn't a time to shout or chastise.'

Cassie took in the words. 'You didn't get any support with your baby, Aunt Aggie, did you?'

Aggie was suddenly silent. She lay back and closed her eyes. But then she spoke, and it was as though she'd fallen back in time.

'I'd been so terrified that my mother would find out. I hid the pregnancy with large baggy jumpers. They'd have sent me away, you see, to the mother and baby home. It was a place where all the girls were sent to have their babies back then.' She gripped Cassie's hand. 'It was a way of hiding the shame from the neighbours, the family and the church. But it was an evil place where the girls were practically slaves and the babies... the babies, they disappeared, adopted they said, sent to good homes and were never seen again.'

'Why would they have sent you away? You'd have given the baby a good home. Why couldn't they look after you, like you did our Lisa?' Cassie thought of how they'd all pulled together. How Marcus had been to visit daily and between them they'd all planned for Becky's arrival. 'And what about John, what did he do?'

'John had taken a job on the railway, trying to earn money for the three of us. But on the night the baby came, it was late, and I was scared. I knew the baby wouldn't wait for its daddy to get home from work and I couldn't risk my parents hearing my screams. They were screams that I knew would come, screams that I'd heard so many times before from the other women in the terrace, including those of my mother. So, I went to the only place I knew that I wouldn't be heard. A place I knew I'd be alone... I went deep into the tunnels, to the catacombs, with only a torch for light.' Aggie's hand once again gripped her stomach and she cried out in pain, making Cassie jump down from the bed.

'I'll get a nurse,' she said. Her hand fumbled to grab at the alarm, but her legs threatened to give way and she sat down heavily onto the chair, just as the curtain opened and a male nurse looked in.

'Are we okay in here, Agatha?' The nurse was in his mid-thirties, tall and he hovered high above the bed. He squirted sanitiser on his hands, held onto Aggie's wrist, checked her pulse, and then picked up the chart that hung from the bottom of the bed.

'Is she okay?' Cassie asked nervously, not knowing what to do.

The nurse looked Cassie up and down. His stare lasting just a little longer than necessary. 'Are you a relation?'

Cassie nodded. 'Yes, I'm her niece.' She stared at his name badge that hung on his jacket: *Todd Bailey, Clinical Nurse Specialist*.

The nurse moved with purpose. Every action was deliberate, and Cassie watched the precision of his movements.

Todd continued to write on the chart. 'And you are Agatha's next of kin, are you?' he questioned her in a firm manner, while looking directly into her eyes. Cassie looked down and stared at the bed's shiny metal undercarriage, the hydraulics, the wheels, the dust ball that floated around on the floor like tumbleweed blowing around in an old western movie. The nurse coughed and broke her thoughts, but she didn't know how to answer. An overwhelming sense of sadness and anxiety overcame her and she squeezed Aggie's hand for support.

'She is, alongside her sister, Lisa,' Aggie whispered, nodded and smiled. But Cassie's eyes filled with tears. Apart from Lisa and the kids, Aggie was all she had and the thought that she could lose her at any given moment was too much to bear.

'OK, so I'll also need your name and address for the chart.' Again, the nurse looked at her and tapped the clipboard.

'It's Cassie, Cassandra Hunt.' She shuffled in the chair. 'I live with my aunt, so... it's the same address.'

'Ahhh, okay,' he said, but then paused before speaking. 'Have you lived together long?' He stared at her, waiting for an answer, all the time hovering over Aggie, holding her wrist, and checking her monitor.

'Yes, since I was eleven.' She looked down at the floor, not knowing what else to say.

'Does anyone else live at this address?' His pen bounced over the address box.

Cassie looked around the room. 'Why... why is that relevant?'

The nurse smiled. 'Just getting an idea of Agatha's lifestyle, that's all. For when she goes home.'

Cassie nodded. 'There's just the two of us.' Again, she watched the nurse; he seemed to stare at the paperwork as though working out his next question. 'Anything else?'

The nurse took in a deep breath. 'No, nothing else.' He stepped away from the bed.

Cassie watched as Agatha moved, once again grabbed at her stomach and stifled a moan. 'Will you be getting her some more pain relief? I think she's in pain.'

Todd smiled. 'I'll ask the doctor to look at Agatha's pain relief, see if there's anything more we can give her.' Again, he looked at her in a way that went through her, not at her. But then as quickly as he'd arrived, he turned to leave.

'I don't need more pain relief, Cass. I'm fine, honest,' Aggie lied. A half smile was forced, but she closed her eyes and Cassie knew that she was waiting for the pain to subside.

Waiting until the nurse's footsteps were in the distance, Aggie tapped the bed covers, imploring that Cassie should climb back up beside her. Cassie held her in a hug and prayed that her pain would go.

'No one really knew the tunnels, not like we did,' Aggie continued her story. 'After all, they'd been our playground for years. But it was 1964 and the tunnels had been all but lost to the world, parts of them had been landfilled. The year before, the council had drilled twenty-one holes trying to find their exact path. The drill holes exposed them, and even though the catacombs had been made unsafe, they still began the excavation.' Aggie spoke with certainty, it was as though it was all happening now, and Cassie could hear the sadness and the anger in her voice.

'So, what happened?'

'As I said, my John had gone to work on the railways. He worked every hour he could to earn money for us both. He promised that once the baby came we would elope, and get married.' She smiled. 'He loved me, Cassie. He loved the both of us.'

'You found him, right?'

Aggie shook her head and once again the tears began to fall. 'John, he'd been in an accident. A bad accident. But I didn't know, all I knew was that he should have been home, but he wasn't. I cursed him so many times and I had no one else, so I went to the embankment, beyond the cemetery, and went through the tunnels, alone.'

Cassie's hand went up to her mouth. 'Oh, Aggie.' She had no other words, nothing she could have said would have made a difference. She tried to imagine what it would have been like to be fifteen and about to give birth in the darkness, alone.

'I crawled on my hands and knees through what was left of the catacombs and made my way until I reached the Elephant and Mahout. The drill holes allowed a little light and I had my old torch to help me. I found my way to the striped blanket that was on the floor of the tunnel. It was a blanket we'd made love on, on so many occasions. But the pains were so bad, and they went on for so long.' She paused and gripped Cassie's hand. 'I knew before she was born that there was something very, very wrong. And then, as she came into the world, and all I heard was a silence that was so deafening it made me scream. I held her for so long, and I waited for her to cry, but it was a cry that didn't come.'

Aggie suddenly went silent, thoughtful and, for a while, Cassie just lay holding onto her, while all the time staring at the curtain surrounding their hiding place. 'I was always going to go back for her, Cassie. But the tunnels were filled and so she's still there, still wrapped in that blanket, tucked under a ledge beneath the Elephant and Mahout.'

Aggie moved out of the hold and sat up, picked up the tea and sipped. 'I felt as though I would die alongside her. Every part of me wanted to sleep, to lie on the floor of the tunnel and allow the darkness to swallow me. But, somehow, I managed to crawl out. The torch battery had died and I managed to pull myself along in the darkness.' Again, she sipped at the tea. 'I went to Ida's,' she paused, 'you remember my cousin Ida, don't you? She used to live further along what was left of Victoria Street, she used to come to our house when you were a child. You see, she'd had twelve children of her own and I knew she'd know what to do. I literally collapsed on her doorstep.'

Cassie moved from the bed to a chair, still holding onto Aggie's hand. 'I'm so pleased she looked after you, Aggie. But... I'm still not sure what you're asking me to do.'

Aggie patted her hand. The heartbreak in her voice was clear. 'It's the whole reason I was keen to study archaeology. I knew that one day the tunnels would be opened, and they were once. It was January 1976. Two boreholes were drilled, this wide.' Aggie held her arms as far apart as she could. 'At least three feet wide.' She nodded. 'So many people came, they went down ladders to inspect the tunnels and all the time I was sure that my secret would be discovered. For days I hid in the cellar, not knowing what to do.' She turned to the window and stared out. 'I wanted to go down the ladder too, and I would have if they'd let me. I'd always wanted to bring her home, you see. But the tunnels, they were filled again, and I finally resigned myself to the fact that I'd lost her forever... until now.'

Cassie's mind was a whirl of sadness and questions, but where to start?

Aggie sniffed and continued. 'After our house on Victoria Street was demolished, I couldn't move too far away, which is why I live on Stirling Street. I could have moved away, I guess. But I chose to stay, I chose to keep renting the house where we live.' She took a deep breath and then whispered with so much emotion in her voice, 'I couldn't leave. I just... I just had to stay close to her.' Again, she paused. For a few moments she closed her eyes, her hands went across herself from one side to the other as though giving herself a much-needed hug. Pain travelled across her face, her brow was now wrinkled, her hair had fallen out and her skin had taken on a different colour. She was seventy years old, and for fifty-five years she had lived with this secret buried deep within her.

'I'm begging you.' Aggie's voice now sounded soft, weak and vulnerable. 'I wouldn't ask. I'd always planned to do it myself, but... look at me...' Aggie held up her arm, the catheter now clearly visible. 'Cassie, help me bring her home.' Her eyes pleaded with Cassie's. 'If it's the last thing I do, I need to bury her properly. I need to lay her to rest.'

The air left Cassie's body all at once. She jumped up from the chair and held onto the bed. Gasping for breath. 'Aggie... my God, I was afraid you'd ask this. Do you know what you're asking me to do? I mean, I can't... I can't remove human remains, it's...' Cassie thought of her training, of how she'd studied remains and it was against all she believed in to remove them from a site. The find would have to be reported. The coroner would have to be called. 'Aggie, you...' she gulped at the air '...you do know that she... that she'll...'

How on earth did she explain to a grieving mother that her baby would be just bones? That there would so be very little left, if anything at all. Especially in tunnels like this where she imagined rats and other animals would have been scouring for food.

Aggie grabbed at her arm. 'My girl, I've never asked anything of you, but I'm begging you to do this for me.' She stared into Cassie's eyes, deep into her soul and, at that moment, Cassie knew she couldn't say no. Somehow, she had to get into those tunnels. She had to find Aggie's baby and she had to do what Aggie wanted: help her to lay her baby to rest. She would do it for Aggie. Whatever danger lay ahead she would face it, regardless of the consequences.

6

'What the hell do you mean, you're gonna ask for a job on the dig?' Lisa turned to the kettle, switched it on and began pulling mugs out of the cupboard with one hand, while the other flicked crumbs off the worktop and into the sink.

'Just what I said.' Cassie looked into the living room where between the settee and chair stood a bright blue pop-up tent. 'Okay, what's going on in there?'

Lisa shrugged her shoulders. 'The boys wanted to camp out. But, obviously, they're only three, so they can't.' She raised her eyebrows and picked up the sugar container. 'I for one don't want to sleep in the garden, so the tent went up in the living room and, according to the boys, tonight I get to sleep on the settee while they get to eat beans and sausages, sleep on the floor and sing camping songs that will annoy us all.'

Lisa leaned on the doorjamb and looked into the lounge where the sound of giggling came from within the tent. 'Up to now they have two sleeping bags, all the cushions off the settee, two pillows off the bed, every teddy bear they possess, and my best snuggle blanket.'

Cassie nodded. 'Don't they like their beds?' She laughed as she thought of the previous night, the night she'd just spent in her childhood bed and of the joy it had brought her.

'Don't be silly, they're three-year-old boys. No three-year-old likes their bed and this is an adventure, Aunty Cassie, and those two just love anything that gets them out of a proper bedtime.' Lisa pulled a face and turned to make the coffee. 'Let's just hope that it isn't too long before they can join the cubs and then someone else can take them off camping in the woods.'

'Do you remember when we were kids and we'd sit really quietly, drinking our hot chocolate so slowly, just so we could stay up for ten minutes longer?'

Lisa laughed and handed Cassie a mug of coffee. 'And after just five minutes our dad would work us out and send us up to our beds anyhow.'

Cassie turned her back on her sister and sighed. The mere mention of her father made her feel tearful and that day in the ginnel came flooding back. Once again, she was crouched behind that wheelie bin and the sound of running footsteps echoed in her ears and then, in her mind's eye, she could clearly see the half-finished snake and its piercing eyes, although now, she could no longer picture the man who it had been tattooed upon.

'Hey, Becks?' Cassie said to her eleven-year-old niece, who entered the living room, then poked her head through the tent flap and pulled a face at the twins. A squeal was followed by giggles and both boys disappeared under a pile of cushions and blankets. Turning to the settee, she took a seat and smiled at Becky, who sat in a big chair in the corner of the room. She had a scowl on her face, her knees pulled up under her chin and her phone in her hand. She seemed to shrink deep into the chair, in an obvious attempt to make herself look small.

'You alright, Becks?' Cassie tried to gain her attention, but saw her chest rise and fall in the biggest of sighs. 'What's up, this isn't like you?' Cassie asked as she stood up, walked over, sat on the arm of the chair, slipped into it beside her niece and playfully bumped her with her shoulder.

Becky shrugged and looked up from her phone. 'Bloody hell, Aunty Cass. What the hell happened to your face?'

'Language,' came Lisa's voice from the kitchen. 'I've told you about swearing, haven't I?'

'Okay, okay, but have you seen the state of Aunty Cass's face? She's had a right battering.'

Lisa suddenly leaned around the door and stared at Cassie who was now squashed into one chair with Becky. 'Cassie. How the hell didn't I notice that?' She moved closer and seemed to suddenly take in the damage to her sister's face.

'I'm fine, it... it was a misunderstanding.' She turned her face away, looking over at the television. 'Are you really watching Jeremy Kyle?' she asked in an attempt to change the subject.

But Lisa raised an eyebrow and stared, just as Becky tried to sit up, caught the tent pole with her foot and then began to laugh as the whole thing collapsed. Screams were heard in unison and the shape of two boys began wriggling within, until both their heads poked out of what had been the entrance.

'Becky, now apologise and put it back up.' Lisa glared at her daughter. 'Come on, before one of them suffocates.'

'Sorry, boys.' Becky laughed as she jumped up and began re-erecting the tent. 'You alright in there?' she asked as she tickled the boys through the tent's opening and then sat back laughing as they both wriggled and screamed.

'Becks, don't do that.' Lisa perched on the chair arm. 'Can you make them some lunch for me while I sort out this tent?' Lisa gave her daughter her best smile and was tutted at by way of reply.

'Whatever.' Becky tipped her head on one side, smirked and left the room. Cassie followed her.

'You okay, hun?' she asked as she leaned against the counter and sipped at her coffee. Cassie watched as Becky began buttering bread, adding cheese spread and then pulled a huge bag of crisps from a drawer. She cut the bread into strips, placed them on plates, added the crisps and then poured some orange juice into two plastic, coloured beakers.

'I'm fine,' she said, but her eyes told a different story.

'Fine? Just fine? It's okay not to be fine, you know.' Cassie pulled out a chair and sat down. Becky was eleven, and even though she seemed so much more grown up than her age, it occurred to Cassie that she was the same age that she'd been when the bullying had begun at school. Thinking quickly, she pointed to her own face. 'I got this because a boy... a man thought it was okay to come onto me, to attack me and he kissed me when I didn't want him to.'

Becky glared. Her eyes as wide as saucers. 'Really? Why would he do that?'

Cassie thought carefully about her answer. 'Well, because sometimes both kids and adults don't always see eye to eye. Sometimes they do things they shouldn't and sometimes they hurt people in the process, people who they normally wouldn't want to hurt.' She paused and saw the words register in the youngster's eyes. 'Has someone hurt you, Becks?'

Becky chewed her bottom lip. 'It's a boy at school. He's really cute, but he doesn't like me,' she whispered and Cassie's heart broke as she heard the pain in her voice. It was more than obvious that Becky had a crush. Which to an eleven-year-old would be both the biggest and most awful thing in the world, especially if the crush wasn't reciprocated. Cassie remembered the feeling.

'Well, it's his loss.' Again, she paused. 'Do you want to hear a story?' She continued without waiting for an answer, 'It's a few years ago now, but when I was at uni I liked this guy. We were friends. I really liked him, and do you know what?' Cassie stood up. She walked over to her niece and pulled her into her arms. 'I wanted him to be more than that... and the short story is, he didn't.' She slowly shook her head. 'But this morning, I saw him for the first time in years and... well, he seemed really happy to see me and... and he invited me to the pub quiz tonight.'

Becky smiled. Her eyes sparkled with excitement. 'What, just like that? Will you go?'

'I guess so. But only because I made a deal. And a deal is a deal, right?' Cassie's hand cupped Becky's chin, her lips dropped a kiss on the end of her niece's nose. 'So, how about I make you a deal.'

Becky looked up. 'I'm listening.'

'How about you come and stay with me. You could come over sometime next week. We could have a girly night, talk, eat pizza, watch soppy films, put face masks on, you know... all the things we haven't done for ages. We could even take the boys for a sleepover, if you'd like that? You know, give your mum and dad a break.' She paused, smiled and squeezed Becky's hand. 'You never know, we might actually have some fun.'

Becky put her arms around Cassie's waist. 'Can we?'

'Of course, we can.' Cassie laughed. 'While you're there, we could talk about this boy you like, and I could give you one of those horrid sex talks.' A look passed between them, Becky blushed, and Cassie knew instinctively that Lisa had already been very up front on the education, especially after she'd become a mum herself at sixteen.

Becky pulled herself out of the hug, rolled her eyes and picked up the two plastic plates. 'Yeah, yeah, I think I know all about it. But you can buy me the pizza. That'd be good.' She walked back into the lounge, Cassie following, carrying the beakers. 'Here you go, brat pack. Have a picnic.'

A squeal came from within the tent. Two tiny hands shot out of the flap and the plates of food and beakers disappeared within.

'That'll keep them happy for at least three minutes,' Lisa said, now sitting in the chair. She sipped at her coffee, then waved the mug in the air. 'Cass, what you said before. You can't go and work on the site. Me and Becky, we need you. Aggie needs you.' She sat back in the chair, looking small, defeated.

Cassie did her best to control her emotions. She closed her eyes, took in the deep aroma of the coffee and then looked down at the floor. 'I can't just sit at home, Lisa. I'd be bored,' she lied. She hated all the deception, but Aggie had insisted that she couldn't mention her secret, not to anyone, especially to Lisa. Nor could she tell her that she was about to break the law by removing human remains from an archaeological dig. There were so many secrets that her mind began to spin, like plates. She just hoped that she could keep them all spinning, without any one of them breaking and knew that she had to form a plan. How was she going to get onto the site, down the tunnels and past Noah?

Shaking her head she realised that she really hadn't thought that far ahead. Damn it – she didn't even have a job on the dig. And without a job, how would she retrieve the bones? What would she put them in? A bag? A box? What if someone else found them first? Would the authorities be informed? Of course, they would. Along with the coroner, and the police. She took in an involuntary gasp, which made Lisa sit up and glare. Smiling

Cassie once again stared into the tent, pretending to concentrate on the boys. Her mind was spinning on an axle. Could she really do it? Could she remove the remains? Could she bury them and, if she could, where? Where in the world do you secretly bury the bones of a baby?

Her whole day had been strange. Nothing had been as she'd expected. After visiting Aggie she'd walked into town, through the Frenchgate Centre, past the cashpoint and made her way to the supermarket, where she'd shopped in a daze. She'd pushed an empty trolley along the aisles and, without really looking at what was displayed, began dropping items into it. Cooking for one wasn't fun and Cassie tried to decide how often she could land on Lisa for dinner before her sister would become wise to her actions. With no plan, she eventually picked up a packet of chicken breasts, some yoghurts, three bananas, a pack of bottled water and a large four-pint carton of milk. Her hand lifted to her lip. Little had she known, just two days ago, how her life was about to change – after all, how could she have predicted that she'd be attacked while buying milk, that Noah would step back into her life, that Aggie would reveal her life-long secret and that she of all people would contemplate going against all that she believed in and retrieve a body that she had no right to touch. But she didn't feel as though she had a choice; they were only bones, similar to all the bones she'd excavated on so many occasions, and just like the ones in Herculaneum, right? But this was not just a set of bones; this was Aggie's baby. Everything was beyond her control and she had no idea how to think or feel. All she really knew was that whatever else happened, she had to help Aggie.

'Cass, hello, are you with us?' Lisa sat forward in her chair and waved a hand in front of Cassie's eyes.

'Yes, sorry.'

'If you work on the dig, you won't get to see Aggie so often, which means it'll be down to me... and as you can see, I have my hands full.' She turned to Thomas who'd emerged from the tent with his plate in his hands. 'Thank you, darling,' she said as he passed her a partially eaten sandwich, which without thought she pushed into her mouth and chewed as Oliver suddenly appeared too.

'Mummy, I spilled my juice,' he said in his smallest voice. 'But don't worry.' He held up her best pink snuggle blanket. 'I wiped it all up with this,' he proudly announced.

Cassie stifled a laugh as Lisa jumped up and grabbed at the blanket. 'Do you see what I mean? You need eyes up your arse. They're always up to something.' She stamped into the kitchen, pulled open the door of the washing machine and threw the blanket in. 'Come on, boys, get your welly boots on. Let's have you playing outside for a while like proper campers.' She began pulling wellington boots from a cupboard and throwing them across the kitchen floor. 'Please, come on, out and play, go make mud cakes for tea or something.'

'Look, I hope you don't mind, but I kind of said that Becks could come over next week for a girly night, said the boys could come too, if it was okay with you?'

Lisa stared at the floor. 'That'd be great. Thanks, hun.' She pulled a soap tablet from a pack, threw it into the washer and turned the dials. 'I'm tired, Cass. It's like Groundhog Day. Every day I get up, I get them dressed, I look after them, feed them and before I know it, it's time to put them to bed and the struggle to get them to sleep begins.'

'Does Marcus help?'

Lisa nodded. 'Of course he does, he's their father and a good father at that. I couldn't wish for better. But he works long hours and by the time he gets home, he's knackered. Some nights he just sits down and falls asleep.' She paused, held her hands up and laughed at the boys who ran into the kitchen and pulled the boots onto their feet. 'Oi, coats,' she called as they both headed for the back garden. She pushed the boys' arms into light summer coats, zipped them up and then opened the back door.

Cassie and Lisa stared out of the window. The boys were playing hide and seek. Cassie began to laugh as she saw Thomas hide behind the tree while Oliver searched and searched. And then it was Oliver's turn to hide, he'd obviously thought that Thomas's hiding place had been a good one because he ran to hide behind the very same tree. The game was repeated over and over.

'Cass, I'm pregnant. Again.' Lisa seemed to crumple on the spot. 'What am I going to do with another baby? I hardly have time for a bath now.'

Cassie didn't know whether to jump up and down in excitement or give sympathy. Lisa looked seriously upset and after a few moments Cassie simply walked over to her sister and pulled her into a hug. 'That's... wow... that's great, Lisa. Seriously. It'll be lovely. You'll see.' She stepped back slightly and looked into Lisa's eyes. 'Does Marcus know?'

Lisa shook her head. 'No one knows, not yet. Except for you.'

'Well, then I really should take the kids to mine one night.' Lisa pulled away, walked to the doorway and leaned against the frame while Cassie really looked at her sister for the first time in years. It was the same Lisa, the same young girl that she'd roomed with, fought with, loved and hated with every other breath. The same girl who at sixteen had come home pregnant, who Aggie had looked after without question. And now, here she was pregnant, and feeling all alone again. Cassie reached out and put a hand on Lisa's shoulder. 'It'll be okay. You'll see.' She paused, turned to the sink and began to wash the cups. 'But you do need to talk to Marcus. Don't you?'

'Mummy, these are for you.' Oliver ran towards Lisa with a handful of twigs. 'They're a present.' He smiled, the sweetest smile in the world as he passed her his precious find.

'Thank you, darling.' Taking the twigs she reached into the kitchen, grabbed at a piece of kitchen roll and wrapped them up. 'Later, he'll ask if I saved them and if I love them... and when he does, I'll have to produce them.' She smiled and dropped the parcel onto the kitchen worktop. 'I'll put them in the bin when he goes to sleep, because by tomorrow he'll have forgotten all about them and he'll set to work collecting new twigs. Because that's how it works.'

A flash of light filled the room, just as the sound of thunder boomed in the sky. Heavy rain suddenly began to fall, and the boys squealed with excitement. Leaping over the step, they ran into the kitchen, threw off their coats, kicked off their wellingtons and headed straight for the living room, where they both dived back into the tent. 'Quick, hide,' one shouted. 'Under there!' screamed the other.

Cassie slammed the back door shut and laughed as she followed the boys back into the living room, where she could hear them hiding under Lisa's precious cushions. The cushions that were normally all in place, all perfectly lined up along the settee and yet today, for the first time in history, they were all thrown on the floor and, unusually, Lisa didn't seem to care.

There was another flash of lightning and as quickly as the twins had hidden, they both emerged. Oliver ran to Lisa and squashed himself so close to her side that he looked almost attached, but Thomas simply ran to the window and stared at the weather. He then mischievously poked Becky in the ribs.

'Bang,' he shouted. 'Tell it, Becks, tell it to bang.' He dived out of the way as Becky grabbed at him, poked him and began tickling. 'Ahhh, get off me, Mammy, tell her.'

'Becks, leave him,' Lisa said as he wriggled out of the hold.

'But Mum, he did it first,' Becky protested, before once again shrinking into the chair with her mobile phone pushed firmly in front of her face.

'And you're eleven, not three, for God's sake,' Lisa chided back. She then screwed up her face, dropped her shoulders, sighed and seemed to rethink the words. 'Sorry, Becks.' There was a moment's silence, but then Becky looked up and gave a small smile in acceptance of the apology.

Thomas had now moved himself across the room. He sat on Cassie's knee where playfully he pulled at her hair, squashed her face between his hands and planted sloppy kisses on her chin. Cassie laughed at the irony. They'd been so identical at birth. Every cry, every meal and every nappy change had been done in unison. But now their personalities had changed, and they couldn't have been more different. She looked from one twin to the other and even though they were beautiful and full of fun, for Lisa's sake she hoped that there wouldn't be a repeat of twins.

The lightning once again flashed and lit up the room, the thunder crashed, and Thomas buried his face in her jumper. 'Ohhh, was that loud, Thomas?'

She felt him wriggle. His arms wrapped themselves tightly around her and he hid his face much further into her jumper. Looking down to see what he was doing, she felt him nod and giggle. 'Aunty Cassie, it's really dark in your jumper, isn't it?' he said as he unburied his face and looked up with a cheeky grin.

Cassie thought of how funny he sounded and of how innocent his words were. 'You're right, Thomas. It is dark in there, isn't it?' She ruffled his hair and watched as he jumped down from her knee and headed back inside his tent, where Cassie could hear him chatting away to the crowd of teddy bears.

Lisa released her hold on Oliver. 'There you go, baby. The lightning's all gone now.' She fussed with his hair, kissed his cheek and then gave him one last squeeze in a protective, motherly way.

Cassie thought of how caring she was of her children, of how all mothers seemed to do this naturally; how after the moment their babies are born, nothing else seemed to matter.

'Is it really awful, you know... giving birth?' Cassie suddenly asked as she continued to watch the interaction between mother and child.

'It's hard, the hardest thing in the world. You feel as though the whole of your insides are bursting out. But somehow—' Lisa began.

'Oh, Mum.' A look of horror crossed Becky's face. 'Do you have to talk about this?' She slinked further back into the chair and with her phone still in her hand, she pulled a cushion up and in front of her face.

Lisa leaned across to where Becky sat and moved a strand of hair from her daughter's face. 'Giving birth is beautiful.' Becky rolled her eyes, shrugged the touch off, stood up and walked through the door and towards the stairs.

'I don't want to know. I'll be in my room,' she said as she padded up the stairs. 'Let me know when you're talking about something that isn't as blah,' she shouted as a door was opened and then promptly slammed.

Lisa stared into the corner of the room with wistful eyes. 'No, Cass. It isn't awful. You have no idea how magical it feels when you hold your baby for the very first time,' she paused and kissed Oliver's head. 'That moment when they give out their first cry and then, in a split second, you know that for the rest of their lives you'll do absolutely everything you can to protect them and keep them safe.'

Cassie bit down on her sore lip. She wanted to sob. She wanted to tell Lisa what Aggie had gone through and how for her it had all been so very different. She hadn't had that beautiful moment. She hadn't heard that first cry and she'd spent the past fifty-five years aching for what she could have had and what should have been. Even though the catacombs had had the boreholes, and Aggie had had a torch, the torch had died, just like her baby, and it would have been dark, gloomy, cold and damp. Locals had often said there was a smell of fungus that had grown up the walls and Cassie thought of how terrified Aggie would have been to crawl through those partially filled tunnels, all alone and then back again after giving birth, with no choice but to leave her dead baby behind.

Lisa frowned. 'Cass, why did you ask about birth?' Lisa tipped her head to one side as Oliver jumped down from her knee and ran across the room to look out of the window. 'Cass, you're not pregnant, are you?' she blurted out as Oliver saw another distant flash of lightning and squealed.

Cassie shook her head. 'Oh no, God no. Don't be daft,' she said as she held her arms out, allowing Oliver to jump up and onto her knee. 'You have to, you know, before that can happen and my life on that front is pretty non-existent.'

Lisa stared at her son. 'They never fail to amaze me. You can buy them all the toys they could ever want, Cass, but today nothing is more important to them than collecting twigs in the back garden or putting up a tent in the lounge. It doesn't take much to make them happy and their lives complete.' She paused. 'So, why do I feel like it's the hardest job in the world?'

Cassie thought back to when she had been happy and her life complete, just a few days ago, in Herculaneum with her skeletons. She wished with all her heart that she could turn back time but, like it or not, she couldn't. She had to stay, she had to persuade Noah to let her work on the dig and she had to make sure that she got to the Elephant and Mahout before anyone else did. Even if that meant finding another way in... hadn't Aggie mentioned another tunnel? An entrance in the graveyard?

7

Noah sat alone in one corner of the crowded bar. He'd gone straight to the pub after work, made his way up to his room on the first floor, showered, changed and then, as he did most nights, he'd gone down to the bar to eat.

But tonight, things felt different. Tonight, he didn't feel hungry at all. His steak pie was barely touched, and he'd moved what was left of it around his plate repeatedly until the gravy had congealed. The spell of continually moving food was broken by the ping of his phone and a message jumped up and onto his screen.

Hi babe. That red dress you bought me last week really needs the matching shoes and they're in the sale. Any chance, it is my birthday soon? x

Sighing at the second request that week, Noah responded.

Sure. £100 enough? X PS: Don't you already have red shoes?

He clicked on the banking app and with a swipe of his finger he reluctantly transferred money from his account to hers. Heaving a sigh, his mind went from Erin to Cassie and back again. The two couldn't be more different. For a start, Erin was tall, blonde, demanding and just a little over confident. Whereas Cassie, well, she was just Cassie. She was around a foot shorter than he was which meant that his arm rested on her shoulder at just the right height. She laughed easily and had dark, glossy hair that glowed. Her eyes sparkled in the sun and she had cute, pixie-type features that lit up with the biggest, most radiant smile every single time she saw him. Shaking his head, he took a slurp of his pint, feeling odd that he could easily describe Cassie in so much more detail than he could his current girlfriend.

The phone pinged again.

Darling, £100, really? You know I like designer things. The cheapest Louis Vuitton are at least £650 these days ;-)

Noah threw the phone down on the table. Her demands were unreasonable, and he picked the phone back up to tell her so, but thought better of it and glanced at his watch.

Cassie was late and he wondered if it were possible that she'd ever worn Louis Vuitton, ever even tried them on or dressed to impress like Erin did.

He laughed at the thought, knowing that Cassie would always be more comfortable in a pair of jeans, T-shirt and boots or flip-flops. She'd answered the door wrapped in a towel, covered in soapsuds and hadn't cared who saw. Au naturel. What you saw was what you got.

All in all, Cassie was comfortable in her own skin; she didn't need props to prove anything, not to anyone. Saying that, he'd also thought her to be the kind of person to keep her word and had been so sure that if he'd delivered the buckets of hot water to her door Cassie would have kept her end of the deal and turn up. If only to do the pub quiz. But now, it was almost 6.45 p.m. and he concluded that she might not turn up at all.

Had he gone about it all the wrong way? Had he blackmailed her into coming out, rather than asking? Seeing her had been such a shock that he hadn't known what to say or do. There had been just a few seconds when she'd first opened the door, a moment between him seeing a partially naked woman standing there, to realising that it was Cassie. His Cassie. He'd felt his whole stomach lurch, his mind had spun somersaults and he'd had no idea where to look or what to say.

His initial thought had been to hug her, invite himself in for coffee and chat with her for hours, just as they used to do. But the fact that she'd been stood before him wrapped only in a bath towel, had caused his temperature to rise, his heart had begun to pound and for the first time that day he was more than happy that he'd had the clipboard in his hands. Having something to hold in front of him had been very much needed, as his instant arousal would have been more than obvious without it. He'd tried to stay calm, tried to act normally, and had tried to control his breathing while doing his best to remember 'the offside rule...' He was sure that someone had once told him that it would work with his predicament. The reality was that there was nothing in the world that would have taken his mind off a naked Cassie, not even the thought of his favourite team. The sight of her had brought back every emotion he'd previously had, and memories of their time together had flooded his mind. Cassie had been his study buddy, his best friend at uni. They'd been in the same classes, had the same lecturers, the same coursework, and studying together had been the perfect solution. But being a friend hadn't been enough. He'd wanted her to be so much more. But he'd been young, stupid and naïve. He'd handled the situation all wrong and had been far too afraid that making a move would ruin their friendship.

Picking up his drink, he took a sip and allowed his eyes to search the crowd, looking for Cassie. He'd missed her. He'd missed everything about her but now, now he felt guilty. He was no longer the young and naïve student, he was a grown man, he was in a long-distance relationship and, as far as he knew, Erin loved him. He pondered the idea and came to the conclusion that Erin might love him, but what she definitely did love was his money.

Which begged the question, why had he bribed another woman into coming to the quiz? Draining the last of his pint, he dropped the glass heavily on the table.

'Because Cassie isn't just another woman. That's why.' He threw his head backwards until it rested against the wall. Everyone had thought them a couple, everyone except the two of them. He'd lost count of the times he'd been just about to kiss her, or just about to tell her how he felt, but something had always stopped him. After all, she'd always be there, there would always be a better day, a better opportunity, or a more appropriate time and place. A perfect moment.

How wrong could he have been?

Cassie had stopped calling. She'd stopped inviting him round. The days turned into weeks and the weeks turned into months. In the end, they barely saw one another at all, but for a wave across the lecture hall or quick hello in the library. Eventually they'd both left university without giving the other a second thought, without promising to keep in touch and as one phone had been exchanged for another, her number had been lost. He kicked out in anger at the table leg and watched as his glass wobbled on the beer mat. He felt angry. Annoyed. He knew that everything should have and could have been different.

'Why didn't you look her up, she'd have been on social media? Someone would have known where to find her,' he inwardly cursed himself, ran his hand through his dark overgrown hair and took in a deep breath as his plate, still full of food was pushed away.

'You finished?' the waitress asked as she walked by. 'Something wrong with the pie tonight, Noah?' She picked up the plate, smiled. 'You normally like the pie?'

Noah shook his head, stood up and walked towards the bar. 'It was fine. I'm not that hungry. But,' he passed his glass to the barmaid, 'I'll have another beer, please.' He didn't normally drink during the week, but tonight he needed something to calm his mood.

'Course you can, my darling. Are you staying for the pub quiz?' The barmaid looked him up and down, pouted her lips and gave him the eye. 'Cos if you are, I finish at eleven if you fancy taking me out for a drink?' The words were more of a statement than a question, but Noah knew for a fact that if he had any sense, he'd make his way up to his room way before she finished work.

'Thanks, but I'm waiting for someone, although it looks like she isn't coming,' he replied and took a long refreshing slurp from his pint.

'Who isn't coming?' Cassie asked as she suddenly appeared next to him, her face lit up with a smile as her hand rested on his shoulder and she reached up to kiss him on the cheek. 'Fantastic, is that a pint of Stella.' She took the drink from his hand, placed it to her lips and drank from it with a cheeky smile. 'Cheers, hun.'

Noah laughed. 'Nothing changes, does it? After all these years, you're still stealing my pint.' He could feel the heat rise up within him, prayed that it didn't reach his cheeks and turned back to the bar, trying to gain his composure and stop himself from grinning like a Cheshire cat. 'I'll be needing another pint, please?' he said to the barmaid. 'Someone seems to have stolen mine.' He raised his eyebrows, and watched Cassie slurp the pint. It was something Erin would never do; her choice of drink tended to fall into the sparkling variety. In fact, it suddenly occurred to him that everything Erin did was done for effect. It wasn't always good, nor was it appealing.

'Another pint, coming up.' The barmaid poured the drink, scowled as she noticed Cassie and placed the drink on the bar.

'So, where is everyone?' Cassie asked as Noah led her back to the table he had just vacated. She threw her bag on the back of a chair, flicked her long dark hair out of her face and sat down. 'I thought you said you'd be here with the lads?' She smiled and picked up the drink. 'Haven't stood you up, have they?' she joked.

Noah didn't answer. His eyes were fixed on her face, on the bruising that was now masked by a thin layer of make-up. He wanted to ask her what had happened, what she was doing back in Doncaster and why she'd left the Herculaneum dig halfway through a contract? He had so many questions, especially the ones that wanted to know why they'd grown apart. He needed to put things right... no... he wanted to put things right. He just didn't know how or where to start. The only thing he really did know was that he still had an overpowering urge to kiss Cassie.

'So, what's the plan if they don't come?' she asked in a matter-of-fact tone as she sat back in the chair and laughed. ''Cos looking at this lot,' she pointed to the crowd that had gathered by the bar, 'we'll need more than just the two of us to win. More brains equal more power, isn't that what you used to say?'

Noah laughed. 'Don't worry, we don't need a plan. They'll be here. They're probably still upstairs getting showered and all that.' He paused and pointed at the ceiling. 'Some of the team, including me, we stay here.' Once again, he studied the bruising that went up one side of her face and stretched from her jawline to her cheekbone. Whoever had done this had really hurt her and he could feel the temper within him boil and he shook as he spoke. 'Cass, I know I asked you earlier and you dodged the question... but your face? What the hell happened?'

He watched as she swallowed and then held her breath. 'It was a guy. He worked on the same dig as me in Italy. He was a bit creepy, watched me all the time and made a move on me down a deserted alley. Made out that he'd liked me and said that I couldn't blame him for having a go.' She was rambling, and her hand lifted to her face. She looked down at the floor. 'I struggled, pushed him away and... well, he lashed out and my face kind of bounced against the wall.'

Noah could see the tears fill her eyes.

'I didn't ask for him to kiss me.' She paused and exhaled. 'I didn't expect it. I didn't want it. He just... well... he just presumed he could... and what made it worse, I was in the maze of alleys that surrounded my flat. All the alleys look the same and I'd taken one turning too many. I was a bit disorientated, unsure of which way to run... and... well...'

'He scared you, didn't he?' Noah asked as he placed his beer back down on the table, his fingers carefully lifted to her face and he traced the line of bruising that ran along her jaw.

Cassie paused and took in a deep breath. 'It made me realise how far away from home I was and that just about anything could have happened to me and when I needed it the most, there was no one to help me.'

Noah watched her as she looked around the pub, at all the people that stood around, her eyes filling with tears.

'I could kill him.' His hand slammed down on the table

beside them both. 'No man should force himself on a woman, not ever.' He began to think of her words, that the man had thought she liked him, thought she'd wanted him to kiss her and, as it turned out, she hadn't. And here he was, wishing his life was different, thinking of telling her how much he'd liked her and wanted to kiss her. Which meant that now, no matter how much he wanted to, he couldn't. Not unless Cassie wanted him to. If he did, he'd be no better than the guy who'd hurt her.

'Hey there, boss?' A tall, broad man of over six feet tall walked up and took a seat at the table, his huge frame dwarfing the chair. 'Not disturbing anything, am I?' He dropped his glass down on the table with a thud, pulled up a second chair and put his feet up on it. 'You ready for the quiz?'

'Cassie, this is Kyle. Kyle, Cassie... Cassie is an archaeologist friend of mine from uni, a bloody good one too. So, you might want to watch your back, or I might just give her your job.' He laughed in an attempt to lighten the atmosphere, but then watched as both Cassie and Kyle exchanged pleasantries, shook hands and began chatting as though they'd known each other for years.

Noah emptied his glass and stood back up. 'Anyone want another drink?' he asked as both nodded but carried on with their conversation as he went to the bar. They were chatting about recent digs, of skeletons, of finds and favourite tools. Noah watched Cassie as she laughed and smiled in all the right places, how she flicked her long dark hair back and out of her face, how she stared into Kyle's eyes, listening intently to his every word with a radiance that glowed and he mentally kicked himself. Maybe the truth was that Cassie Hunt would never have been interested in him romantically, maybe the friendzone had been the right place to be. He nodded. 'Well, I can be a friend, that I can,' he thought and gulped at the same time, knowing deep inside how difficult that would be.

'Here you go.' He placed the glasses on the table and then stepped to one side as a burly looking man approached the table. 'Hi, Joe. I didn't know you were coming. You want a drink?' he asked as the man stopped in his tracks, stared at Cassie, and then nodded.

'Sure. Just Coke.' His voice was more of a grunt than words. He shuffled on the spot and looked at his watch. 'Thought I'd have a quick one. I'm working in just under an hour.' He seemed to study the table. 'So, we have a visitor...?' He tipped his head to one side as he directed the question at Cassie. 'I'm Joe.' He held a hand out and shook hers. But Noah noticed how Cassie had moved her chair backwards before visibly taking in a deep breath. She glanced between Kyle and Noah, looking for support.

'Joe's the night security on site,' Noah said, placing Joe's drink on the table. 'Knows more about the tunnels than most of us do.' He sat back down and motioned for Joe to do so too. 'And Cassie, she's an archaeologist, best in her field.'

Joe acknowledged her, grunted once again and began muttering under his breath. 'A dig is no place for a woman, you mark my words. Women bring trouble they do.' His words were harsh, unwarranted and uncalled for and Noah noticed how he turned his chair away and arrogantly sipped at his drink.

Cassie caught Noah's eye. She gave him a nervous, hesitant smile. It was the kind of smile she used to give him at uni, the one that said, 'Let's go, the party's over.' And Noah knew that for Cassie's sake he needed to take the hint.

'Cass, you got a minute?' He raised an eyebrow. 'We've just about got time to pop up and get that book you wanted to borrow.' He hoped she'd take the hint and realise he was giving her an out.

Cassie looked relieved.

'Hey, boss, that was the smoothest "come to my room" I've ever heard, best not to let Erin hear you say that,' Kyle chipped in, laughing loudly.

Cassie froze, her whole body went rigid and Noah noticed how for a few seconds she stared at a beer mat. Not moving any part of her, not even her eyes.

'I'll keep hold of your beer, shall I?' Kyle continued with a smile and pulled the two pints of beer towards him. 'If you're not back when the quiz starts, they're mine, right?'

Cassie gave a mock smile and slapped Kyle on the top of the arm. 'Hey, cheeky, we'll be back in a minute. And don't you dare drink my pint, no one gets away with doing that. Not even you.'

8

'You okay?' Noah asked, his eyes full of concern as Cassie walked up the staircase behind him, taking in great gulps of air and holding onto the banister for support.

'That Joe. Who is he?' She hadn't liked the way he'd glared, the way he'd hovered, grunted and stared at her for just a little too long. 'He seems really familiar, but I don't know why.'

'Joe's alright. He's security, works in the Portakabin at night, watches the site, the cameras and makes sure no one breaks in, falls down the shaft or takes off with the plant hire. Why?'

Cassie shrugged, sighed and pulled a face. 'I don't know. He just gave me the creeps and I feel as though I've seen him somewhere before. But...'

'You've probably seen him about, he used to work on security at the shopping centre and I'm sure he lives around here, so he does.'

Cassie took Noah's explanation on board. So many people lived in or around the flats that it would be easy to acknowledge someone for years without really knowing them. 'Yeah, maybe that's where I've seen him. Doesn't like women much though, does he?'

Noah laughed. 'Nope, he thinks that women are bad news, especially on site.'

'I guess he thinks we should all be at home, rocking a baby, does he?'

Noah shrugged, walked across the corridor and stood in front of a white wooden door. The number seven hung upside down, swivelling on a single pin nail. He moved the number the right way round and then began to laugh as it immediately dropped the moment his finger moved.

Tipping her head to one side Cassie reached her hand up to playfully ruffle his beard. 'So, what's this all about? How long have you had it?'

Noah laughed. 'Well, it keeps out the cold, razors are expensive and, if I'm honest, I've kind of gotten attached to it.' His own hand went up to the beard. He rubbed it affectionately and then puckered his lips. 'Everyone seems to like it.' A broad smile lit up his face and Cassie felt herself blush.

'Look, before we go in there, my room's a bit of a mess. I wasn't planning on inviting anyone up here, but I saw that look on your face and, well... this was all I could think to do.' He turned the key in the door and pushed it open.

Cassie laughed. 'You know me so well.' She stepped past him and automatically began picking his clothes up off the floor, as she'd done so many times in the past. 'So you still haven't learned what a wardrobe is for, have you?' She folded the items and placed them in a pile on the bed. She then turned around on the spot before walking across the room. 'This... you see this piece of furniture.' She pointed to the small wardrobe that was fitted into one corner. 'This, my friend, is a wardrobe.'

'Okay, okay, you've made your point.' Noah picked up the

clothes, opened the wardrobe door and dropped them inside. 'There you go, they're in the wardrobe.' His Irish tone was music to her ears. His eyes sparkled in the artificial light and Cassie purposely took slow deliberate breaths. He was far too good-looking, and far too cheeky.

'Now then, a book...' Noah stood before a bookshelf, searching.

'What?' Cassie was confused. 'What book?'

'Well, we came up here on the pretence that you wanted to borrow a book, so I thought it'd be a good idea if you at least went down with one in your hand.'

Catching on, Cassie suddenly realised what he meant, dropped her bag on the floor and sat on the bed. 'Okay, I guess that'd make sense.' Her eyes scanned his bookshelf and took in the framed photograph of a woman. She had long, blonde hair and was wearing a bright yellow dress, a fedora hat and sunglasses that would have stopped an eclipse. Taking in a deep breath Cassie struggled with what to say. 'Wow, you... you still read a lot.'

'Of course I do. We have a pub quiz once a week. Most other nights I'm up here, all alone and there's only so much rubbish on the telly you can watch.' He began running a finger along the books. 'Besides, you know I prefer to read.'

'I do.' She laughed. 'So which book do you think I should borrow? I could always give it you back tomorrow.'

His eyes lit up. 'Tomorrow? So, I'll be seeing you tomorrow, will I?'

Cassie laughed nervously. 'Well, I thought I might make an official visit to the site, and...' She paused and looked at the floor. 'Well, I was going to ask you for a job. That's if you have anything going?'

Noah sat on the bed beside her. 'Cass, you know I'd love to

give you a job. But,' he sighed, 'budgets, they're a bit tight.' He handed her a book. 'Here, try this. It's all about the Sand House,' he continued, 'written by one of the house's descendants, Richard Bell.'

Cassie felt her heart sink and she closed her eyes, trying to think. How many times had she heard that, especially on digs. But 'a tight budget' wasn't going to get her into that shaft. She had to go through the tunnels, she had to get to the Elephant and Mahout, and she had to get there before anyone else did.

'Having someone with your experience down there would be amazing. Honestly. I just...' She heard the words that Noah was saying, while her mind whirled. She had to find a way; she had to be part of the dig.

'What if... what if I donate my services for free.' She paused, opened her eyes and stared into his. His deep brown eyes seemed to penetrate her very soul. She'd forgotten how mesmerising they were and how handsome Noah was, even with the beard. 'I have to be here, my aunt is sick, and, you know me, I can't just sit at home worrying about her. It'd drive me insane. Besides...' She had a trump card and, girlfriend or not, she knew she had to use it. 'It'd be good to spend some time with you. You know, catch up on old times, I've missed you. You were once my best friend and I haven't seen you in forever.' She watched him, waiting for a response.

Every emotion seemed to pass across Noah's face. He seemed to be struggling with the decision as he pushed his hands through his overgrown hair.

'Come on, Noah... you can't say no, not to me, can you?' Closing her eyes she prayed that using the trump card had been the right thing to do and it was true, she had missed him. But now, seeing his indecision, she wondered how much he'd missed her and whether or not he'd be happy seeing her again on a daily basis. She tried a new approach. 'Noah. I've grown up with these tunnels. They're literally right outside my back door. I've been immersed in their history since I was eleven years old. They're the whole reason I became an archaeologist and I... well, I just have to be a part of it. Even if I have to work for free and starve in the process.' She gave him a hopeful smile and looked down at the book, her finger tracing the picture of the Elephant and Mahout on the front. 'I just have to see this.' She held the book up.

'Okay, okay. I'll find a way,' he said. 'I'll talk to the powers that be, try and get some extra funding from somewhere, tell them you're an expert in the field and that... well, that we just have to pay you something, even if that's just some kind of expenses.' He raised an eyebrow. 'How does that sound?'

Cassie smirked and bounced up and down. 'Sounds great, besides expenses would be small, wouldn't they? It's not like they'd have to pay me any mileage or car parking. They don't even have to pay for my digs.' She laughed. 'I could almost fall out of bed and straight down the shaft.' She stared at the book, at the Elephant and Mahout on the front, hardly daring to believe that she'd finally get to see it. It was right there, just nine metres below the pavement, right next to where she lived. 'If only the tunnels had survived,' she said with a sigh, while staring at the picture, knowing that beneath the Elephant and Mahout was an unmarked grave. A grave that only her and her aunt knew about.

Noah stood up and began to scribble on a piece of paper. 'That was a big sigh from such a small person,' he said as he looked down and passed the paper to her. 'My number, in case you have any problems in the morning.' He smiled. The deep, darkness of his eyes sparkled like granite and Cassie could feel herself being dragged into them. To break the tension, she turned to her phone, added his number and sent him hers.

'Do you know you're sat on my best jumper?' His words broke the moment and he pulled at the jumper. But Cassie playfully and without thought grabbed hold and held on tight, pulling Noah forward to land on the bed beside her, where they both lay in a heap, giggling.

'It's so good to see you again, Noah,' she finally said. But then turned and poked him in the ribs. A familiar tickling fest began, and loud shrieks and giggles came from them both until tears of laughter fell down their faces. It was something they'd done so many times in the past. But without warning the laughing stopped and Noah stared into her eyes. She could feel his breathing, deep, slow and laboured.

'I want to kill the man who did this to you.' His fingers went up to her face and she felt a heat beneath them as they traced the line of her jaw. He stared deeply into her eyes and Cassie caught her breath, as she hoped that he was about to kiss her. But Noah jumped up from the bed.

'Come on, the others will wonder what we're up to, especially if they just heard all that giggling.' He held a hand out to her and pulled her towards him. 'Look, about the book. Keep it for a while, especially if you're starting work at the dig tomorrow.' He gave her a smile. 'You know, you might need to do some late-night reading for research.' At that, he opened the bedroom door and the sound of the noisy bar once again filled the room. 'The quiz will be starting in...' he looked at his watch '...three minutes.' He held out a hand, which Cassie took and together they walked down the stairs and back into the busy bar.

Squeezing herself between the queue of men that stood waiting to be served, Cassie recognised one or two women from the estate, said hello and then made her way to the table where Kyle was now surrounded. More of the men from the site had now joined them, and as she and Noah took their seats she watched as Kyle laughed, joked and handed out pieces of paper.

'There you go, Cass. Write down what you think the answer is and why and pass them back to me and I'll fill in the master copy.' He tapped his pen on his piece of paper. 'We tend to go with the majority and we don't shout our answers out as the other teams are cheating bastards and might hear us.'

Cassie laughed. But Kyle's face was more than serious, and she immediately knew that the archaeologists were out to win. 'Are you always this competitive?' she asked as he pushed his hand through his unruly blond hair.

Kyle nodded and gave her a cheeky grin. 'Of course, no point in entering if you don't plan on winning, now is there?' He continued to pass the pencils around the table.

Cassie settled herself into her seat. The whole bar had a buzz about it, the atmosphere felt electric. It was an old spit and sawdust style pub and typically almost everyone seemed to know everyone else. The friendly banter had begun and was now being passed across the pub between different groups.

'How about we just shout out the wrong answers?' Cassie said, making the others laugh. But Kyle just stared. 'Talk like that will get you a beer fine, young lady.' He raised both eyebrows and slapped the back of his hand as though telling her off from a distance.

Another man had joined them. 'Hi, I'm Johnny,' he shouted. 'I'll introduce myself seeing as the boss here seems to have lost his tongue.' Cassie lifted a hand up to give him a wave. She recognised him from earlier that morning. He'd been one of the young men that'd been stood to one side, giggling with two of the other men at the sight of a half-naked woman. It was more than obvious that he hadn't recognised her and seeing as by tomorrow she'd be a work colleague, she didn't feel the need to enlighten him. Two middle-aged men were sat beside Joe, neither of which looked happy. Both held pint glasses in front of their mouths and chatted between themselves in soft but growling whispers, while all the time their eyes darted around the table, often staring at Cassie, making her feel uneasy and she wondered what they were talking about.

'Right, I'll be off.' Joe stood up, his chair scraping across the floor. 'Work calls.' He shook the hand of the man he'd been chatting to and nodded at one or two of the others, while completely ignoring Cassie, before turning and disappearing into the crowd. But Cassie didn't feel insulted, more a sense of relief. She was pleased that he'd left, and she took in a deep breath, just as a man's voice came over the speakers.

'Right, we have twenty questions...' She watched everyone around the table, their faces now serious, their manner determined. Even Noah had pulled a pair of glasses from his pocket, pushed them up his nose and sat with his pencil at the ready. She took a moment to study his face. Had it really been three years since they'd left university? She counted back. Yes, 2015. That's when they'd left. She allowed her thoughts to wander. The few minutes they'd just spent together had brought back so many emotions. The tickling had been something they'd often done, especially as Noah was unbelievably ticklish and all she'd ever had to do was poke a finger within an inch of him to send him flying in the air, and for the giggles to begin. She now looked at his angular jaw, the stubble that grew on his chin, the piercing eyes. Nothing had changed, it was still Noah, but now... now he'd grown up. This was Noah the man that sat beside her... not the boy that she'd known at uni.

'Cassie, Tavares or Bee Gees, we've got six of each answer, we need a deciding vote,' Kyle whispered as he kicked her ankle under the table. 'Come on, are you with us?'

Cassie tried to think back to the song that had just been played. She'd taken in the familiarity without taking much notice of what it had been. She turned to Noah, hoping for some kind of help, but Noah had stood up and was now at the bar, ordering more drinks. She could feel panic rise within her. What if she got it wrong? It was fifty-fifty. Her mind spun around like a food mixer on low speed, she desperately wanted the speed to increase and to get the right answer. Bee Gees... She took a guess, scribbled it on the piece of paper and passed it to Kyle, vowing to pay more attention to the rest of the questions.

9

Cassie stepped out of the lively pub, leaving both Noah and the party behind, along with a whole table of archaeologists who still sat, drinking, laughing and celebrating. The Bee Gees answer had been correct and much to everyone's delight it had gained them a point along with four gallons of beer which they were all now trying to devour between them.

The pub door once again opened. A blast of sound suddenly burst out, but the noise disappeared as soon as it banged behind her. In its place came the sound of traffic, pelican crossings, singing and general joviality that came from somewhere in the distance. 'Everyone's having a party,' she thought. The majority of the noise seemed to be coming from the town centre just across the road and for a moment she stood at the side of the dual carriageway and looked across to where groups of people went in and out of the busy bars that lined St Sepulchre Gate. It surprised her that so many people were out on a Thursday night and she fondly remembered many a night that she too had patrolled the streets, with groups of friends, doing the traditional Doncaster pub crawl, all looking for fun. But now, tonight, she felt sad and alone. Sad that she had to go back to an empty house and alone because she now wished that she hadn't refused Noah's offer to walk her home.

'Why, why did you do that?' she berated herself, kicked out at the railings and then yelped. 'Ouch. That was stupid.' She crouched down to rub her foot but while doing so, she glanced back at the pub and the bedroom window behind which Noah was staying. His light flashed on and his curtains swished to a close, which meant that even though the others were still downstairs having fun, he'd gone up to bed just as soon as she'd left and for a moment she thought about going back in, going up to the room and asking him to walk her home, just as he'd wanted to. But something stopped her.

The pub door once again swung open and Cassie clearly heard one of the men shouting across the room, 'Bee Gees, who'd have thought we'd win a pub quiz with a bloody Bee Gees question.' The statement made her smile, as had the look on both Noah and Kyle's face, and she whispered a silent prayer in thanks that she'd guessed the answer correctly.

'You can come again,' Kyle had said to her, while slurping his beer. 'First time we've won in ages, so you... you must have been our lucky charm.' He'd patted her on the back and while everyone was chatting and drinking, she'd reluctantly kissed Noah on the cheek and made her way to the exit.

'What are you going so early for?' Johnny had asked. 'Surely you've got time for another one?' He pushed the beer card towards her. 'You did contribute.'

But Cassie shook her head. 'Can't, I'm afraid. I've got to be up early tomorrow. Work, you know how it is, and it's a new job. Besides, I've heard the boss is a bit of an ogre.' She winked at Noah making Johnny and Kyle look between them both. It took a few seconds for the penny to drop, but the moment it did, they both jumped up to give her a hug.

'Welcome to the team,' Kyle had said, his words genuine as a huge grin crossed his face. 'Be nice to have a woman around the place, you might keep this messy lot under control.' He indicated the younger boys. 'They need someone to sort them out and none of them ever listen to me.'

'Hey, I'm not their mother. I'm an archaeologist, a good one and I'm planning on getting down that hole and bringing the past to life.' She'd stood up straight, proud of what she'd done with her life, proud of her achievements and she just knew how happy Aggie would be, once she heard that she'd landed the job. Which reminded her. She'd have to let Lisa know too and ask her to take on the afternoon visits to Aggie in her place but swear her to secrecy. Not only did she want to see the look on Aggie's face when she told her about the job, she wanted to see the relief in her eyes when she realised that her baby would be coming home, that Cassie would do what she'd asked and that the past would finally be laid to rest.

She'd enjoyed her night, and, what's more, she'd loved spending time with Noah again. But, as of tomorrow, the dynamics would be different. He'd become her boss, which made everything just a little bit more difficult. The last thing she ever wanted to do was lie to him or deceive him, which meant that from now on she had to keep a low profile. Just get on with her work and say as little as possible to the rest of the group. After all, none of them could know her real agenda, especially Noah. She couldn't allow him to become involved. It was bad enough that she'd be risking her own reputation, without risking his too.

Cassie began to walk along the street and past the shops but stopped to pull at her boots. Not only was her toe now sore, but also her feet were hurting. They were still not used to being confined and they were currently screaming at being restricted within the leather. Sighing, she continued to walk, but noticed that the street lights had begun to flicker. It gave an eerie feel to the road and she pulled her jacket more tightly around her. Hesitating, she looked back at the pub. It was all in darkness, including Noah's bedroom.

'At least the street lights are still on,' she whispered as they gave a final flicker and went out. 'Oh great,' she growled at the lights, but then stood, frozen to the spot, not daring to move forward or to run back. Feeling her heart beat wildly in her chest, Cassie knew she had to make a decision. Which way would she go? Inching along the pavement she made her way past the deserted car park. It was a road she knew well, although in the darkness it looked more eerie, different, and shadows appeared where she'd never previously noticed them. She felt alone, and more than a little vulnerable. Unlike the alleys in Italy, no one lived along this street. Other than a bridge that went across the train lines, it was full of shops, some were thriving businesses, others had long since been boarded up and the rest looked like they should have been.

The sound of footsteps on tarmac came from behind her. She spun around, turning to the left and then to the right, staring blindly into the darkness. She stood with her back to the wall, not daring to move, while waiting for the noise to happen again.

Holding her breath, she bit down on her lip, winced with pain and only allowed herself to breathe as and when she had to. Still she waited, watched and tried to focus. The shadows all began to blend into one. She was sure she could see someone. The tall, broad, shape of a man.

'Is someone there?' she shouted all the time pulling at her bag. She rummaged inside, pulled out her mobile and flicked the screen, using the torch to light up the way ahead. But the noise had stopped, the shape had disappeared and then she heard the scurry of a cat that suddenly burst out from behind a wall and sped across her path, making her jump.

Grabbing hold of the railings, Cassie began to laugh nervously. But still she waited and stared at the darkness. 'Not far now,' she whispered, before turning and trying to judge how many minutes it would take her to run home if she had to. She knew she'd have to go past the construction site, past Joe in the Portakabin and for a split second she wondered if Joe was friend or foe. Should she go to him? Would he help her if she needed him? Surely he would.

Increasing her pace, she headed towards the dual carriageway, and to where car headlights travelled past at speed. At least here she felt a little safer. A little more visible. Plus, she could see the subway that led under the road. But the thought of the subway troubled her and once again she stopped abruptly.

'Subway or road? Subway or road?' she questioned herself. The thought of going down into the darkness didn't appeal to her. She didn't like the subway on the best of days. But if someone was following her it would be the perfect place to attack and for a moment she wondered when she had started to think in this way. She could never before remember having worried about being attacked, robbed or jumped on, especially not here, not in her home town. She pondered the thought as she made for the road. 'Best to be safe...' She stood to the side of the dual carriageway and looked at the barrier along on the central reservation, knowing that she'd have to jump over it. But right now, even that felt preferable to going through the subway. 'Bet you're glad you wore jeans now, aren't you?' she asked herself as she mentally prepared to leap over the barrier, while hoping she'd keep her dignity and not end up flat on her face on the tarmac at the other side.

Decision made, Cassie ran between the cars, threw her bag over the barrier and jumped. A sense of relief crossed her mind as she landed perfectly and, once again, she dodged the cars that travelled along the other side of the road.

Safely on the pavement, she could easily make out the high-rise flats that rose up before her, and the construction fencing that surrounded her street. Leaving the footpath, she went between the houses. Joe's Portakabin came into view, standing in darkness. Not even Joe's torch could be seen and she carefully made her way towards it, just as the lights came on. Showing it to be empty.

Nervously, Cassie turned and looked over her shoulder, searching the darkness. She was sure she'd heard footsteps; and was sure that someone was still walking behind her. 'Joe... Joe... is that you?' she shouted into the darkness. She looked again at the Portakabin, wondering where Joe had gone? Noah had mentioned that he walked the site each evening but right now, she couldn't see him at all, nor could she see his torch and her caring instinct took over. What if he'd had an accident? What if he was lying on the floor, waiting for help? Quickly walking across the road, she glanced through the Portakabin window. But the room was empty, just as she'd thought.

Turning, she stopped in her tracks as Aggie's terraced house came into view; the back gate was open. A light was on in the kitchen and smoke bellowed out of the chimney.

'The fire... I... I didn't light the fire,' she whispered to herself as she began to move slowly, taking one step after the other. Her eyes were constantly fixed on the back window as she rummaged in her bag. She pulled out her mobile phone but wasn't sure what to do or who to call. Did she phone the police, Lisa or Noah? She thought through the options.

'Who would light a fire?' Her whole body trembled with

uncertainty and she began thinking back over her movements. During the hour she'd had in the house before going to the pub, she'd had a proper shower and washed her hair. She had moved her suitcase and as she'd felt the weight it had occurred to her that her hand tools were still packed and still dirty. Leaving Italy in a hurry, hadn't left her enough time to clean them as thoroughly as she'd have liked, so she'd quickly washed them under the bathroom tap, before placing them back in the bedroom and leaving them out to dry. She couldn't remember spending any time in the living room at all. She'd simply passed through, so why was the fire lit?

Shaking her head, she began to doubt her actions. 'Maybe I'm going crazy. Maybe it was me. Maybe I did light the fire. But the lights...' It had still been daylight when she'd left.

Then a thought crossed her mind, and a huge grin lit up her face. Aggie? Of course. They must have sent Aggie home. She pushed her phone into her pocket and ran as fast as she could. Pulling her key from her bag, she ran through the open gate, into the yard and then stopped as though she'd been nailed to the spot.

The back door was open.

The kitchen had been turned upside down. Every drawer was open, their contents spilled out. She grabbed at the wall and felt her stomach turn as she stared into the lounge. There were so many books littering the floor. Aggie's chair had been turned on its side. The china cabinet doors were wide open, Aggie's ornaments lay smashed to pieces on the floor.

Still holding on, she made her way along the wall and grabbed hold of the door frame. Then, both horror and terror hit her at the same time and she took sharp, rapid breaths, her eyes darting around. She looked through the lounge, towards the front where the staircase stood. A noise. She couldn't move. She listened and held her breath. She had to get out but didn't know which way to run. Front door or back door.

Turning, she made her decision and sped through the kitchen. Her jacket caught on an open drawer. She yanked at the material, lost her footing, stumbled, fell to her knees and stifled a yelp. But as quickly as she'd gone down, she jumped up, grabbed at a chair and for a second, she held onto it, like a lion tamer waiting to be attacked. She waited and listened. But the only sound she could hear was the beating of her own heart and finally she dropped the chair, turned and ran. Launching herself towards the pavement and into the street, Cassie scrambled across the road. Her legs had turned to jelly, and she gripped onto the fence for support while searching the road hoping to see a neighbour or friend. But like in Italy, the street was eerily empty.

'Think. Think quickly. Where to hide?' Her mind spiralled as all the games of hide and seek she'd ever played came back. But one game had outplayed them all and she ran along the ginnel and into a gate hole to cower behind a tall grey wheelie bin. Her whole body shook with fear and she took in deep, measured breaths as she peered out, watching the back of her house, once again waiting for her life to change. She shook her head and gasped at the air. 'Come on... come on... get a grip, it can't happen again, it just can't, can it?'

Who had been in the house? There was nothing much worth stealing but she supposed every one knew that Aggie was in hospital and the house empty. Was someone still in there? Had she really been followed? Nothing made sense.

She waited and listened. But all was quiet. Too quiet. She felt as though she was in a bubble, a single solitary bubble where the world had gone silent. The bubble seemed to spin on its own axis, round and round without direction. She tried to shake off the feeling, tried to decide what to do, just as the bubble burst and the noise around her suddenly boomed in her ears. The world had been set back in motion and everything felt as though it were suddenly coming at her through a loud and out of tune speaker. A man shouted from one balcony to the other, a dog barked, and a baby screamed incessantly, while trains thundered past in the distance.

Pulling her mobile from her pocket. She looked down at it and with shaking fingers she flicked the screen until she saw Noah's name and pressed.

'I'm so sorry... I shouldn't have called, but...' She suddenly didn't know what to say, didn't know what Noah could do; she wasn't his family, or his responsibility. But it was simple. She had no one else. There was no one that could get to her quickly. No one except for Lisa, but she wasn't in the next street, she also had three children to look after and, being pregnant again, she was hardly someone who needed to be stressed out so late in the evening.

'Cass, what's wrong?' Noah asked as she inched forward until her eyes became fixed on the Portakabin. Joe was back. He stood in the doorway, cigarette in hand, staring in her direction.

'Where have you been?' she whispered suspiciously.

'Cass, where has who been?' Noah questioned. 'Cass... are you there?'

'Noah... I'm here,' she said as her whole body shook. 'Why, Noah? Why did they do it... why?' she shrieked.

'Cassie, what's happened? Where are you?'

'Aggie's. I'm at Aggie's. Someone broke in.' Her voice was now less than a whisper. She leaned her head against the wall as the tears began to fall. 'I... I daren't go back in. The place has been ransacked.' A sob left her throat. 'I'm so sorry. I didn't know who else to call.'

10

Cassie turned over, punched the pillow and moved it to a more comfortable position. She then tossed, turned and finally propelled herself into a sitting position to look at the clock. It was just ten minutes since the last time she'd looked and, for the hundredth time, she threw herself back on the mattress where she resigned herself to the fact that no matter how tired she felt, sleep was not going to happen.

Lying back down, she stared at the ceiling. The bed wasn't as comfortable as her own, but with both Noah and Kyle sleeping in the single beds in her room, she'd had no choice but to sleep in Aggie's. It had been a choice between that or sleeping at the pub and instinct had told her that she needed to be home. She'd wanted to be home. While Aggie was in the hospital the house was her responsibility.

'Cass, you awake?' Noah's voice came from the hallway.

She glanced towards the door. 'Yeah, sure. I'm awake.' She pulled the covers over herself and sat up against the pillows. 'You can come in.'

The wooden door creaked, and Cassie watched as Noah

made an attempt to push it open. But as it normally did, it stopped halfway. The numerous dressing gowns that were hung behind it bounced against the wall, almost springing the door backwards, but Noah managed to swerve, just before it knocked both mugs of tea out of his hand. He walked across to the bed, placed one of the mugs on the bedside cabinet, but kept the other for himself.

'Right, I'll drink this and then I'm off to work,' he said, sipping at the tea. 'Kyle has secured the back door and we ate some of your bananas and yoghurt for breakfast.' He gave her an apologetic smile and once again she realised that living on milk, yoghurt and bananas really couldn't go on for too much longer.

Picking up the mug, she glanced across at the digital clock, its luminous numbers shining back at her. Eight o'clock. She was sure the time had altered, that it had been much earlier just a few seconds before and she blinked repeatedly, trying to work out how that had happened.

'Wow, it's later than I thought. Give me a minute. I'll get ready for work.' She threw a leg out of bed. 'With all the excitement last night, I forgot to ask about a start time.' It was supposed to be her first day on the dig, her first chance to see how far they'd excavated the tunnels and she had no intention of missing a minute.

'Hey, take your time.' Noah smiled. 'Things are still all over the place down there and you might want to tidy up before you come into work.'

Cassie closed her eyes and remembered the devastation of the ransacked house; the books, belongings, paperwork and furniture that had been thrown haphazardly around after it had been searched. 'What do you think they were looking for?'

'I dunno. But Kyle and I lifted the chairs, the dresser and the table back into place right after the police had gone, but we didn't really want to touch any of Aggie's personal stuff. So, we just stacked it all on the table.' He gave her another apologetic glance. 'Thought you'd kind of want to deal with all of that yourself.'

She nodded. 'The police said that I have to try and work out if there's anything missing.' She shrugged her shoulders. 'Not sure how I'm supposed to do that as I haven't really lived here that much for the past few years.' She had a puzzled look on her face as she tried to remember those mad few minutes after she'd realised that someone had broken into the house. There had been the call to Noah followed by the wait as she'd crouched in the gate hole. The wait had gone on for what seemed like forever, when in reality it had most probably only been just a few minutes before both Noah and Kyle had bounded around the corner at speed.

'I'm here, I'm here,' Noah had whispered as he'd pulled her to her feet and into his arms, while Kyle had practically vaulted into the house. In and around every room at speed, like a marine on a mission.

'Place is clear,' he'd shouted as he'd launched himself back down the stairs to where Cassie and Noah stood in the doorway. 'Right, the police. Did you call them?' Kyle already had his mobile to his ear. 'I'll do it and then I'll walk across and have a word with Joe. Check the CCTV and all that.' He was so precise, everything was done in order, all bases were covered and at that moment Cassie immediately knew why Noah employed him.

She remembered how she and Noah had walked back into the house and of how they'd stood together staring at the mess and damage. But this time the shock had gone, and anger had replaced it as Cassie told Noah all about her walk home, the street lights and the person she'd thought she'd seen in the darkness. It had been at that moment that her legs had turned to jelly, the shaking had taken over, and Noah had practically caught her in mid-air as the room had spun around her.

'Hey. Come on, sit down. I've got you,' he'd whispered, while pulling her into his arms and for a moment, she'd felt safe, protected and sheltered from the world. Right now, it was a world she hated. So many things seemed to be going wrong and every one of them out of her control. 'No arguments... both me and Kyle, we'll be staying with you tonight. I won't leave you,' Noah had said as his phone had bleeped and he'd released his hold to look at his mobile and read the text. 'That was Kyle, police are on their way.'

It had been around an hour later when the police had arrived. They'd marched from one room to another, looking suspiciously at the mess. 'And how do you think they got in, miss?'

Cassie had felt her shoulders drop as she'd sighed. 'I don't know. There's no sign of a break-in, the back door was open, no locks have been broken, but they lit the fire? Why... why did they do that?' Her eyes had travelled across the floor. 'And this, why did they do this? What were they looking for?' Drawers had been emptied and their contents strewn across the floor, books had been tossed to the ground, some left open as though waiting to be read, amongst them her dad's sketchbook. It lay on its side with his doodles and drawings clear to see, and she picked it up and began flicking through the pages. Every tattoo she ever remembered him doing was in this book. She'd spent hours cuddled up to him as a child watching him draw and design the most intricate of pictures on pieces of paper. But then, once perfected, they were always copied into his book. Some pages had more than one picture; some of the drawings were miniature examples of the actual tattoo, yet others covered more than one page. He'd always ensured that all his designs were in one place; in this small book, as though to have them elsewhere would bring bad luck. Cassie huffed at the irony, knowing that his luck couldn't have got any worse on the day that he was stabbed. But then, as she turned a page, she gasped. A page was missing, torn out and Cassie knew that her perfectionist dad would never have done this. Not to this book.

'This... this page, it's been torn out, hasn't it?'

The policeman raised an eyebrow. 'Maybe you could tell us, miss?' He smirked, pressed his lips together in a mock smile and turned to his colleague. 'Hey. Looks like we've found what's missing. Someone tore a page out of an old notebook.' His words were said in a sarcastic and matter-of-fact way, giving Cassie the impression that he wasn't taking her seriously.

But then again, why would he? Even she knew that criminals didn't normally let themselves in, make a mess and then light the fire. Why would they do that? Did they suddenly get a conscience and decide to make the place all warm and homely? Stamping out of the room, she headed up the stairs where she stood at her bedroom window and stared out. Someone out there had followed her home from the pub, she was certain of that. Someone wanted to know exactly where she was and what time she'd get home, and had been looking for something beforehand, she just didn't know what.

Whatever the answer, Cassie knew that she couldn't be distracted, she'd made a promise to her beloved aunt and to fulfil it meant getting herself on site and into the tunnels to find the remains.

11

Cassie couldn't help but feel an immense sense of pride as she watched Noah shuffle the polypropylene chair into place. He pushed his hands through his hair and began unzipping his waterproof jacket as he stared down at the site map that covered the whole table before him.

'These are two sets of plans that I've merged so that you can see the position of the dig, the tunnels and the catacombs, as well as showing exactly what's built above,' he said as she studied the map alongside him.

Kyle walked in, a tray in his hand full of Styrofoam cups. 'Here, one of the lads made a drink.'

'Great... coffee, just what I need.' Noah smiled as he took one of the cups and placed it before him on the canteen style table.

Cassie smiled too as she also took one of the drinks that was offered. 'Thanks, Kyle.' She'd quickly worked out that Kyle was one of the good guys. What you saw was what you got and not only had he stayed overnight to look out for her, he'd also got up early and fitted new locks to both the front and the back door.

Even though it was mid-August, the Portakabin was cold. Joe hadn't had the heaters on overnight and Cassie wondered why.

'Here you go, buddy, take a seat.' Noah kicked a chair towards Kyle who pulled it backwards and sat down. His huge frame dwarfed the chair and for a split-second Cassie held her breath to stop herself giggling. The whole scene reminded her of the day she'd gone to Becky's infant school and had had to sit on one of the children's chairs. Not only had the chair been much too small for an adult, but she'd had to jump up quickly before all four legs had buckled beneath her.

Kyle studied her. 'You okay?' he asked, with a genuine look of concern. His hand moved to rest on her shoulder and he gave it a gentle, caring squeeze.

Cassie nodded. 'Yep, I'm fine.' She thought of the night before. 'Just tired. I'm sure you both feel the same. It was around two thirty when we all got to bed, wasn't it?' She gave them both a lacklustre smile. 'Look, I really appreciate what you did for me last night.'

Kyle tipped his head to one side. 'Hey, any friend of Noah's is a friend of mine, if you know what I mean?' He gave her a genuine smile. 'And according to Noah, we're staying at yours tonight too. So, the pizzas are on you.'

Cassie laughed. 'Oh, okay.' She felt relieved. 'But I have to go to the hospital after work. There's no food in the house and I'm sure you'd be happier to eat at the pub.' She didn't want to impose, nor did she expect them to babysit her, but deep down she kind of hoped they'd insist.

'Well, the offer's there. I was kind of looking forward to pizza.' His hand dropped onto the table and Cassie smiled, leaned forward and once again began to carefully study the map. Both Kyle and Noah sat next to each other and Cassie found it amusing how their bodies seemed to move together as one, their heads tipped from one side to the other in unison and their eyes following the course of the tunnel.

'We need to get from here to here; this is where the Elephant and Mahout is situated. Labourers are almost there, but the crawling tunnels need widening if we have any hope of getting the equipment through.' Noah stabbed his finger at the map, to a point where the shaft was and then to an area that he estimated to be around forty feet away, right next to the entrance to the car park that served the seventeen-storey block of flats.

'So, what's this?' Cassie pointed to the circular shape that was central to the tunnels.

'That, that's the "Ceiling Rose"; we're going in just a few metres away from it.' Noah pointed. 'There were eight western windows, the Ceiling Rose is exactly where the fourth window was.' He moved his finger to one side. 'Our shaft is south-west of the Ceiling Rose. This is an area where there were no recorded carvings, it's a good twenty metres away from the Elephant and Mahout.'

'And our objective is?' Whenever a site was dug, there was always a reason why they were there in the first place and Cassie needed to fully understand what that was and what her role would be.

'We need to take a latex moulding of the other carvings while the labourers dig out the tunnel. Once we get to the Elephant and Mahout, we take the most intricate of latex mouldings ever. This is the one they really want and then, and only if it's safe, we take mouldings of these two statues, situated here and here. Of Pat and Biddy.' He pointed to the very first window of the catacombs. 'This is where they stand. Both are of huge archaeological interest.'

Cassie looked to the other side of the map to the north-east of the catacombs. 'What about these two carvings?'

'The Cherub and the Clown... I wish,' said Kyle as he pointed to an area to the north-east of the tunnel. They stood to the opposite side of the tunnel to where the carvings of Pat and Biddy were located. 'History says that both were badly eroded the last time they were seen, so there won't be much left of them now. Therefore, it's probably pointless uncovering them. Shame though, would have been amazing if we could have got moulds of them too.'

Cassie continued to follow the tunnels back and forth with her finger. 'That's one hell of a dig. Do you have any idea how long it will take to get from our entrance point to the Elephant?' Cassie needed to be prepared. She knew it was a race against time, but whatever happened, she had to get to Aggie's baby, she had to bring her home and then... then she had to do her job, make sure she followed the brief, get the latex moulds and chart the tunnels as best as she could.

She watched as Noah took in a deep breath, followed by a sigh. 'We're almost there.' The job was immense and just by looking at the map she knew what a difficult task they had ahead of them. Her finger ran itself across the cream-coloured architect paper, where she traced the path of the catacombs, where they had been, then the edge of where the Sand House had once stood and finally, she stopped at the Elephant and Mahout. That was where Aggie's baby lay, right there, right under its ledge.

'Do you think it'll still be intact, boss?' Kyle questioned. He ruffled his overgrown mop of blond hair with both hands, while his vivid blue eyes stared intently at the map. 'I mean, the tunnel was filled in with some kind of concrete, wasn't it? So it won't be easy, will it?'

Noah didn't reply, just sat staring at the map, deep in thought.

Cassie watched as Kyle reached across and pulled at a box that stood on the corner of the table. He then lifted one photograph at a time from inside and spread them around the map. Each picture was carefully put in its rightful place, one of the Sand House itself, one of a doorway, with the original owner Mr Senior standing outside, and then another of the catacombs, showing how vast they'd originally been. Finally, he came to a picture of the Elephant and Mahout and stared at it for much longer than the others.

Cassie gasped.

'It's beautiful, isn't it?' Kyle murmured. His finger gently touched the picture's surface before placing it on the map, right above the car park of Silverwood House. 'You say that the crawling tunnels need to be wider. How much access do we actually need to get to this?' He pointed to the photograph.

Noah pondered the question. 'Well, the Elephant was around nine feet tall and we need to bear that in mind. Of course, we can section the moulds, but I'd rather not unless we have to.'

'And the point of getting them is?' Cassie asked.

Noah shook his head in exasperation. 'Truth is, none of this should ever have been buried. This site was bought by the corporation. You'd have thought that they would have preserved it. So... whatever the cost, we have to get to it.' He paused, stood up and walked around the table. 'We just need to find a way through what's down there. It'll be hard going and we'll be cutting through concrete that surrounds the sandstone carving.' He leaned on the table with both hands. 'Not an easy task.'

'So, the objective is to reach the Elephant and Mahout, take the mouldings, capture all of the details and get the hell out of there. Got it.' Cassie sipped at her coffee. 'But where will the moulds go after?'

'They're building a new museum, on the corner of Waterdale. It's going on the site of the old girls' school and will have a full exhibition and a virtual tour. All because we did this.' Noah's

Irish accent had become stronger with excitement but then softened as he tapped on the map with a finger. 'The other half of the tunnel, this half, will stay buried.'

Kyle stood up, walked to the door and looked at the high-rise flats that towered above them. He chewed his cheek, pondering. 'A lot of spoil came out of that hole. Really wish I could have got the shaft closer.' He shook his head. 'Would have been too risky though. We really didn't want a problem with the flats' foundations or with the claims that no doubt would have followed.'

Cassie agreed. 'Plus, the shaft could have ruined too much of the history that we're battling to keep.'

Noah took a sip of coffee and almost spat it out, pulling a face. 'God, that's disgusting, don't we have any sugar?' He waved the Styrofoam cup around in the air. 'Can someone make some fresh coffee, white, one sugar, please?' he shouted out of the door. One of the young labourers nodded as Noah turned his attention back to the map. 'We dropped the shaft in exactly the right place. Once we have enough of a passage to get ourselves through, the job will get done. Especially with Cassie on board.' His eye caught hers. 'I certainly think we've now got all the expertise we need.'

'I'll drink to that,' Kyle said as he returned to his seat, lifted the coffee to his lips and sipped. 'And, for safety's sake, I've got the lads shoring up the tunnel as we go, inch by inch, just in case.' He raised an eyebrow in affirmation.

Noah nodded. 'Perfect, and we need some cheap local labour, all the spoil that we're bringing out, it all needs sorting.'

Cassie stood up. 'Where will the shaker boxes, and sifts go?' She looked out of the window and onto the roads she'd grown up on. 'We'll need access to water, and preferably not the water that serves my shower.' She took note of the skips full of debris. 'Does all of that still need sorting?'

Noah laughed. 'No. It's being sorted as we go. Anything of interest has been boxed, labelled and stored. Once the tents go up, we'll start looking at the contents of those boxes really carefully. We've got tables to do the sorting on, water organised, but we need to put someone in charge of cataloguing and photographing the finds. So, if anything of archaeological interest comes out of that hole, we'll know about it.' He paused. 'Most of it was just concrete and landfill, so will probably be worthless, all grotty, and smelly. But I need someone who knows their stuff to sort the wheat from the chaff.'

'I can organise the cataloguing.' Kyle held his hand in the air as though at school and then laughed at his own actions.

Noah checked his watch. 'And Kyle, try and get me a few community service guys down there that need a few hours. They'd be cheap.'

Again Cassie took note at how intently he stared at the map and of how he drummed his fingers on the table. Noah was no longer the boy she'd known, he was now a man with knowledge, skill and power. She smiled and again she felt proud. Responsibility suited him.

'Just so you know, there's pumping equipment in place too. We couldn't risk it flooding, not once we had people down there,' Noah said as he walked around the table and moved his attention to the cemetery. It was at the far edge of the map, standing at the other side of the bypass and Cassie knew it shouldn't be an area of significance, but was aware that local gossip had more than stirred up interest.

'What is it, boss?' Kyle asked.

'Rumour has it that the tunnels travelled right under the cemetery and that there used to be an entrance somewhere over here.' Once again, he tapped the map and tipped his head to one side. 'Let's get on the internet or go down to the library. Try and trace some old maps or get someone asking round the locals, see if anyone knows anything?'

'I heard that a local teenager was killed in that tunnel,' Kyle said. 'Word had it that it was sealed and that no one's been through it since.'

'Can we maybe find out what happened? Find out who the kid was and why he was in the tunnel in the first place?' Noah looked across the table at where both Kyle and Cassie sat.

'Or we could just go down there and take a look. If the tunnels were sealed, there must be some sort of evidence to show us where they were,' Kyle chipped in, nudged Cassie and gave her a cheeky smile. 'Do you like graveyards?'

Cassie held her breath. Aggie had told her of the tunnels. She'd mentioned an entrance in the graveyard, but she hadn't thought to press her on its exact location. She got up, walked to the door and looked across at the cemetery. Would that be a faster way in? She wondered if she could get in that way and get to the Elephant first? Immediately she shook her head at the thought. If there had still been an entrance there, if it had been possible, then surely Aggie would have used it. She dismissed the idea but made a note to ask her aunt all about them, because if anyone knew of another way in, Aggie would.

12

'Aggie, how are you...?' Cassie almost bounced into the ward, dropped her bag by the hospital bed and threw herself into the waiting arms of her aunt. She breathed in deeply and smiled. Even in the hospital, her aunt wore her favourite signature perfume. The smell of Vivienne Westwood's Boudoir filled her nostrils, just as it had so many times in the past.

'I've brought you some yummy goodies.' She reached down for her bag and began pulling out a bottle of squash, packets of biscuits and the biggest bag of boiled sweets that the shop had to offer. 'You said your mouth was always dry, I thought these might help.' She shook the sweets in the air before placing them on the bedside cabinet. Moving the chair closer to the bed, Cassie pointed to the bottle. 'This lemon drink is really fresh tasting.' She poured some juice into a glass and added the water. 'There you go. Try that, because I have so much to tell you.'

Sitting down by the bedside Cassie suddenly stared at the floor and took in a deep breath, not knowing where to start. Such a lot had happened. But the question was, how much did she tell Aggie? Did she mention the break-in, the fire being lit, the books?

Did she tell her that her father's tattoo sketchbook had had a page torn out, or not? These questions had flashed back and forth through her mind the whole day, but, on reflection, she knew how much the news would upset her aunt and eventually she'd decided against it.

'You'll never guess what's happened?' she finally whispered. 'I got a job on the dig. I've been there all day.' Her face lit up as she spoke. 'Noah's the boss, do you remember me talking of Noah?'

Aggie physically gasped. 'Really?' She inched forward on the bed with such a look of hope on her face. Her hand immediately grabbed hold of Cassie's. 'Did they finish digging the shaft? Did you see it, did you see the Elephant… his Mahout?'

Cassie looked away. She was almost afraid to speak and took a moment to look around the ward while she considered how to answer. Nurses moved from bed to bed in the ward opposite. One female nurse and one male; Todd.

'I see Todd's here again. Is he looking after you?' she asked Aggie.

Aggie shook her head from side to side. 'He only works on the ward two or three days a week, so the others look after me too. I think he works in the community the rest of the week.'

'What going to people's houses?'

Aggie nodded. 'Says he'll be on the team that looks after me, as and when I get to go home. They wanted me to go to a hospice but I don't want to do that. I want to go home.'

Cassie almost bounced on the spot. 'When might that be?'

Aggie frowned. 'Soon, I hope. I can't bear it here for much longer. But I know how much there is to organise. So…' She paused and Cassie felt her heart sink as she realised once again how sick her aunt was. She wanted Aggie to get out of the hospital, wanted to see her sat in her chair by a roaring fire and, above all else, she simply wanted her to be there, at home.

Sighing, Cassie looked across at the bed opposite. It was empty. All the clutter that had been by the bedside was now missing and the bedding had been changed. Cassie thought of the lady that had been there and of the woman who'd been with her, caring for her. Cassie hoped that she'd been taken elsewhere, to a hospice or maybe she'd gone home too and was now sitting in an armchair with a nice cup of tea, and a piece of cake. She felt her heart lurch as she turned back to Aggie, who was now sat forward, watching her.

'Her daughter, she wanted to take her home, but...' Aggie said as though reading Cassie's mind. She shook her head, a tear rolled down her face as she swallowed hard, shut her eyes and for a long time after, Cassie simply stared at their conjoined hands.

Finally, Aggie opened her eyes and smiled at Cassie. 'Now, tell me about the dig. Have you been down the shaft, have you seen the Elephant?'

'Oh, Aggie. I don't know where to start. I really wish it was that easy, I wish I'd already been down there.' Cassie paused and squeezed her hand. She didn't want to lie. 'I did get to stare down the shaft though and we studied all of the maps that we have available. But we have to wait. Once they break through, we'll send a camera down and then, and only if all is safe, then and only then, we get to go down.'

Aggie's hand went to her stomach, the pain on her face more than obvious and for a few moments she sat back and took slow deep breaths, until the pain had passed.

'Aggie, are you okay?' Cassie asked.

She nodded. 'You will be careful, when you're in the tunnels, won't you?' The words were full of concern and Aggie sat forward as she said them. 'They're not safe. They haven't been safe for years. That's why I never went back down there myself. Because if I could have, trust me, I would have.' She dabbed at her eyes with a tissue. 'I don't want you getting hurt, my girl. It's the last thing I'd ever want, you know that I'd never forgive myself, don't you?' She patted Cassie's hand.

Cassie thought of the tales she'd been told, of the hours she'd sat by Aggie's feet listening to how she'd spent her childhood down in the tunnels, of how the local children had played hide and seek. And how beautiful the carvings had been. But now Aggie sounded afraid; she no longer had the same enthusiasm or that magical childlike look on her face that Cassie remembered seeing so many times before.

'But the shaft, it wouldn't be the only way in, would it? When you went in as children, didn't you have another entrance, a way in through the cemetery?'

Cassie's mind went back to what Noah had asked earlier that day, when he'd said they should ask the locals.

But Aggie sat bolt upright. 'Oh no. Don't you dare. You don't go in that way.' Her voice shook with a temper that Cassie had never heard before. 'Do you hear me. It's far too dangerous,' she hollered as a buzzer went off somewhere down the corridor. All the nurses began to run in its direction, all at once, making Cassie hold her breath. Someone close by was in trouble and the reality of life on the ward – and death – suddenly hit her. She turned back to Aggie, searching her eyes for answers, knowing that time was most probably running out and that she had to ask the difficult questions, while she still could.

'Aggie...' Cassie searched the pain-filled eyes that looked back at her. 'There is still a way through, isn't there? I mean, do you think I could go in that way and get to the Elephant before the workforce do?'

Aggie shook her head from side to side and her breathing got faster and faster. 'You can't... promise me. That tunnel... it collapsed many years ago.' A sob left her throat and her eyes seemed to search the air for the words. 'Some of the graveyard remains, they fell into the tunnels.' She nodded. 'If one grave can fall through, then so can the others.' She yelled out in pain as she tried to move closer. 'You mustn't go in that way; do you hear me? You'll get hurt just like...' Aggie flopped back against the pillows and began to sob.

'Hey there, Agatha.' The male nurse, Todd, walked up to the bedside, squirted antibacterial gel onto his hands, picked up Aggie's wrist and took her pulse. 'Now, are you okay? Do you need some pain relief?' He moved to the bottom of the bed, picked up the chart and began flicking through the pages.

'I'm fine,' Aggie lied, lying back and closing her eyes. Cassie watched how he moved, how his eyes seemed to search every inch of Aggie's bed, her side cabinet. He looked down at where Cassie had dropped her bag, then looked her up and down. 'I want to go home,' Aggie suddenly announced. 'You said it might be possible. Well, I've decided, I really want to go home.'

Cassie gasped. 'Can she? Can she come home?' She directed the question at Todd who stood back, looking thoughtful.

'Well, we'd have to speak to the doctors and to the Macmillan team,' Todd spoke without looking up.

But Aggie's face lit up. 'But it is possible, isn't it?' The words were heartbreaking. Of course Aggie would want to be at home, of course she'd want to sleep in her own bed, sit in her own living room and drink a cup of tea that wasn't served in a plastic beaker. Cassie stared at Todd, but her heart sank. He didn't look up or at them as he spoke, which didn't give Cassie much hope.

'You'd need daily visits by the Macmillan nurses. There'd be a lot to arrange and, as I've said before, I would also go out as part of the team myself. The first thing we'd have to do is get you a hospital bed. It'd be delivered to your home.' He paused. 'Your living room is big enough, isn't it?'

Aggie's hand went up to her mouth, and the tears once again began to fall. 'My living room? Why can't it go in my bedroom?' She asked the question, but then patted Cassie's hand. 'I guess it'd be too heavy. Wouldn't it?' She paused. 'Oh, I'd love to go home,' she whispered and then turned to Cassie. 'That is okay, isn't it?'

Cassie looked from Aggie to the nurse. 'Of course, it's okay. We'd love for you to be at home.' Cassie meant what she said but frowned and supressed a sob. She knew that by taking Aggie home, she'd be taking her home to die.

Todd hung the clipboard back on the end of the bed. 'Okay, I'll get onto the office. See what we can do.' He tapped the end of the bed with his hand and then looked directly at Cassie. 'Agatha would need constant care, you do realise that, right?' His eyes pierced hers.

Cassie sat back. She didn't like the way he glared and she began to fidget in her seat. He was waiting for her to answer, but she didn't dare speak and simply nodded in agreement to his question. 'Keep calm, keep calm,' the words went over and over in her mind. 'Let's just get Aggie home. Then we'll work out all the logistics.' She looked at the floor, hoping that he'd leave.

'Did you hear that, Aggie? I'm going to take you home. I'll organise the bed, the nurses, everything. I might even try to cook something nice for when you get there,' she rambled on at a hundred miles an hour all the time smiling, but Aggie looked anxious and as soon as the nurse had gone, she grabbed hold of Cassie's hand.

'Promise me,' she whispered. 'Promise me you won't go through those tunnels, not the ones in the cemetery.'

Cassie sat back. In her excitement about taking Aggie home, she'd forgotten the earlier conversation. 'But... I thought that's what you wanted... it would be a way into the tunnels. I could get in without being seen and you used it yourself, you said so.'

'Oh, my girl. That was over fifty years ago and even then, it was terribly unsafe.' She swung her legs over the edge of the bed and sat forward. She began to tremble, and Cassie suddenly remembered Kyle's words about a local man being killed.

'I didn't tell you the whole story.' Aggie held onto her hand. 'My John, he'd been badly hurt on the railways and had spent months in the hospital.' She shrugged her shoulders. 'There were no mobile phones back then. It wasn't easy to get in touch, and he was in one of the hospitals in Sheffield, so I couldn't visit, not without catching two or three buses that barely ran. It could take a whole day to go just a few miles up the road and back.' She reached for her lemon drink and picked up the glass with a shaking hand. 'The moment he got home, he came to see me. He was so excited, he thought he'd get to meet his baby, you see.' Aggie pulled a tissue from the box and wiped her eyes. 'But then, I had to tell him the truth. I had to tell him what had happened. I'd never seen him so angry. Said that I should have got word to him. Said I should have written. But... but... Oh, Cassie,' she paused and sobbed, 'I wouldn't have known where to start; I mean how do you tell someone something like that in a letter?' Aggie blew her nose. Her legs were hanging off the side of the bed and Cassie tried to cover them back up with the sheet to keep her warm.

'What did John do?'

'He was so angry. He said it wasn't right, her being alone in that tunnel without a grave, and he was insistent that he had to go and get her and that she had to be buried, properly. I tried to stop him, but he set off running as fast as he could towards the graveyard.' She moved her hands as though running in motion. 'Without any thought, he went straight into the tunnel. I shouted.

I screamed. I swear to God I tried to get him to stop. I begged him not to go and then, I held my breath, the smell of fungus had gotten stronger. It was overwhelming, and even though it made me gag, I tried to follow. I couldn't let him go alone, could I? So, I followed him.'

Cassie listened in silence.

'He was quite a distance ahead of me and it was dark, so very dark. I couldn't see. The boreholes had gone and we hadn't had time to collect a torch. I had to squint to keep track of his shadow. But we went deeper and deeper. The light disappeared fast. It was pitch black and then... there was a thunderous noise. At first, I didn't know what had happened.' A sob left her throat, 'I could feel the mounds of earth, rocks, bones and pieces of rotten wood, the parts of a coffin blocking the tunnel and I knew, it had all fallen right on top of him.'

Aggie had taken a hold of a corner of the bed sheet and she'd begun to twist it around and around until she could twist no more, her eyes were fixed on the window and she stared out as the memory flooded her mind. 'I couldn't stop screaming and I tried... I tried so hard to pull him out. I dug and dug all the debris with my hands and kept going till they bled,' she grabbed at the air as she spoke, 'but there were concrete blocks, pieces of gravestone...' She stopped speaking as the nightmare once again crossed her face. 'I couldn't move them, they were so heavy, and I was so scared. I could just feel my John's leg beneath the earth. It was so cold and he wasn't moving, not at all. And then, then there was another deafening noise as more of the tunnel began to cave in; more human remains came down with the dirt. I was terrified. I knew I had to go and get help, before I was buried too and I ran back to the house as quickly as I could.' Her voice went faster and faster, her breath becoming laboured and, for a moment, Aggie just sat and grabbed at the air. 'All the way there I prayed. I prayed so hard that he'd live. But it was some hours later when the men finally dug him out. And then, and only to me... it became very obvious that my John had died within a few metres of his baby girl.'

Aggie began to cough, and Cassie quickly stood up, poured some more of the juice into a glass and passed it to her aunt who took in deep breaths as she sipped at the drink. 'The authorities, they sealed the entrance and the graves that had fallen in are now just grass.'

Cassie sat down on the bed beside her aunt and pulled her into a hug. 'Oh my God... you... you lost them both... in those tunnels.' She paused and realised what her aunt had gone through. 'Aggie, how did you explain what had happened? What did you tell his family?' Tears stung her eyes.

'It didn't surprise his family that we'd been down there. You see, we'd spent years going there, all the children did.' She shook her head. 'So, I never told them the truth. They never knew about the baby. There wouldn't have been any point. John was still gone and them knowing why he'd died wouldn't have helped them, it wouldn't have helped anyone.'

Cassie could feel a heat rise up within her and she moved to the open window, wafted air into her face and then stood with her back to it. She knew what she had to do. She also knew how hard it would be for Aggie to think of anyone else she loved going into those tunnels. Stepping forward, she took hold of Aggie's hand. 'I'll find her for you. I'll find her for John. I swear to God; I'll bring her home to you Aggie. I'm gonna bring her home for the both of you.'

Cassie knew the promise was a big one and that getting to the Elephant and Mahout first would be a challenge in itself. But, with luck on her side, she prayed that she'd find a way to do it. And while she hoped that everyone else would be taking in the beauty of the Elephant and Mahout, her main focus would be on retrieving what was left of the blanket and the remains within.

Cassie helped Aggie lay back against the pillows. She suddenly seemed to relax, and her eyes closed as her breathing became slow, and almost rhythmic.

'It's the morphine,' Todd whispered as once again he appeared at the bottom of the bed, picked up the clipboard and began checking the monitor by Aggie's bed. 'She drifts in and out of sleep all day. Chatting to you must have exhausted her.' His lips formed a forced smile.

Cassie turned and looked over her shoulder. How long had he been there? And how much had he heard of Aggie's story?

He moved away and Cassie looked at her watch. It was six thirty. She'd been at the dig all day, and, after a quick change, she'd gone to the supermarket to get Aggie some treats and had caught the bus directly to the hospital, which meant that she still hadn't eaten. Her stomach now grumbled relentlessly. Pulling her mobile from her bag she stared at the screen, wondering what Noah was doing.

Fancy some company at dinner? I'm starving! Cass x

She pressed 'send' on the text and sat back in the chair and waited. Aggie still slept, and Cassie reluctantly made the decision to leave. 'I'll see you tomorrow,' she whispered as she stood up, kissed her on the cheek and left. Checking her mobile, she homed in on the small number one at the corner of her phone and hurriedly tapped the screen. But instead of the response coming from Noah, as she'd expected, it was from Sasha.

Hi honey, the excavation of our bones is going well. The legs are now exposed and I'm cataloguing everything, waiting for you to come back. I miss you so much, our flat isn't the same without you. Tabitha says hello and I'm sorry, but I think I may have killed Bill, the tomato plant. He's kind of drooped and fallen off the balcony x ps: Thought you'd want to know, Declan was sacked and left the site early yesterday morning, last seen heading for the airport.

Declan had left Italy. She let out a sigh of relief, before reading the text again. The words 'early yesterday morning' jumped out from the text. Declan had left 'yesterday'. She closed her eyes. The break-in had happened 'yesterday'. She shook her head. It couldn't have been, could it? Did he know where she lived? Her stomach turned and she quickly replied.

Oh, hun. I miss you too. But, poor Bill, what happened, did you forget to water him? Don't forget to give Tabitha her treats. We hid extra in the top cupboard. Fuss her for me. And as for Declan, let's hope that's the last we see of him. x

She wanted to tell Sasha about Aggie. About meeting up with Noah, the night in the pub. The feeling of being followed and the break-in. So much had happened, but she knew that now was not the time as she picked up her bag and walked out of the ward.

13

It was just after seven when the overcrowded bus pulled into the station. Cassie had spent most of the journey with her eyes closed praying for it to end as the overwhelming smell of body odour and cheap perfume hit the back of her throat. She got off the bus, shivered and immediately pulled her coat tightly around her. The bus station had never changed and for as long as she could remember it had been the most perfect wind tunnel, no matter what the time of year. She headed to the exit, made her way past the Frenchgate Centre and looked up to the balcony of The Mallard, which was already full of people drinking, laughing and already having Friday night fun.

Making her way along the dual carriageway and past the busy train station, she noticed all the construction and the amount of people that dashed in and out, and the taxis that stood, engines revving, in front of the main doors, while the constant sound of trains sped up and down on the main line.

Cassie ran her hand along the cold metal railings that edged the dual carriageway, forming a barrier between pavement and road, as she walked. At least today it was still daylight and after the night before, she felt grateful. Checking her mobile, she noticed that Sasha hadn't replied, and neither had Noah. As she approached the pub where he was staying, she allowed herself to glance up at his bedroom window. The curtains were still open and she tried to decide what to do. Sighing, she wondered if he was in the bar eating dinner with Kyle? Or lying on his bed, chatting to his girlfriend? What if she'd arrived for a visit? Shaking her head, she looked back down at her phone and decided that he'd have texted her if he'd wanted her to join him. She didn't want to impose so carried on walking along the road towards the subway. 'Chicken, I have chicken in the fridge. Hot chicken sandwich. That'll do,' she thought as she kept looking over her shoulder and then stopped and stood quietly for a few minutes by the railings. She could feel herself trembling, her stomach churning, as her eyes searched the road, the shop doorways and the car park. The events of the night before had left her feeling nervous, but, as far as she could tell, there was no one about. No one was following her. Convinced she was alone she headed for the subway's ramp. As normal, it smelled of urine and she held her breath as she ran down, through and then back out and into the open air at other side where she gasped for breath.

'Hey, Cassie,' came Kyle's voice. 'What you up to?' He was heading towards her, in jeans and a clean shirt, with a huge disarming smile on his face and a carrier bag in hand.

'Just going home. Been to the hospital to visit my aunt and now... well, now, I'm debating what to do about food. I'm starving.' She thought of the fridge, and of its unappetising contents. There was still some milk and the chicken, but she sighed, knowing that that would mean cooking. Her shoulders dropped, and she looked back across the road to where the Chinese takeaway stood. 'Did you get all dressed up to go to the chippy?' She laughed and pointed to the bag.

Kyle smiled. 'Nah. We had a breakthrough. Noah has sent the cameras down and I'd just got changed when he called me and I couldn't miss it, could I? I just had to be there to see the Elephant for the very first time.' His whole face lit up. 'We're right in there, Cass. You can almost make out the size of the carving now, the Mahout's foot has been exposed, it's amazing.'

Cassie bounced on the spot. She felt the excitement and nerves all at once. 'That's fantastic. Is... is Noah still over there? I wouldn't mind seeing it for myself.' Her hands began to shake. 'Kyle, was the carving intact? Did... did you see anything else?' She didn't know why she'd asked, but felt desperate to know if the remains had been spotted.

Kyle took a step closer to the subway. 'Nah. Just the shape and the size. Argh, Cassie, it's going to be beautiful, stunning in fact and Noah, well he was still chatting to Joe when I left. I went to the chippy and, once I've had these, I'm going to be the one soaking in the tub for the next hour, at least.' He rubbed his back and yawned, but then stopped in his tracks and threw his head backwards. 'Actually... Jesus... what am I thinking.' He dragged his boot across the edge of the grass. 'I forgot about the idea of staying at yours. I'll collect my things, meet you over there. Might even let you share the chips.'

She felt grateful for the offer but had noted the smile and enthusiasm on his face when he'd mentioned the soak in the tub. She knew that he'd help her if she wanted him to and for that she felt grateful, but tonight it was the last thing she'd ask. Tonight, she had to get used to the idea of going home alone.

'Thanks, Kyle, but you go and enjoy your food and your bath. I'll be fine, honestly,' she lied, anxiety already threatening to overwhelm her. 'I have to be home alone sometime.' She smiled. 'Besides, the police want me to sort through everything, make sure nothing is missing and, to be honest, I'm knackered. So I think I might just have a bath and an early night too.'

Kyle nodded. 'Well, you have my number. Any problems, call me.' He turned, headed for the subway and disappeared underground.

Taking a deep inward breath, she hurried towards the site. This was it. They'd reached the Elephant chamber and by the sound of it, it was all still there, looking just as it had over fifty years ago. Kyle had said that Noah had been chatting to Joe and maybe, if she hurried, he'd still be there and he'd let her see the footage too. She quickened her steps, made her way through the maisonettes and turned the corner to see the Portakabin all lit up. Inside sat Joe. Alone. He was staring at the CCTV screens and Cassie felt a hypothetical tidal wave of disappointment splash her heavily in the face. Noah had already left and now she wouldn't get to see the him or the carving. Both, she realised, were equally disappointing and she turned to her left, between the maisonettes to walk home.

As Aggie's house came into view the fear that had gripped her the night before came flooding back, and as she walked through the garden, her stride slowed. She took a deep breath before putting the key into the new lock that Kyle had kindly fitted and, turning it, she carefully peered into the kitchen and sighed with relief. Everything was as she'd left it. The three mugs that Noah had washed still sat on the draining board. Her coat still hung on the back of the kitchen chair and in the living room, the full coal scuttle still stood by the fire, along with lumps of wood and firelighters. 'Thanks, Noah,' she whispered to the walls, swallowing hard. She then stood by the door, sizing up the room, trying to work out where a hospital bed would fit and what furniture would need to be removed. After all, the house was terraced and the room really wasn't that big.

Cassie was deep in thought when a sudden knocking thundered through the house, making her jump. Her breathing accelerated and she scanned the room before grabbing the long-handled poker. Standing behind the living room door she peeped through the crack and into the kitchen. 'Who is it?' she shouted, with the poker held up in the air.

'Cass, it's me, Noah.'

Cassie breathed a huge sigh of relief, quickly put the poker back by the fire and ran to the back door. 'Noah, what... what are you doing here?' Her face lit up, her delight obvious.

'Well, I was down the chippy when Kyle phoned me. He told me he'd seen you and that you were starving. So...' he passed her two parcels out of the bag '...I bought a couple of kebabs. Hope you still like them?'

14

'Oh my God, do you remember that lecturer, the one that really hated us?' Cassie pushed the kitchen door closed and sat on the carpet with her back resting against Aggie's chair. She waved her bare feet around in front of the fire, as bright yellow and orange flames hovered around what was left of a log, before flying up the chimney.

Noah was sat on the floor beside her. He too was leaning against the furniture and Cassie watched the way he picked at the last pieces of kebab, dipped the meat in what was left of the chilli sauce and then, with a satisfied grin on his face, pushed it into his mouth.

'Mr Parkinson,' he said while chewing. 'It was... it was Mr Parkinson. He used to say, "You children, I just know you'll be the death of me", didn't he?'

They both laughed as their outstretched feet began to tussle and prod, until both big toes began wrestling with determined but friendly aggression.

'Not sure how old he thought we were. Most of us had seen the back of eighteen at least, which makes me think that he can't have liked kids very much. Or young adults. Ouch...!' Cassie yelped and pulled her toe up and away from Noah's. 'That hurt.' She quickly returned her foot to the floor and the battle of toe wars continued, until they were both sat in a checkmate situation with the bottom of their feet pressed tightly together. It was a move of submission, which meant that neither had won and she smiled, an automatic, comfortable smile, as she looked up and caught his eye.

'He probably didn't like anyone,' Noah said. 'I've no idea why he ever became a lecturer.' He rubbed her foot with his by way of apology. 'Sorry, I didn't mean to hurt you.'

Cassie took in Noah's good looks. 'Well, he certainly wouldn't be able to call you a kid now, would he? You're quite the grown-up, digging all those tunnels, unearthing the past and in charge of the whole bloody archaeological dig.' She paused, 'I'm so proud of you, Noah.'

Noah stared into the flames with a wistful look, before glancing back at her with a smile. 'It was so amazing today, when we sent the cameras down,' he said, lost in the memory of the moment. 'The only people who'd actually seen any part of the Elephant in the last fifty years had been the labourers and now... now they're in its chamber. They'd all been down there with breathing apparatus at the ready, just in case they needed it. Us mere mortals, well, we have to wait until the worst of the spoil is out. But come Monday, we'll get to see it all. It should be our turn. We get to do the intricate stuff.'

Cassie sat up on her knees. 'So... what did it look like?'

Noah's eyes lit up. 'It was amazing. I could see the shape of the first chamber, a huge circular ceiling, the cameras picked out the carving of The Pope, it was standing perfectly to the side of the room as though the past years hadn't happened, as though it had been sat there just waiting for us to find it.' His hands moved around in an animated way as he spoke, and Cassie could see the passion he had for the subject. One of the first things she'd ever noticed about Noah had been his love of archaeology. He'd respected the subject just as much as she had. And between them, they'd had more enthusiasm than most of the other students combined. They'd often laughed between themselves and wondered if the others had chosen the degree simply because they'd had no other choice or maybe they'd been pushed into it by a parent or teacher.

'And then, and although we can't quite see the Elephant itself, we got to the chamber. The crawling tunnel isn't wide enough yet and that'll be what the guys will work on next.' He nodded. 'The access needs shoring up properly and then...' He rubbed his hands together in excitement, making Cassie sit forward to listen. She had a hundred questions that she wanted to ask, but right now, it didn't seem right to ask them.

'Oh, Cassie, I can't wait for you to see it,' Noah's voice broke into her thoughts and he gave her an apologetic look. 'I'd have told you about us putting the camera down there tonight, but you'd been excited all day about going to see your aunt. I knew you'd have been torn and didn't want you to have to make that choice.' He took hold of her hand. 'I knew that seeing the tunnels could wait for another day, but from what you've told me your aunt might not have too many more left and I didn't want you to miss a single minute with her.' He looked genuinely sorry, but Cassie focused on their hands. They were linked together, so innocently, yet so naturally too. But Noah realised what he'd done and let go of her hand, purposely moving to one side to create a space between them.

'I have to admit, she isn't good,' she chewed her lip, unsure of what to say. 'She... she's always loved the tunnels, she used to play down there as a child and she'd always wanted the chance to go down there again.' She looked up and directly into Noah's eyes. 'But she knows that that won't happen. Not now. So, I'm kind of living that dream for her and she insists that I tell her every detail of what I see.' The words were true, and Cassie was satisfied with her explanation. The last thing she wanted to do was lie to Noah. But a promise was a promise and to tell him the whole truth would betray the love and loyalty she felt for Aggie. 'And the Elephant. Well, that's the goal. I just have to see it. I have to tell her absolutely everything about it.'

'You really love her, don't you?' he whispered as his phone pinged, but he ignored it.

Cassie nodded. 'She brought me up, did everything for me. And, not that I'd have realised it at the time, on many occasions she went without, just so Lisa and I could have things.' She pointed to the room. 'She didn't have very much, as you can see, but she shared it with both of us and we all kind of muddled along together. So, yes, I love her.'

She sighed, picked up the plastic trays that the kebabs had been in and stood up. 'Anyhow, thanks for this,' she said, changing the subject and pointing to the tray. 'Kyle was right, I really was hungry and...' she walked into the kitchen '...as you saw this morning, my fridge is pretty bare.' She switched on the kettle. 'Right, do you want tea, or coffee?' she asked as she pulled two mugs from the cupboard. Cassie stared out of the window. Something was wrong. 'Noah. Did you leave the gate open?'

'Nope, not after what happened last night, I locked it and checked it. Why?' He got up and followed her into the kitchen. 'And tea, tea would be good.' He stood behind her, resting his elbows on the draining board as he looked under the blind. The gate was clearly open, and he straightened up, moved to the back door, opened it and walked down the path. He stood for a moment, looking up and down the ginnel. He then reached up and pushed the lock back across on the gate. 'I've secured it again, but it doesn't make sense. I'm certain I did that earlier,' Noah said as he came back into the kitchen. He flicked the Yale into a locked position, turned the second key and then pulled at the door handle to ensure it couldn't open. He then went to the front door and repeated the exercise.

Cassie finished making the tea and then carried the mugs into the living room.

'Probably nothing, but...' he looked at the settee '...I'll sleep on there tonight.' He paced up and down and once again looked towards the back door. 'If anyone gets in, they'll have to get past me first.'

'Don't be daft. You can't sleep on there. It'd be really uncomfortable. We're just being paranoid. Somebody might have simply popped by. The neighbours do it all the time around here.' Cassie tried to think the situation through. 'Maybe they looked in through the back window, saw us sat by the fire, decided against disturbing us and went again?' She could hear the wobble and uncertainty in her voice. It was unconvincing. It was a voice that even she didn't believe. 'Maybe it was Kyle,' she said, even though she doubted that Kyle would have turned up. Not when he'd been looking forward to his dinner, a hot bath and a pint. But then an uneasiness crossed her mind and she looked up at Noah with raised eyebrows. 'You don't think...' She stopped while she thought of the text that Sasha had sent and shook her head. 'Look, sorry. Now I really am being a bit silly, paranoid even.' She turned and threw herself at the settee.

'Cass, it was only last night that your house got broken into. Someone was in here, so right now, I don't think anything is silly or paranoid.' He sat down on the settee beside her and his arm automatically went around her in a hug. A hug that Cassie gratefully sank into. It was as though they'd turned the clock back,

back to a time when life was simple. With Noah she was always happy, comfortable. In fact, she was probably a little too comfortable.

'My friend, Sasha, the one in Italy that I told you about, she sent me a text.' Cassie pointed to the side of her face, to the bruising that had now begun to fade. 'The guy that attacked me, Sasha says that he left Italy yesterday. Said he was last seen heading for the airport.'

'Do you think he'd come here?'

Cassie shook her head. 'I don't think so. I don't think he knows where here is. But then I wouldn't have thought he'd chase me down an alley either.'

'Awww, Cassie. Put it into perspective. He literally could have gone anywhere in the world, couldn't he? There's thousands of other airports, not just the one in Doncaster.'

As always, Noah was the voice of reason and she could feel his breath on her cheek, the warmth of his arms and the underlying smell of his aftershave. A subtle, musky, manly scent. Closing her eyes, her breathing slowed. Her mind began to drift. She felt warm, content and thought of happier days. Days when she and Noah had spent hours studying together, followed by long walks along the canal, chatting to other walkers and watching the narrowboats as they floated gracefully by, adorned with plant pots, brass nameplates and beautifully painted decks. She smiled as a warm glow overtook her and, for the first time since she'd set foot back in England, she felt happy and safe.

15

Noah's eyes flicked open. Something had disturbed his sleep and for a few seconds he simply lay on the settee, listening. His eyes were half closed, he felt warm, content and he tried to stretch but couldn't. At first, he felt confused. But then he smiled, remembering the hug he'd shared with Cassie and took great pleasure in the fact that she was still there, fast asleep in his arms where she'd snuggled in as close to his body as she could possibly get.

He could feel the warmth of her breath on his skin and carefully he moved his hand up to her face. His finger slowly began to draw a line along her cheek, down her jawbone and finally he came to a stop just by her lip. This was where the bruising still showed, and he glanced from her eyes to her lips. He took in a deep measured breath as he fought the urge to lower his lips to hers. He so desperately wanted to kiss her but knew it was wrong. Being here, like this, this was wrong. So why did it feel so right?

He thought of Erin, of how he'd slept in the same bed as her so many times. He'd been sure he'd loved her. He'd been sure she'd make him happy, that they'd make each other happy, but recently she had changed. All she seemed interested in was money and how he could provide the lifestyle she wished for. Closing his eyes, he tried to see where they'd be in five, ten, twenty years' time, but couldn't. He couldn't ever imagine them sat by the fire, eating kebabs, playing at toe wrestling or just laughing about anything and nothing, just because they could.

Reaching down and into his pocket with his free hand he pulled out his mobile, saw the four missed calls, the numerous texts and began reading through them, one by one.

Babe. Call me. It's important x

Noah, hello… are you getting my messages. Call me as soon as you get this xx

I've called you twice. Where r u? xx

Babe, I managed to get some shoes for £352 online. Not the ones I wanted. But I suppose they'll be okay. Any chance you fancy treating me to the other £252. Xx

Noah. I'm getting annoyed. You need to call me back. That's four times I've called and I don't like being ignored. I need the money transferring, or I'll go into my overdraft and I can't afford to do that, not three days before I go on holibobs with the girls and you don't want me to be the only one who doesn't look nice, do you? xx

Throwing the phone to the bottom of the settee, he lay back down and took pleasure in the contentment he felt. He was in exactly the right place, with exactly the right person and at that moment, he felt more at home than he'd probably ever felt in his entire life. Was that what this was? Was being with Cass like going home?

Noah stared down at the pixie nose, the eyes that fluttered occasionally while she slept and the way her hands were slipped under her face as though in prayer, in a sweet and childlike manner. He felt the anger surge through him. 'How could anyone hurt you, Cass?' he whispered as his fingers began to move a strand of hair from in front of her face, but then stopped as she twitched and turned, burying her face in his jumper.

A scraping noise disturbed his thoughts. Unsure what had made the sound or where it had come from, Noah carefully began to disentangle himself. He gently used one hand to support Cassie's head, while he pulled at a cushion with the other. Laying her down, he watched as she curled up tightly into a ball. Her fingers slid back to where they'd been, underneath her cheek to make a temporary pillow and, for just a moment, her eyes flickered, making Noah hold his breath in case he had woken her.

Standing up, he forced himself to look away, then moved from the living room to the kitchen, listening intently. There was the sound of the couple next door, shouting at their children. 'I've told you two to get to bed. I'm warning you, if you don't get to sleep, I'm gonna turn off the Wi-Fi.' He clearly heard the rant and smirked at the thought that most children these days were living their lives on the internet.

He wondered if the noise could have come from the terraced house on the other side and once again found himself peering out and under the blind. Again, the gate was open. It blew back and forth in the wind. Banging against the wall. Another noise that could have woken him.

'Who the hell keeps doing that?'

He went to open the back door, but a noise from above stopped him. Walking through the living room, he moved towards the stairs, glancing at Cassie as he passed. Should he wake her? She looked so beautiful, so at peace and after the night before, the break-in and the upset, he was more than certain that she needed the sleep. But then again, if someone was in the house, she needed to be alert. He needed to decide what to do and stood for a moment, listening and waiting for the house to give him a clue.

After a few minutes of hearing nothing and deciding that his imagination was running wild, Noah left Cassie to sleep and crept up the stairs, one step at a time, with the sound of his own heartbeat echoing in his ears. He took long slow breaths, all the time listening, and on high alert, expecting something to happen.

Pushing the bathroom door open, he felt a sudden rush of air. The window was open. It rattled in its frame and a reed air freshener had fallen from the windowsill and into the bath. 'So, that's what it was.' Noah breathed a sigh of relief.

Pulling the window closed Noah felt satisfied that the house was safe, but decided to look around. He turned and headed for Cassie's bedroom, pushed open the door and stood in the entrance. The room was in darkness, the curtains were open, and the moon partially lit the room. He stared at the bed in which he'd slept the night before. But tonight it felt wrong to go in and he respectfully pulled the door to a close and turned. Stepping across the landing he checked Aggie's room.

The door was open, as was the wardrobe. Items of clothing had been dropped on the floor, along with shoes, handbags and hats. All looked as though they'd been dragged out and left where they'd dropped. 'Cassie Hunt, you dare to walk into my room and tell me that I'm messy,' he whispered as he picked up the items, pushed them in the wardrobe and closed the door. But as he stepped to one side, he glanced at the perfectly made bed. Cassie had put so much effort into making it, placing each of the decorative cushions in exactly the right place. Even the curtains had been positioned, rather than just opened. So, for her to throw things on the floor didn't seem to make sense at all? He shook his head.

Closing his eyes, he took a deep breath in and a strange odour filled his nostrils. He tried to place the smell but couldn't. He thought of Cassie, of her movements and of what she'd said earlier about going to the hospital to visit Aggie. 'Would Aggie have needed clothes?' He moved the shoes to the side of the room and put them in a row by the skirting board.

Leaning against the bed, Noah sighed, his eyes were heavy and he needed sleep, but the noise, the gate, the window, the break-in, and the mess – it was all bothering him far too much. What was he missing?

His thoughts went back to the night before. To being at the pub and to lying on his bed, thinking of Cassie. Of how she'd called him, her distress obvious and of how two minutes later he'd been hammering on Kyle's door. The two of them had run across the estate at speed. He'd grown to know the estate over the past few weeks. It was normally busy, people walking up and down the streets. For a street so close to the town centre, it had been unusually quiet, and dark. The street lights had been out, and he'd got quite close to her aunt's house before he'd heard Cassie shout. Standing for a moment, he'd stood and searched the ginnel and then he'd seen her, crouched down in a gate hole, on the floor, in the dirt, behind a tall grey wheelie bin. Noah's heart had gone out to her. He'd never seen her look so very small or vulnerable before and even though she'd jumped up the moment he'd approached her, he could physically see her whole body violently trembling in the darkness and without thought had pulled her into his arms, closed his eyes and thought of how right it felt for her to be there.

As for Kyle, he'd done exactly what Noah had thought he'd

do. He'd gone straight into military mode. He'd quickly checked the house for intruders, before running around the site, phoning police and checking CCTV, while Noah had simply cared for Cassie.

It had been a good while later when they'd followed Kyle into the house, to wait for the police. So, what had the break-in been all about? Nothing of value had been taken. He raised an eyebrow, knowing that there was nothing of value to take. The only thing that the intruder had been bothered about was the books. Noah allowed his head to drop back, he looked up at the ceiling as though it would give him the answers. Did it have something to do with the books? And the fire? Someone had lit it. But why? He thought of the book that Cassie had picked up. She'd looked through it carefully and with every turn of the page a noticeable memory had crossed her face. The book had obviously meant something to her and the fact that it had had a page torn out had visibly upset her. But again, why? Had the page been burned or taken? And above all else, wouldn't it have been easier to throw the whole book into the flames? Or had the book meant something to the intruder too?

Noah made his way back down the stairs and began to tiptoe through the living room. Cassie was still fast asleep, her hand still resting under her cheek, and he carefully leaned forward and without thought, he placed a kiss on her lips. Shocked by his own actions, Noah stood back. 'So, why can't you be the big man and do that when she's awake... eh?' Again, he thought of Erin. 'Because it's wrong, that's why.' He wasn't that kind of a man and berated himself as he moved away and picked up the small pile of books from where they'd been left the night before. He stepped into the kitchen and, one by one, he looked over the books before placing them down on the small kitchen table. It was a table that looked as though it had been there for many years. It was just big enough for two people to sit at, similar to one you'd see in a café, and he could imagine both Cassie and Lisa sitting here as children, laughing, eating, and playfully toe wrestling under the table. There was a farmyard salt and pepper pot stood to one corner. A chicken and a cow and he picked the chicken up, turned it over in his hand and then cursed as salt spilled out and onto the table.

Aware that he might disturb Cassie, he closed the door, turned on the light and quickly swept the salt into his hand. 'Best be safe than sorry,' he whispered as he threw a pinch of the salt over his shoulder. He mouthed a wish. It was a wish that he knew would cause some initial pain, but also a wish that he hoped would make him happy.

Picking up the first of the books, he pulled out the old wooden chair and sat down to leaf through its pages. 'One of you has the answer I need, and for Cassie's sake, I intend to find it.'

16

Cassie moved awkwardly. Her back ached, her shoulder screamed out in pain and as she cautiously stretched out, she felt the arm of the settee connect with her foot. Opening her eyes, she realised that it was still dark. She was cold and alone. Yawning, she sat up, and squinted. The fire embers were now barely visible, and a frown crossed her face.

'Noah?'

She sat up and listened. A soft gentle snoring sound seemed to come from the kitchen. Pulling open the door she saw Noah, fast asleep, childlike, with his head on the table amidst a pile of books. The sight melted her heart.

'Hey. Come on, sleepy. Come to bed.' The words slipped out. A blush crossed her cheeks and a hand went up to her mouth. 'I mean... come on, you can take my bed, again. I'll take Aggie's.' She pulled at his arm and watched as his eyes flickered, recognition crossing his face as he gave her a huge smile.

'What time is it?' he asked, pushing himself up into a sitting position, yawning and blinking as he took in his surroundings.

'Half eleven.' Cassie moved around the kitchen, placing the cups in the sink and running the hot water. 'I'll give these a quick wash, save doing them in the morning.'

Noah pointed to the books. 'Do you want to see what I found?' He yawned again, picked up one of the books and took a deep breath. 'This sketchbook, the one with all the illustrations, am I right in thinking it's the one that was found by the fireside. It's had a page torn out.'

Cassie frowned. 'It is. Go on.' She took the book from his hands and slowly turned it over in her own. Her fingertips affectionately grazed the cover. It was the book that contained her dad's tattoo designs and was a keepsake her mother had loved and kept for years, and because her mother had loved it, Aggie would have loved it too, refusing to throw it out, no matter what.

'I looked the whole way through it and remembered your telling the police that it had all your dad's tattoos in it. Yet I don't see any that resemble the snake tattoo you told me about at uni.'

Cassie stepped back, puzzled. 'But it was definitely in there. I remember it.' She flicked the pages over, one by one. 'So, where did it go?'

Noah stood up and turned off the light, picked up his mobile and flicked on the torch. He then turned to the place where the page was missing and shone the torch directly at the page. 'Also, do you see what I see...?'

Cassie squinted. She tried to concentrate on the page and at the point where the beam of light had landed on what seemed to be a blank page. All she could make out were a few slight indentions on the page. 'See what?'

Noah altered the position of the torch. 'Look carefully. You can just see the words. These words would have been written on the page above. The page that was torn out. But look, whoever wrote the words had pressed on the page hard with a biro and it's made a mark on the page below.'

Again, Cassie stared, turned the page and stared again. Noah was right. There were two names, she could just make out. Two scribbled names.

'What do they say?' she asked, looking up at Noah for support.

Noah shrugged. 'I've been trying to work it out.'

'Can't you do that thing we used to do in school with wax crayons?' She waved her hand around in the air as though she was taking a bark rubbing against a tree. 'Would that work?' Walking behind Noah, she watched over his shoulder as he moved the notebook from one position to the other in order that the names might stand out more clearly.

'I think the top name says Mar... Margaret Smith... or Smithson. Definitely more than just Smith.' He pointed with a pencil to the curvature of the letters. 'Then I think it says, Peter something, Peter Boote or Booth, maybe.'

Cassie shook her head. The names meant nothing to her. She sighed and studied Noah with amusement. 'Anyhow.' She poked him in the ribs making him jump up and out of his seat. 'Answer me this, how the hell do you go from being fast asleep to wide awake in three seconds flat?'

He tapped his pencil on the piece of paper. 'Cass, these names are important. I just know it. We just have to find out why they're important.'

'Or maybe, they just wanted the picture of the snake tattoo?' She flicked from one page to the other.

He turned the torch off. They stood in darkness and only the fire's embers gave a glow to the room. 'These names, they were written on the page that was torn out, the page above this one, the one of the snake tattoo. It has to be relevant and someone thought it important enough to break into your house for. So, my guess is, if we find out who these people are, we might discover who broke in and why.' He paused, yawned and stretched. 'Now, did I hear you say the words "come to bed"?'

17

Noah wanted to kick the wall but didn't. Throwing himself at the single bed that had once been Cassie's, he lay looking up at the ceiling and listened intently for noises in the house but all was quiet.

Picking up his mobile, he went over his messages from Erin, word for word. Including a new one.

Hey. Can't believe you didn't call me back. Maybe I'll forget to call you next week while I'm living it up in Majorca x

He read between the lines knowing that the message was a poke. This was Erin's way of making sure he knew exactly where he stood and for the next week, she'd be in the sun, with the girls, having fun and because he hadn't jumped as soon as she'd expected him to, he was now well and truly in the doghouse.

The question was, did he care?

He lay motionless. The thought of her being abroad and living it up really didn't bother him and he waited for a streak of jealousy to sear through him. Normally he'd have phoned her immediately, made a fuss, calmed the waters and told her he loved her. But instead, he placed the phone on the bedside cabinet and felt a stab of remorse as he realised that not only had he stopped missing Erin, he'd stopped being affected by what she did or did not do. He sat upright against the pillows. Was he wrong not to care? Was he wrong not to feel jealous? Was he wrong to love Cassie?

'You need to get a set of balls, my friend,' he whispered into the darkness, knowing that just a few moments before he'd been stood looking into Cassie's eyes. They were eyes that he'd looked into before, eyes that were always pleased to see him, eyes that he could easily stare into for the rest of his life. Which begged the question, why was he still with Erin?

He moved to the edge of the bed, knowing what he now had to do. Picking his phone back up, he flicked onto the browser. 'Flights to Dublin from Doncaster,' he murmured, knowing that he needed to go back home. He needed to see Erin before she went on holiday and he needed to end their relationship. He looked up at the ceiling and said a silent prayer of thanks that there were no houses or children involved.

He lay back down and turned onto his side, frowning. Looking at the other bed, alongside the pretty pink curtains, he could imagine Cassie lying here as a little girl, chatting to her sister. They'd have chatted about their hopes and dreams, and the kind of man they'd want to spend the rest of their lives with. With a sudden realisation, Noah's frown turned into a smile. Cassie was the one he wanted to spend his life with. He sighed. 'But what if she doesn't want you? What if you missed your chance? What then?'

Questions flew around his mind and seemed to bounce back off the walls. But when he closed his eyes a picture of Cassie's face calmed him. 'Well, how I see it, Noah my friend, you can either be a man and follow your heart. Or you can stay friends, risk losing touch again and miss out on what could be the best years of your life with the woman you love. Either way, being with Erin is wrong, for you and for her, and that needs sorting out sooner, rather than later.'

18

'Lisa, please stop worrying. Everything is fine.' Cassie threw her head back for the tenth time and went over every aspect of the past two days with her sister. She was leaning against the pillows on her bed and punched one of the decorative cushions each time Lisa screeched down the phone at her.

'Why, why didn't you call me?' Lisa insisted. 'I would have come over. I could have helped.' Cassie could imagine her stood at the other end of the phone with her arms flaying around in the air, lips pursed and toe tapping up and down on the kitchen floor.

'Lisa, there was nothing you could do. You have the kids to worry about, you don't need to worry about me too.' Cassie smiled at the irony; Lisa had worried about her every day of her life and she had no idea why she expected her to stop now. 'Besides, Noah stayed over. He was a true gentleman. Looked after me, even brought me a mug of tea before he went to work.'

She sighed. It was Saturday morning, and reluctantly Noah had had to go down to the site. Another meeting that just couldn't wait. But, for her and the others, there was no work until

Monday and she didn't know whether to feel happy or sad because no work meant no time with Noah.

Cassie heard Lisa giggle. 'So why do you sound just a little bit too disappointed about him being a gentleman?'

It was a fair question and Lisa was right. She was disappointed. 'Oh, Lisa. You know how it always was with me and Noah. I always thought it would be more, but obviously he never felt the same. Besides, he has a girlfriend.' Once again, she pulled the decorative cushion onto her knee and punched it repeatedly.

Looking across the room, Cassie spotted Noah's shirt and laughed at the irony that Noah's clothes were hanging up in her bedroom and that last night he'd slept in her bed. 'I think I must have "friendzone" stamped to my forehead. The guys I like stay well away and the guys I don't seem to jump on me from a great height.'

Cassie threw her head back in frustration, banged her head on the headboard and yelped. 'Ouch.' She pushed her tongue against the back of her teeth and her hand automatically went to her lips that still felt sore. 'So, what do I do, Lisa? Stand in front of him naked, do you think that would give him the bloody hint?'

'Oh, honey. I don't know. Seriously I'm the last person to ask about relationships. Me and Marcus, we met so long ago that I'm not sure I remember anything about the dating game or the signals that men do or don't give.' She began to laugh.

'Actually,' Cassie changed the subject, 'talking of Marcus, have you told him about the baby yet?' Cassie waited for an answer, but the silence on the other end of the phone spoke volumes. 'Lisa, you have got to tell him, come on, he's bound to think that something's going on when you drag the cot down from the loft.' Cassie pushed her hair away from her face.

'Cass, it's difficult. The kids, they're always around. If it isn't one of them, it's the other. Oliver has had a stinking cold and

Thomas has far too much energy. He won't sleep. I swear he must be fitted with batteries. And as for Marcus, he's been coming home late most nights. It's been either eight or nine o'clock every night and, quite honestly, if he's late home much more often, he might as well sleep at the damned office.'

The phone line went quiet. Cassie could hear her sister breathing and took comfort in the fact that whatever happened in life, Lisa was always there, even if at times, like in the playground that day, she'd wished she hadn't been.

She changed the subject again. 'Lisa, in Dad's old sketchbook, the one with all his tattoo drawings, I found some names. Margaret Smithson and Peter Booth. Do you remember him ever mentioning them or names like them?'

'Nope, means nothing. Have you tried the internet?' Lisa's voice went distant, the handset had been covered and she could hear her muffled voice shouting at the boys, 'No, Oliver, don't do that and leave your brother alone.'

Cassie continued to listen, breathing in deeply. She could smell Noah's aftershave. It had lingered on her pillow from the night before and she briefly closed her eyes as the aroma stimulated her senses. Had it really only been three days since she'd arrived home from Italy? Was it only three nights since she'd walked into this very room and dumped her bags in the corner – the same bags that she still hadn't finished unpacking? She sat up and stared at the corner. 'Where the hell's my mattock?'

'No idea,' Lisa replied in answer. 'What's a mattock?'

Cassie jumped up from the bed. She was now tearing around the room, looking inside wardrobes, under the beds and behind the curtains. 'It's one of my tools. A hand tool, long, pink handle with a metal curved head. One side is like a pick, the other side's an axe. I'd washed it and left it out to dry. But... but it's gone.' She continued to search.

'Maybe Noah moved it,' Lisa suggested, but Cassie shook her head. She remembered getting home, dragging both cases up the stairs, where they'd sat unopened overnight. But the following day, she'd pulled the tool roll out of the case, retrieved the mattock and washed it. Then, she'd left it on top of the tool bag to dry and now, now it was nowhere to be seen.

19

After putting the phone down, Cassie had paced around the house in a daze. She'd picked up and put her phone down at least a dozen times, spent at least an hour wondering if she should phone Noah, but knew that he was still in a meeting. Not wanting to disturb him, she walked out the door, locked up and left the house that she no longer felt safe in, heading for the library. It was just a short walk from home, but the heavens opened, and rain began to bounce all around her like gobstoppers landing heavily on the pavement. Running past the site, Cassie glanced at the Portakabin. The meeting was still in full swing and she could see a man, pacing up and down as he spoke to the group.

The sky turned from grey to black, thunder roared somewhere in the distance and Cassie pulled an umbrella from her bag, but the wind repeatedly blew it inside out and she found herself running between the puddles in an attempt to dodge the worst of the weather. At first, she'd run towards the subway, thinking that the tunnel would give her some shelter, but the rain cascaded down the ramp like a waterfall and she quickly changed direction and headed for the pelican crossing. Here she stood, waiting for the crossing to change, while the buses and cars sped past, splashing water up and over her boots, making her feet squelch as she ran. She was beginning to wish she'd stayed in Italy. Since she'd been home, everything had gone wrong and she felt in need of comfort, which was why she'd automatically set off to the library. It had been one of the first places she'd gone to after moving to Aggie's house when she was eleven. Over the years it had become her very own refuge from the rest of the world, a place where she'd quite often managed to disappear from everyday life and into her safety net of books.

Entering the library foyer, Cassie stood for a moment on the coir doormat to catch her breath. Stamping her feet, she waited for some of the water to drip off, before removing her coat and running her hands through her dripping wet hair. She passed the umbrella from one hand to the other, opened the door back to outside and shook it. For a moment, she considered throwing the umbrella into the corner by the door, but then changed her mind, pulled a plastic carrier out of her bag and placed it inside. 'Can't have you stolen too, can I?' The thought shocked her. Was that what she really thought? Had her mattock been stolen? And if so, why? Why were the only two things missing after the break-in the sketch of the snake tattoo torn from her dad's sketchbook and her mattock? It didn't make sense.

Fumbling in her pocket for her phone, she decided to send Noah a message.

Hi Noah. Did you or Kyle move my mattock the other night? It was on the dressing table. Bit worried that it's disappeared x

She read the text back, the text looked like an accusation, which made her cringe and she quickly deleted it and started again.

Hi Noah. I've misplaced my mattock. Felt sure that I'd left it in my bedroom (I know, stupid place to leave tools) I can't remember moving it, but… I can't find it anywhere… you didn't push it in a cupboard or anything for safekeeping, did you? xx ps: I've gone to the library, house felt strange without you. Call me when you can xx

Cassie considered the text. Did it sound okay? Taking a deep breath, she concluded that it wouldn't get any better and quickly pressed the 'send' button.

She continued up the stairs and onto the first floor where the computers were. There was no Wi-Fi at Aggie's house and she needed to do some research to see if she could find any further information about the tunnels, Aggie's boyfriend John, or about her two mystery names.

Filling out the relevant form, Cassie paid for the computer usage. She then sat down at the desk and began keying in the log in detail. The screen immediately kicked into life and she opened a browser and keyed the name 'Margaret Smithson' into the search engine. Sitting back, she was amazed by how many people obviously had the same name. There was one social media account, ten different LinkedIn pages and a third option, 'Margaret Smithson Obituary Notices'.

Raising her eyebrows, Cassie considered the possibility. The sketchbook had been her dad's. He'd drawn his pictures in it since he first began his trade so, yes, there was a distinct possibility that both Margaret Smithson and Peter Booth could have died.

Cassie tipped her head to one side. 'Okay, let's try Peter Booth...' she whispered, punching his name into a separate window. Again, she stared at the screen as the results came through. There was an artist by that name, half a dozen accountants, followed by multiple social media accounts, LinkedIn profiles and again, obituary notices. 'Come on. Come on. Give me a clue? Are you alive or dead?' She clicked on one or two profiles and studied the images. 'Are you him, are you *my* Peter Booth?' She threw the question at the screen before checking her watch. It was already lunchtime and she tutted at the computer.

'What to do next...' Chewing on her fingers, she debated which lead to chase, eventually going back to Margaret Smithson and to a site she'd spotted earlier. 'Search Cemeteries.' Spotting the 'register for free' symbol, Cassie began filling in her details. She hit the enter key with enthusiasm and waited. The anticipation was killing her. She began looking through the spreadsheet of over a hundred Margaret Smithsons that had immediately appeared. 'Wow... so many.' There were at least six that were born in Doncaster. 'What do I do? Do I go through them one by one? And if I do, how do I know what I'm looking for?' She clicked on the first name that appeared in the search, but then without warning her screen disappeared, and another screen replaced it. 'No, damn you, I don't want to take out priority membership.' She sighed and slammed her hand down on the desk, then quickly looked over her shoulder and apologised to the three older men that had spun around in their chairs. 'Sorry,' she whispered.

Cassie sat back in her chair. 'It should be easier than this,' she thought and stared down at the keyboard. 'Okay, come on, think logically.' Her fingertips drummed on the desk. 'How about...?' She tried to remember what Aggie had told her about the accident. Had she given John a surname? What year had he died? She stared up at the ceiling and then typed, 'Accident, Balby Bridge.' She sat back as a list of results filled the page. 'Wow, fourteen killed, incident at the tower block.' Her eyes moved down the screen as she once again checked her watch. Her internet time was being quickly eaten into. She couldn't stay much longer and flicked through the screen as fast as she could.

'Next, next, next...' She scanned the pages. Then she saw the headline. 'On this day in history. Tunnel collapses killing local boy 1963.' Opening the screen, Cassie could feel the anticipation inside her build. This was it. This was the article that told of John's death. But as the page opened, she felt an overwhelming wave of sadness. Sadness for Aggie, for how her life had turned out and for the man she'd loved.

She began reading.

Man Dies After Sandstone Tunnel Collapses.

Sixteen-year-old, John Foster, a Doncaster man has died in Balby when one of the old cemetery entrances to the famous Sand House tunnels collapsed on top of him. It's said that the former tunnels had in recent years been used as a playground for local children and it took many friends, family and bystanders to pull Foster out. He was unresponsive when the emergency crew arrived and pronounced dead at the scene.

The tunnels were vast and had gone between Green Dyke Lane and the far edge of Hyde Park Cemetery. It is thought that Foster died when the section of tunnels that led under the cemetery collapsed and the aged grave of Margaret Joan Smithson fell into the void, leaving a substantial hole in the graveyard. Doncaster council will landscape the area in due course.

'Oh, my God.' Cassie couldn't believe her eyes. It was all there, including the names. 'I... I found her. She's here.' Elation filled her mind, but her enthusiasm was soon diminished. 'Okay, one down, one to go... Peter Booth, your turn?'

20

Noah paced around his bedroom at the pub, picked up his phone and reread Cassie's text. I've misplaced my mattock. Felt sure that I'd left it in my bedroom.

He chewed at his bottom lip. He'd thought back to the night before ever since the text had landed and he was certain that he'd seen the mattock lying on top of the tool roll. He remembered picking it up. He'd admired how clean it had been and laughed that only Cassie would clean her tools to such a degree. Then he'd placed it back on top of the roll, on the dressing table, exactly where he'd found it. He could visualise it perfectly and knew that it had definitely been there, along with a set of metal spikes that had been lying beside it.

Sitting down on the bed, he closed his eyes and went through everything that had happened the day before, step by step. Kyle had gone back to the digs early, maybe around six. He'd returned about eight, with new locks in hand, which he'd put on both the front and back doors while Noah had taken Cassie a mug of tea. And, because Cassie was upstairs and getting ready for work,

Kyle had stayed downstairs because he hadn't had any reason to go back up.

'But then Kyle had left, hadn't he?' he said to himself and nodded as he remembered looking at his watch. It had been just after eight thirty when he'd shouted up and asked Cassie if he could grab his stuff, before running to the top of the stairs where he'd found her stood in the bathroom doorway with her toothbrush protruding from her mouth. He remembered laughing at her, before running into the room, drawing the curtains, grabbing his bag and spotting the tool. It had been on the dressing table, half hidden by the curtain. Then he'd left and neither he nor Kyle had been back to the house all day, not until he'd turned up that evening with the kebabs.

He paced back and forth. The mattock had definitely been there that morning and now it was missing. He swallowed and held his breath while slowly shaking his head. That noise, the one that had woken him. There had been nothing to see, nothing except the bathroom window being open. But why was it open? He'd stood in the doorway of Cassie's room. Why hadn't he gone in? He remembered having an uneasy feeling about the room, the odd aroma and had just stood in the doorway staring in but couldn't remember focusing on anything in particular. Had the mattock been there?

He picked up his mobile. 'Hi, Cass. Just got your text, so I did.' He didn't know what else to say to her and tried to sound cheerful. The last thing he wanted was to frighten her but knew that at some point he had to tell her what he thought. 'Can you meet me? I need to run something by you.' He looked at his watch. 'Yeah, sure, twenty mins at yours. See you there.'

Clicking the phone off, Noah threw it on the bed, ran a hand through his hair and checked his appearance in the mirror. He smiled at himself, checked his teeth for food and headed out of his room.

Stepping outside, he saw the rain and considered turning around. He really needed a coat, but adrenaline was now coursing through him and he set off running through the estate, towards where Cassie lived.

* * *

Cassie continued to battle with her umbrella. It had turned inside out on numerous occasions and now, just minutes from home, she finally gave up, put it down, tossed it into her carrier bag and rounded the corner to see Noah, patrolling her back gate.

'Noah, what on earth, you're soaked.' He looked agitated as he paced up and down and Cassie immediately knew that something was troubling him.

'Can we go in?' Noah's voice trembled and for a few seconds, Cassie just stood and stared.

'Of course. What's wrong?' She headed towards the door. 'Where's your coat?'

She opened the back door and watched as Noah pushed past her. 'Cassie, let me go first.' He gave her an apologetic look, kicked off his wet shoes and stamped through the kitchen. He moved quickly, his eyes looking in every direction, reminding Cassie of the security dogs that had often patrolled around the site in Herculaneum, checking every corner, every stone and historic building before moving on.

'Noah, what are you doing?' She watched him move from kitchen to living room.

'Come with me.' He grabbed hold of her hand and dragged her towards the stairs.

'Noah. Stop. What the hell?' She pulled her hand from his, took a step backwards and hovered around the bottom of the stairs. 'You're frightening me.'

'Cassie. You need to trust me. This is really important. Please...' He ran upstairs and disappeared into the bathroom. 'Cassie...'

Confused and worried, Cassie followed him and watched as he exited the bathroom, then walked into Aggie's room. 'What are you doing?' She went in to find Noah standing in front of Aggie's wardrobe, moving clothes, shoes and handbags and carefully positioning them on the floor.

'Cassie. Last night, either before I got here or while we slept on the couch...' He paused, his hand went through his hair and he pulled at it with frustration. 'Did you...' he pointed towards the bathroom '...did you open the window, in there, like that?' He stared at her, waiting for her reaction.

'No, why would I?' Cassie could feel her anxiety rising. She looked from one room to the other. She felt scared and took a step backwards. 'Noah, what do you know that I don't, because right now, you're really scaring me?'

Noah sat down on Aggie's bed. His eyes were closed, and he began taking deep breaths. 'Please, humour me.' He paused. 'Cassie, look at Aggie's room.' Again, he went quiet, sighed and his shoulders dropped as a look of defeat crossed his face. 'Cassie, think really carefully. Before I got here last night, did you by any chance leave the clothes, the shoes, the bags all over Aggie's floor, just like this?'

Cassie looked at Noah and slowly shook her head.

'Right, next question.' He stood up and walked to her bedroom, pushed the door open and walked inside. 'The mattock. It was there, right?' He pointed to the dressing table.

Cassie nodded. 'Yes, that's where I left it,' she said as Noah turned and stared at the open door, the colour draining from his face.

'Cassie. While we were sleeping on the settee, I heard a noise. It came from up here. Everything looked like this.' He pointed into the bathroom and then at Aggie's door. 'I stood in your doorway and stared into the room. But I didn't go in. Something didn't feel right. There was a strange aroma, like the smell of a cleaning product. The question is, Cass, why didn't I go in? And why...' His hand reached out and took hers in his, as his eyes scanned between rooms as though adding up a sequence of events. 'Oh, Jesus, Cassie, I think I know what happened.' His voice had gone up an octave, the colour drained from his face and he hesitated before carrying on.

'What?' She looked from bedroom to bathroom. 'What are you thinking?'

'When you were kids, Cass, did you ever play hide and seek?' He stared at the door. 'Did you ever use the door to hide behind?' He pulled her across the room and Cassie watched as he slowly closed the bedroom door behind them. Both their eyes immediately went to the carpet behind the door, where her levelling pins and chisel lay discarded by the skirting board.

'That's... they're my...' Her hand went up to her mouth. 'They were in my tool roll. So, what the hell are they doing behind the door?'

Noah took in a deep breath and sat down on the bed. 'Cass, I think someone was up here.' He pointed to the area behind the door. 'I don't know why, but I felt uneasy. I stood in the doorway, but didn't come in. And... and I think they were stood right there, with your tools in hand, ready to use if they'd had to.'

'But you slept in here.'

'I know, but the noise, the things all over the floor had bothered me and last night I slept with the door open, so I could hear if you shouted. I wouldn't have noticed the chisel or the pins, not without closing the door.'

'So, where did they go? How did they get out?' Cassie asked.

They both stared down at the two long metal spikes that were around eight-inches long, the sharp chisel that had been sharpened regularly. Along with the mattock, the intruder had held the perfect weapons.

'I guess the intruder left the same way they had come in – through the bathroom window – before we came up to bed,' Noah replied.

Walking to her bedroom window, Cassie pushed it open and pulled in deep gasps of air.

But Noah shook his head and began scanning the room. 'So, what did they do with the mattock?'

21

The bedroom at the pub was clean, but it wasn't home. The walls were plain, bare, painted in a neutral cream emulsion and the windows had chocolate brown curtains that had long since seen better days. Cassie's hand grazed the bedding that wasn't hers. She didn't want to be there. But didn't feel as though she could be at home either.

The distant noise of the pub was creeping up the staircase; the sound of pool balls could be heard dropping down the chute, rattling and clanking as shot after shot was taken. Darts were fired at a board, men cheered, a slot machine pinged, and the occasional clatter of coins crashed into its metal tray. She glanced at the television that had been bolted to the wall and tried to pay attention to the meaningless noise that came from it, but failed. Sighing, she eventually picked up the remote and turned it off.

Throwing the remote at the bed, she followed it, and buried her face in the pillow. Her body heaved with a sob. Why was everything going wrong? She pulled at a tissue from its box, wiped her eyes and then blew her nose. 'Who had been in the house, and what the hell had they been looking for?' She turned over, shook her head and stared at the ceiling, looking for answers.

Since coming home from Italy, her whole life had turned into a turbulent mess. In fact, apart from finding Noah again, she couldn't think of one single thing that had gone right, and now, after what appeared to be another break-in, she was hiding herself away in the pub's B&B while the police searched her home, dusted it for fingerprints and looked for clues, when all she really wanted was for everything to go back to how it was.

She took in deep breaths in order that she might try and control her tears.

'Please, please just let one day be easy, let one day be normal and, for God's sake, let Noah kiss me,' she growled. Her mind was back in that playground, to that day when she prayed for her life to change. Since that day, she'd always been careful never to wish for another dramatic change, not after what had happened, and re-thinking her wish, she revised it. 'Okay, please, just let me get to sleep in my own bed tomorrow and all will be good.' She pulled the pillow from under her head. Her mobile buzzed and she turned over to grab it. Sitting up, she wiped her eyes and read the text.

You okay? Noah x

Cassie read the message and smiled. Noah was most probably just a few inches away from her. 'Are you there?' she questioned the wall as her hand touched the paintwork. She closed her eyes, imagining that he might be doing the same. His room was a mirror image of hers, which meant that tonight he'd be right there, at the other side of the wall, sleeping in his own bed, just inches from her.

She turned on her bed to face the wall. 'You didn't expect to be sleeping here tonight, did you?' she asked herself but thought of the alternative. 'I guess I could have stayed home. Waited for the police to leave and for Kyle to attach the window locks, just as he'd promised.' She imagined trying to sleep. It would have been close to impossible with one eye open, watching, waiting, while hugging a kitchen knife, ready to strike, just in case.

'House'll be like a bloody fortress once Kyle's finished,' Noah had said. 'By tomorrow, you mark my words, even the British army would find it hard to get in.'

She was worried about her tools, about who had taken the mattock, what they were doing with it and about how the policewoman had rolled her eyes while placing the levelling pins and chisel in a clear plastic bag.

'I will get them back, won't I? They were a gift from my aunt,' Cassie had said as the officer had simply turned on her heel and left the house, taking the tools with her. 'I'm an archaeologist, I need them,' she'd shouted to the policewoman's back. But then she'd sighed. She'd looked from the bedroom to the landing, and directly at the spot where Noah would have been standing.

'I can't bear to think that you could have been hurt. What if...?' she whispered through the wall. She began to shake, nothing felt real, bile rose in her throat and she dashed to the bathroom. Running the cold water, she splashed her face and the rest of the sentence hit her with force. 'What if... I never get to tell you how I feel? What if you go back to Dublin and marry Erin? What if I've messed everything up?' She tried not to think of his planned trip home, of the early flight he'd booked for the following day, along with the promise of being back before work on Monday. She'd overheard a whispered conversation with Kyle, the mention of Erin's holiday and of how he just had to see her before she went. 'He must really love her,' Cassie thought, while remembering how she'd fallen to sleep in his arms, of how comfortable and safe she'd felt. But, above all, of how she wanted to fall to sleep there again.

In fact, she just wanted him to hold her over and over again. Just as he'd done earlier, at Aggie's while they'd waited for the police. 'Hun, it's far too dangerous for you to stay here tonight. I have to leave really early in the morning. Which means you'd be alone for half the night,' Noah had said. 'What if the intruder comes back? What if, without me here, he takes his chance and has another go at you?' He'd paused. 'If it wasn't so important, I wouldn't go. But I really do have to see Erin. She goes away on Monday and I really need to see her before she goes.' He'd looked her in the eye as he spoke. 'I think we should see if the pub has a spare room. If not, you can have my room till I get back, I could go share with Kyle for tonight, sleep on his floor. Or maybe you could call your sister and stay with her.' His arms had tightened, all the time whispering in her ear. 'Please. Do it for me, at least till I get back from Dublin.' The hug had seemed to last forever, then, slowly and carefully he'd lifted his fingers to her face to move a strand of long dark hair away from her face, where they'd lingered on her cheek and burned a path across her skin.

Cassie turned the tap water off, walked back to the bed, picked up the phone and replied to the text.

I'm okay, I guess. What time do you leave tomorrow? x

She was sick of crying and sick of feeling angry at the world. 'Whatever happens, it isn't going to change anything and no amount of wishing will change it either.' She stood by the window, looking out. She needed to alter her mood. 'Okay, time for a shower.'

Moving to the bathroom doorway, she pulled a face. The

bathroom was so small that she could quite literally sit on the toilet, wash her hands and put her feet in the shower tray, all at the same time. She reached into the shower to study the dials and then turned the water to hot. Leaving it to run, she stepped back into the bedroom. Her rucksack still sat on the carpet by the door. Its zip was torn, as was the pocket and she lifted it onto the bed, pulled it open and looked inside for pyjamas, shower gel and shampoo.

Her phone pinged again.

You only guess?? That doesn't sound good. Anything I can do? x

Steam was billowing out of the bathroom and Cassie went in, pulled the shower door open and stepped inside. Closing her eyes, she allowed the water to splash her face, the lemon shower gel again reminding her of Italy, of lemon groves and of all she'd left behind – and of her beloved Aggie. Allowing the water to soak her hair, she washed it quickly, jumped out of the shower and wrapped herself in her oversized bath towel. But then she sighed with frustration as once again she dug through the contents of her bag, looking for her hairdryer.

Her phone pinged again.

Hun, seriously, are you okay? Flights early, 6.30 – taxi booked for 4 x

Cassie shook her head. She wasn't okay. She wanted to go home, she wanted all of her things around her and right now, she really wanted to dry her hair. But none of that was Noah's fault. Trying to keep the tone light, she responded.

Sorry, was taking a shower, you don't have a hairdryer, do you?
Forgot mine x

She clicked on send and then remembered her trip to the library.

ps: Forgot to tell you. I went to the library and I found Margaret Smithson. Margaret Joan Smithson to be precise x

Less than three seconds later Cassie heard a loud knocking on her door. She laughed and pulled the towel tightly around herself. 'Wow, that was fast. I knew you'd be interested but—' The door was flung open and her smile disintegrated. 'Declan, what the hell?'

Stepping back, she grabbed at the door. One of her worst nightmares was right there, in that doorway and she didn't know whether to slam the door, scream or phone the police. She looked over his shoulder towards Noah's room. Could he hear?

Declan took a step forward, making Cassie gasp. 'Can I...' He smiled a lopsided smile, moving nervously from foot to foot. 'Can I come in?'

Cassie froze. She literally couldn't move or speak. She knew that any fast movement could result in the towel dropping to the floor, leaving her naked and vulnerable. She began to feel panic and light-headed. The floor began to move, and she had to force herself to breathe.

'You... you need to leave, right now,' she managed to whisper through gritted teeth.

But Declan just stood there, stepping back and forth. He looked nervous, awkward and unpredictable and Cassie stepped back, all the time getting closer to where her phone lay on the bed.

'I never meant to hurt you. It wasn't...' He paused, all the time staring down at the floor. 'It wasn't supposed to go like that.' His eyes never once looked up at her and she noticed how his hands shook uncontrollably.

'Declan, what the hell are you doing here?' Inching closer to the bed and to the phone, Cassie once again tightened the towel, but noticed the flash of confusion cross Declan's face.

He pointed over his shoulder. 'I live here, and my dad, Joe, he works here on security... and... and he's not right happy that you got me sacked.' He paused. 'I've always lived up there, in the flats, seventeenth floor. I... I thought you knew me...' His shaking hands seemed to fidget for no reason as he stepped from foot to foot. He looked agitated, distant and upset.

Cassie once again grabbed at the towel. She felt as though her whole life depended on her keeping hold of it and she felt her stomach begin to somersault like an orangutan doing back flips. Every inch of her trembled as a sudden rush of recognition flooded her mind. All the time they'd been in Herculaneum she known he'd looked familiar. The way he'd stood, stared, and smiled awkwardly and she'd recognised Joe too, but hadn't realised where from. And now she understood why Joe had been so rude. It all added up. Declan was probably the sort to have phoned his dad and told him what had happened, which was why Joe had dropped in the comment about women causing trouble, especially on a site.

'I need you to help me,' he continued, almost in tears. 'Please...'

'Why would I help you?' Her voice was barely a whisper, she couldn't breathe, couldn't think, and her mind spun like a fairground ride.

Once again, Declan took a step towards her. "Cos I need a job and—'

'And what? Did you think I'd give you one... well, think again? Besides, it wouldn't be my decision. So...'

'Please, Cassie.' Again, Declan stepped forward. His foot had now crossed the doorway and Cassie stared at his feet.

'One more step and I swear to God, I'll...' Cassie felt her whole body shake. She could feel the water dripping down her back and legs, forming puddles by her feet on the carpet, but as she stared down at the water the anger seared through her. 'I've told you. You need to leave, right now.' A million thoughts flew through her mind, starting with the break-in at her house and ending with the mattock. Had he been responsible? Had it been Declan that had followed her home that night?

Suddenly Declan's body flew backwards. One second, he was stood there. The next he was pinned up against the wall. 'The lady asked you to fucking leave,' Noah growled. 'And I suggest you do that right now.' Declan was thrown across the landing and Cassie saw him scramble towards the stairs. 'Ever go near her again and I'll kill you. You got that?' Noah shouted, but Declan had already gone.

'He didn't hurt you, did he?' Noah asked as he looked searchingly at Cassie, making sure that she was okay.

'No,' Cassie replied. 'It was just such a shock, seeing him at my door...'

For a moment, Noah leaned on the wall. He looked deep in thought, then picked something up from the floor, and turned towards her with a hairdryer hanging loosely in his hand. 'Madam requested a hairdryer,' he said with a disarming smile.

In the last few minutes Cassie had gone through a tumult of emotions – from fear to relief to lust – and now she couldn't speak. She simply stood and stared, taking in the sight of Noah with his shirt open, the buckle of his belt undone and his black jeans barely hanging on his hips. Gone was the slight frame of a teenager that she'd known and in its place was the toned, muscular chest, strong arms and perfectly shaped body of a grown man. She felt a blush rise on her cheeks and lifted a hand to her face in the hope that he wouldn't see.

'And... turning up at your door to find you dressed in a towel is becoming quite a habit,' he whispered. His eyes searched hers as though looking for answers.

Cassie stood riveted to the spot, every part of her tense.

'Cass...' He finally stepped towards her and, with one hand carefully reaching out, placed his fingers under her chin. 'Cass, I don't want anyone to ever hurt you, least of all me.' He took another step towards her.

Cassie smiled and raised her face towards his. 'Why would you hurt me?' They stood, just inches apart. Their eyes locked, her breathing slowed, and she waited, confused, as she saw the indecision cross his face.

But Noah shook his head. 'Oh, Cassie.' His hands rested on her shoulders and he pulled her into a hug. 'You have no idea how much I want to kiss you right now, no idea how much I want you. Jesus, Cass. I've always wanted you. I've just been too big a coward to say it.'

'But...' She pulled herself out of his grip and grabbed at the towel.

Noah ran his hands through his hair. 'But... what...?'

Cassie turned away. 'There's always a but, Noah... and I could hear one coming.'

'Cass, I'm not a cheat. It's not my way and... well, you're far too special to be the other woman. I can't do that to you. I won't do that to you.' He shook his head, slowly.

Cassie wanted the floor to open, for it to swallow her whole. She didn't know what he meant or what he wanted. She suddenly didn't care. All she knew was that Noah had almost kissed her, he'd wanted to kiss her and then, he hadn't, he'd pulled away. She turned and sat on the bed, her face burned, and she closed her eyes. 'Noah...'

'What?'

'Please don't go to Dublin.' She whispered the words so quietly; they were almost a wish. She didn't know what else to say or why she'd said it. The only thing she did know was that she didn't want him to go. She didn't want him to be with Erin, and she certainly didn't want him to kiss her, hold her or make love to her.

'I... I'm so sorry, I...' his words were stuttered '...I have to.' He took a step backwards and turned to stand on the landing. Both hands raked through his hair and Cassie could see the heave of his shoulders as he took in huge breaths of air and then the reality that he really was walking away hit her.

She stood up and stepped towards the door. Taking a moment, she tried to think of something to say, something that would make him stay. But couldn't. 'Fine. I... I'll see you Monday,' she eventually managed to say and, with shaking hands, she slammed the door behind him.

22

Cassie tossed and turned in the darkness. The bed was narrow and lumpy. The pillows were thin, and her foot constantly caught against the footboard. She'd tried everything from counting sheep, to singing songs. But nothing took away the spinning, the constantly flashing images, that went from Noah, to Declan, then back to Noah. Seeing Declan had bothered her more than she cared to admit. He'd dropped back into her life like a tidal wave, without warning. She didn't like it, nor did she like him.

Sitting up, she looked at the luminous digits of the clock, realised that it was still far too early to be up and threw herself back at the pillows. The thought that Noah was just a few inches away, at the other side of the wall, didn't give her any comfort and she turned her back on both Noah and the wall, all the time hoping that the embarrassing memories of the night before would fade and disappear. Every time she closed her eyes, she could see his face, his eyes, his lips. Eventually sleep had overtaken her, until a distant bleeping noise woke her. A few minutes later the noise bleeped again, and she could imagine Noah hitting the snooze and then turning back over. Her heart rate rose and she turned over, punched the pillow, closed her eyes and waited until she heard the sound of his door open and close.

At some point soon after Noah had left, she'd fallen into a deep sleep and the rain that had poured the day before had stopped. The sun had broken through the clouds and it was now shining through the gap in the chocolate brown curtains. Walking to the window, Cassie parted the curtains, looked up to the sky and began counting down the minutes until the clock said six thirty. 'Fly safe...' she whispered, but then sighed as she thought of the look that he'd given her, of the way he'd almost kissed her and of the way she'd felt, deep inside.

Dressing quickly, she grabbed her bag and headed out of the room and down the stairs. It was still early. Still not quite 7 a.m. But today she was determined to keep busy. She wanted to keep her mind off Noah and of what he was doing in Dublin and had every intention of going home, whether he liked it or not. After the invasion of the police, the sniffer dogs and the fingerprint powder, the whole house would all need cleaning.

Walking the long way back to Aggie's, Cassie kept half an eye on the Portakabin. The site had suddenly filled with large white tents. They'd been erected along the roadside in the shadow of the flats. It was as though Kyle had single-handedly built a whole production line overnight. And now everything was ready for clearing and sorting.

Cassie's stomach turned with excitement at the thought of going down the tunnel. She was due to go down the shaft the following morning. Both she and Noah would be the first, apart from the labourers who would continue to move the spoil. Time was now ticking, and the moment it started, their work wouldn't stop until the carvings were reached and the precious latex moulds had been taken.

'Cass,' Kyle shouted. 'Here you go.' He held out a set of keys.

'All the windows have locks; the doors have two. I know it seems a bit over the top, but with all that's happened, I had to be sure. Noah would kill me if anything happened to you.' He gave her a knowing smile and looked over his shoulder. 'And... Noah called me. Told me the guy who hurt you in Herculaneum turns out to be Joe's son. He lives here, well up there.' He pointed to the highrise flats. 'So I can't stop him being here. But I saw Declan last night and warned him to stay away from you and Joe's promised to keep an eye on him. He won't bother you again,' he said apologetically, paused and looked down at his boots.

'Thank you,' Cassie said. 'I knew I'd seen Joe before, but couldn't place him. He'd been to the relatives' week in Herculaneum, came out there for a week along with loads of other relatives. We got to show them the site, walk them around and at night, everyone ate together at one of the local restaurants.' Sighing, she remembered how jealous she'd felt, that she'd been one of the only workers to have no visitors and now realised that the lame excuse Aggie had given her about why she hadn't been able to come was due to her illness. Cassie had spent the whole week working, while almost everyone else had taken time out to be with their families.

'I'll be watching Declan,' Kyle continued, while screwing his hands into fists. 'If he goes near you, Cass... you scream and I'll...' Again, he gave a determined smile. 'Well, I don't think you need to know what I'd do.' Turning towards Aggie's, he began to walk. 'Come on, I'll check the place over, make sure it's safe before you go in.'

Just a few minutes later, Cassie was stood, alone, in Aggie's house. Kyle had left after checking every room, including the cellar and had even gone as far as to lift the loft hatch to peer in there too.

'Everything's going to be okay now,' Cassie thought in a silent promise. 'You'll see.' She ran a hand across the windowsill where silver white dust covered the surface. Tutting, she went into the kitchen, pulled a bucket and cloths from under the sink and began to clean.

Determined that Aggie would come home one more time, she began pulling and tugging at the furniture. The two fireside chairs and small table were dragged up the stairs and placed in Aggie's room, the china cabinet was emptied, cleaned and moved into the corner of the room before Cassie placed each ornament that had not been broken in the break-in on the shelves. Standing back, she felt pleased. The hospital bed now had somewhere to go, and she felt just a little satisfied that she'd done as much as she could in the battle to get Aggie home.

23

Cassie sat beside Aggie's bed, with heavy eyes while listening to the commotion of the ward. Patients shouted and nurses tried to help as hurried footsteps went up and down the corridors. The drinks trolley was on its second round of the day and a different, but equally friendly lady chatted to patients while pouring tea. Though, Aggie slept through it all.

Cassie leaned back in the chair, closed her eyes and allowed herself to drift. In her mind, she ran through the trees, she was running towards Noah. He was stood, waiting, but Declan stood in her way. She moved to one side, tried to swerve around him, but couldn't and then suddenly, she was falling, falling down the shaft. The floor was speedily coming towards her. She could see the snake tattoo. The Elephant. His Mahout. A baby. All the images flashed repeatedly. Then, there was her father's voice, a voice that halted her fall and suddenly she was drifting slowly, but purposely through the tunnel. She was flying without wings and no one could catch her.

The voice came again and Cassie's eyes shot open.

'Are you okay?' Todd, the male nurse stood beside her, his

hand clasped tightly to her wrist. 'You were having a nightmare.' He dropped her hand and Cassie quickly moved her chair backwards. Knuckle rubbing her eyes, she began to pull herself out of the sleep, but the drowsy feeling remained, and she picked up Aggie's glass to sip at her water.

'There you are, my beautiful girl,' Aggie's voice whispered, and Cassie turned to see her aunt sitting up against the pillows. Her smile melted Cassie's heart.

'Hey, you're awake.' Cassie managed to say as she inched the chair forward and once again, she knuckle rubbed her eyes. But as she looked back up, Aggie's eyes were closed, and it was more than obvious that she was asleep, and Cassie began to doubt that she'd ever been awake.

During the hours that followed, Aggie woke for just a few minutes at a time. She'd smiled and listened just long enough for Cassie to tell her about the site, about the progression, and their plan to go down the tunnels. 'Tomorrow, Aggie. I'll go down the shaft. And tomorrow night, when I visit, I'll tell you all about it,' she'd whispered, all the time holding onto her aunt's frail shaking fingers.

'And Noah...' Aggie had asked. 'What about Noah?'

'He'll be coming down the shaft too.' She'd tried to sound positive, but her voice had wobbled at the thought of seeing him, the thought of having to work with him, of looking him in the eye. She cringed, knowing that right at this moment she was imagining him with Erin, kissing her, making love to her. Cassie hated the thought that she'd be touching him back, holding him and that it would be her eyes that would be taking in the sight of his naked chest. The same chest that had tormented Cassie's thoughts since he'd stood partially naked outside her bedroom door and she bit down on her lip, shook her head and tried to dispel the image.

Aggie had leaned forward to give Cassie a piercing look. Her words had been slow and deliberate. 'Fight for him if you have to, my girl. You were there first and he's yours to take back. Do you hear me?' She'd held her gaze, before she'd continued. 'Don't ever forget, where love is lost, it can also be found.' Then she'd slumped back against the pillows, closed her eyes and a deep, but troubled sleep had once again overtaken her.

Cassie had sat and waited. She'd hoped that Aggie would wake, that she'd tell her what she'd meant and give her the advice that she needed. But the bell had rung, visiting was over and reluctantly Cassie had picked up her bag, kissed Aggie on the cheek and left. Not wanting to go back to an empty house, Cassie had ignored the bus and had set off at a pace to walk the two miles home.

Walking past Aggie's, she made her way through the subway that led to the cemetery. Here, a pair of metal gates stood over six foot high. They were old, rusty and permanently open after having years of grass growing through their fixings. Looking up and over them, Cassie noticed the sky beginning to darken, clouds turned from white to grey, as though the mood in the cemetery had changed and an eeriness enveloped the surroundings.

Trying to ignore the weather and staring into the vastness beyond the gates, she followed the line of the headstones and noticed that they were of every shape and size. Some still stood upright, but most were old, broken and lay in disrepair. Others were just pieces that lay forgotten. Most pieces had been placed along the wall and between the bushes and trees, where ivy had grown over them and now hid all but their shape from view. Puzzled, Cassie moved between the stones. The normal feet to the east rule didn't seem to apply and she spun around, confused. 'Maybe it's a class thing,' she whispered to herself, without knowing the answer. All she did know, and according to the date above the gates, was that the pattern of the graves would have been decided back in 1856, and at a time when the cemetery would have only been around half its current size. Keeping her eye on the ever-darkening sky, she nervously meandered down the path, towards the wall. Most of the stones in this part of the cemetery were old, pale and crumbling, with inscriptions that could barely be read.

Her phone buzzed and she answered it without thinking. 'Hello?'

'Hey...' Noah's voice came through the handset. 'I've just landed, where are you?'

'Why?' Although happy to hear his voice, the memory of the night before was still at the forefront of her mind and her cheeks immediately burned with embarrassment. Plus, a big part of her felt hurt that even though she'd asked him not to go to Dublin, he'd still gone.

'Come on, Cass.' She could hear an eagerness in his voice. 'Tell me where you are.'

'I'm looking for Margaret,' she answered bluntly, sighed and continued her walk between the stones. 'Margaret Smithson. I'm in the cemetery.'

'Wait there,' he said. 'Don't move an inch. I'm jumping in a taxi. I'll be with you in five.'

The phone clicked off and Cassie stared at the screen. Noah was here, back in Doncaster, in a taxi. She looked at her watch. 'Six thirty.' He'd been to Dublin and back in exactly twelve hours. Which meant that he hadn't stayed over with Erin. It was a thought that made her smile.

But then, a roar of thunder broke her mood. A flash of lightning tore viciously across the sky and she flinched with fear. The clouds that had been darkening were now black and she ran towards the wall and one of the trees that stood beside it. Cassie stood below its branches as they blew violently in the storm and the rain began, slowly at first, but within just a few minutes it fell in torrents and both the path and the headstones that she'd just walked past could barely be seen as a bleak uncertainty surrounded the graveyard.

Cassie pressed herself close to the wall, her eyes searching for a better place to shelter. She should go home but Noah had said to wait; if she moved he wouldn't find her and even though the rain continued to fall, her mind buzzed with excitement.

Another crash of thunder roared, a little more distant than it had been, but still the rain poured with no intention of stopping. Her soaked clothes clung to her and she found herself standing on her tiptoes to peer over the wall like a meerkat. She tried to see the road and the roundabout that Noah's taxi would undoubtedly cross, but her vision was blurred and suddenly her mind filled with fear. All she could focus on was the figure of a man in the distance standing on the bridge in the pouring rain. Watching her. Just like Declan had done back in Herculaneum. Was it Declan? She squinted and tried hard to make him out. All she knew for certain was that it wasn't Noah and instinct told her to hide. Feeling nervous, she breathed in, ran to stand under the biggest tree, using it for shelter, and tried to make herself as small as possible, keeping the broad trunk of the old tree between her and the man.

Then, without warning, there was a noise behind her. Someone was running and then, they stopped. For a moment she held her breath, her heart pounding in her chest and she didn't know whether to turn or run. Was Aggie right, was Noah hers to take? Would she have to fight for him? Her eyes were fixed to the floor and then, she felt his hand gently touch her shoulder.

'Cass...'

In a second, Cassie had turned. She'd closed the slight gap that was left between them and looked up and into his eyes, where the raindrops hung precariously on his lashes, before running down his cheeks. His shirt clung to his body and her hands went up to his chest as she saw the desire cross his face and in a single moment his lips moved forward to graze hers. It was as though he were waiting for permission to kiss her, but as she eagerly responded, Cassie felt Noah's lips part, and his tongue seductively began to tease. Her breathing became laboured, she could feel every single heartbeat as it pounded within. Every touch of his lips filled her with short sharp bursts of desire. Then his hands began to move up and over her rain-soaked blouse and he caught the back of her neck and pulled her firmly towards him as rivulets of water ran down her spine. And then, as quickly as it had begun, his lips unexpectedly left hers. They began searing a path across her cheek, down her neck and back to her lips. Cassie felt his hands pull her tightly to him while all the time his breaths were coming faster and faster.

Stepping back, his hand touched her face as between laboured breaths he spoke, his eyes locking with hers. 'Oh, Cass, I've wanted to kiss you forever.' He shook his head. 'I can think of a million times that I almost did. But didn't dare.'

Cassie felt confused. 'So why did you leave? Why go back to Dublin? I... I asked you not to go.'

He ran his fingers through her hair to tenderly move it back from her face. 'Jesus, Cassie. Don't you know me better than that?' he questioned. 'I had to go. I had to end it with Erin face to face, I couldn't just send a text.' He shook his head, 'Now that wouldn't be my way, would it?' He pulled her as close to the tree as he could as his body pressed against hers, his arousal now more than apparent, making Cassie give an involuntary gasp. His mouth once again began to sear a path down her neck. 'I've always loved you,' he whispered. 'I just didn't realise how much until I saw you again and, well... I just knew I had to step up. I had to be the man and tell you how I felt, before... before I lost you again.'

Cassie felt the heat rise in her cheeks. His hand lifted and momentarily touched her face. Every caress, every movement was as though he were asking permission to touch her. It was as though the years of waiting were almost too much, as though longing and anticipation had taken the place of an immediate passion and as though Noah had every intention of savouring every single moment, even in the midst of a storm.

'Kiss me again,' she encouraged as she melted in and out of his kisses. She thought that after all the years she'd know every contour of his body, and every beat of his heart. But his lips gave off tiny electric shocks, each touch made her feel as though she'd never been touched before and every slow, but deliberate movement made her chest constrict. It was as though she were breathing for the very first time, taking each breath as though it were something new, something precious. Yet, deep down, his touch was perfect and exactly as she'd imagined.

Pulling away, Cassie searched his eyes. 'Take me home,' she mouthed between kisses. 'Take me to bed.'

A cheeky smile crossed his face, 'You have no idea how much —' He stopped talking, his eyes suddenly focused on a small piece of gravestone that was half buried by the wall. 'Oh my God, Cassie, it's him, look. Do you see that piece of stone? You can just make out the first letters of the name. I'd say that it's a piece of Peter Albert Booth's headstone, and where he is, Margaret is.' He almost bounced on the spot. 'They've both been here, right next to where we kissed, the whole time.'

All that was left of the grave was a small piece of stone. It stood, right there by the wall, the letters 'Pet' and 'Boot'. And a freshly mown piece of grass was all that marked the true position of where his and Margaret Smithson's graves had originally been.

Cassie looked up to the sky; the rain still poured relentlessly, her hair, body and face were now soaked, as was Noah's, but she didn't care. All she could do was think of Aggie's words. 'Where love is lost, it can also be found.'

She thought of the tunnel, of John and of Aggie. Of their love and of Aggie's desperation as she'd watched the tunnel collapse and every dream of a happy ever after had been shattered for her, right here, on this spot. Yet for Cassie, as she pulled Noah back towards her, she would always know that for her, here was where it all began.

24

With a necessity that Cassie had never previously experienced, she and Noah had run as fast as they could through both the rain and the puddles, only stopping as they reached Aggie's back door. Cassie fumbled with the new keys, laughing as she tried to open the door and then as it finally did fly open, they practically fell through it and into the house.

Her hands moved over his rain-soaked T-shirt and in one swift movement she pulled it up and over his head and threw it to the floor. And again, she felt his lips fall upon hers. The urgency increased, his tongue teased and his eyes gleamed. The force of his lips against hers sent shock waves flying through her and every inch of her body cried out for more.

'Noah. Make love to me.' She lifted her arms and hooked them behind his neck.

But Noah stopped. His lips left hers, he could barely breathe and as he stared deep into her eyes, she saw the question within them. 'Cass, tell me you're sure. Tell me...' He watched waited for her to nod.

'I'm sure.'

Noah pulled her towards him, and with an urgency she didn't know existed, her lips were crushed beneath his. She could feel every single contour of his body as he pressed passionately against her, his arousal, once again, fully apparent as they inched up the stairs one by one. She wanted him so much, she couldn't breathe, her heart pounded violently in her chest and she was sure that at any moment the spell would break, that the kiss, the passion wouldn't exist, and she wished as hard as she could that it could last forever.

'I want this so much,' he whispered between kisses as he moved them from stairs to bedroom. 'I've always wanted this... us.'

He pulled her tightly into the curvature of his body and Cassie felt his fingers on the button of her jeans. Moving them downward over her soaked skin, his hand skimmed her hips and thighs as the other began a gentle massage of her spine, sending currents of desire spiralling through her. But then he slowed and laid her down beside him. His fingers began skimming her skin, slowly at first but then his mouth left hers and a torrent of gentle, soft kisses were dropped the whole way down her stomach and onto her thighs.

Instinctively, her body arched toward him and she gasped as the kisses stopped and once again Noah hovered above her. His eyes locked with hers and without saying a word she gave him all the permission he needed. Cassie felt herself surrender to his touch, as Noah's fingers carefully moved over her, each touch was pure, sensual and arousing and each kiss was carefully placed for maximum explosive pleasure. But then, Cassie took control, knowing that she wouldn't be satisfied until she'd given the pleasure back and she moved onto her side, leaning on one arm as the other hand began touching him, kissing him and caressing him until he too cried out with desire.

'Noah, I think we've waited long enough, don't you?' She gave him a cheeky wink. 'Do you have...?' She didn't need to finish the sentence and watched as Noah hurriedly grabbed at his jeans, pulled a condom from his wallet, while all the time Cassie stared at his naked body.

The deep sparkle of his eyes shone back at her, as he momentarily moved away, only to return seconds later. His mouth immediately took over hers and within seconds, and finally, after all the years of waiting, of loving him, she felt him push himself deep inside her. The world sped up, their bodies moved in unison, one scream after the other left Cassie's lips and a crescendo of multiple explosions escalated through them both. Noah moaned with pleasure and Cassie finally allowed the release to leave her body with a long, surrendering sigh.

'I love you,' he whispered in her ear as he pivoted above her. 'I've loved you since that first day we met.'

Cassie giggled, suddenly aware and pulled the sheet up and over her body. 'Hey, did we just...?'

Noah nodded. His hand protectively cupped her chin as he dropped a light kiss on her lips. 'You have no idea how long I've wanted to do that.' She saw him blush. 'I was always too afraid, too scared that if I made a move, we'd stop being friends.'

Cassie felt her heart reach out. 'Noah, whatever happens, we'll always be friends,' she whispered. 'And, like you, I've always wanted this too.'

Curling into the shape of his body. Cassie relaxed and allowed herself to drift into sleep. Finally, she was where she wanted to be and, just for now, there was nothing more she could wish for.

25

Cassie woke early. An early meeting on site meant that Noah was needed, and she'd heard him making an attempt to sneak out of the room, only to turn, walk back to the bed and place a gentle kiss on her lips before he'd gone. Turning in the single bed, she smiled seductively and moved her naked body to one side, as though making room and waiting for Noah to come back. But then, the thought of the tunnels stirred her, and she leapt from the bed and began running around, dressing and cleaning her teeth.

With a new-found energy she ran out of the house and towards the site.

'Now then, what have we got?' Cassie asked as she stared over the metal edge of the shaft. But then jumped back, gasping as she held a hand over her mouth and gagged. 'Jesus, Kyle, I know they said it stunk down there, but wow, it really does, doesn't it?'

Kyle laughed. He'd obviously taken in the smell before and had known exactly what her reaction would be. 'Yeah, sorry, should have warned you about that,' he said as he tapped away on his iPad.

With a free hand she dug around in her rucksack until she retrieved a small bottle of fluid. 'Lavender oil,' she said as she opened it and put a single drop onto the collar of her jacket. She turned her head and sniffed at the oil. 'Wow. That's better. Now...' She once again looked over the shaft, took in the depth, the supports and the safety equipment that now surrounded her. 'How deep have we gone?'

'The floor is around nine metres below ground level,' Kyle said. 'I've had cameras down the shaft. We've taken air samples every hour and yes it smells, but it's nothing lethal. So, are you ready to go?' He moved from one side of the shaft to the other, looked across the car park and to the marquee-sized tents. At least six men, all in Tyvek suits, stood with long rubber gloves on and their arms in huge buckets full of mud and debris.

Cassie could almost see the cogs turning in Kyle's mind. He had full control of the site. Every single movement, every person, every bucket of spoil was being washed, sorted and categorised. Cassie knew that nothing got by him, which made her nervous. If Kyle was down in the shaft when they walked into the Elephant chamber, he'd be watching everything, and everyone, her included.

The shaft had been boarded out with long lengths of wood, metal scaffold holding them in place. Between the wood she could see the clearly defined stratums, as though time had stood still just for her to observe. One more look down the shaft made her whole body begin to shake. She didn't know whether to bounce with an edgy excitement or throw up with nerves. Her hand went up to her hair and with a single fluid movement she whisked the dark mass upwards and into a bobble that she'd had looped around her wrist. 'The gases they're on a constant monitor, right?'

Kyle nodded and passed her the iPad. 'Of course, and as you'd expect we have fresh air pumping down there on a constant flow.'

'Ratio?'

'Normal, twenty-one, seventy-nine.' He held his hands up indicating the air around him. 'Same as the air we breathe. I can increase the oxygen levels should we need to.' Again, he looked at the iPad. 'We've also put pumping equipment in place, just in case the heavens open again today, and the tunnels decide to flood. Obviously, we'd get you out before that happened.' He moved to one side and passed her a harness. 'Now then, you ready to go down?'

Cassie nodded. 'You bet.' She climbed into a set of white, paper Tyvek overalls before pulling the harness around herself and clipping herself onto the wire. Turning her back to where Kyle stood, she rummaged in her rucksack, grabbed at a small plastic bag and quickly pushed it down the front of her suit. She felt nervous, hoping he hadn't seen and took in the deepest of breaths. 'Where's Noah?' She smiled and searched the site. 'I was hoping we'd go down there together.'

Kyle smiled. 'Are you kidding? He couldn't wait. He's been down there for the past hour.' Kyle pointed downward and Cassie felt her stomach lurch at the thought that Noah was down there in the same tunnels that had collapsed on top of John. 'Is he alone?' The thought made her breathing accelerate and she began speedily pulling at the harness, ensuring it was tightly fastened.

'He has two of the labourers with him.' He paused and looked her up and down. 'What's the problem, Cass?'

She swallowed hard and remembered the night before. She'd finally got her wish and she'd made love to the man she loved.

'There is no problem. I'm just excited. I need to get down

there.' She tried to smile but couldn't wait. The thought that Noah was underground made her hyperventilate. It had only been the day before in the cemetery that she and Noah had discussed how unsafe the tunnels could be, and how easily a collapse could happen.

Standing beside Noah, she'd picked a few wild flowers and placed them by the wall, lowered her eyes and prayed silently, while holding tightly to his hand. Together, they'd marked the spot where both Peter and Margaret had been laid to rest. But privately, she'd thought of how Aggie had watched the tunnel collapse on top of the man she'd loved and of how easily his life had been extinguished like the blowing out of a candle.

She couldn't allow that to happen again, not today, not to Noah.

'Can I go now?' She quickly climbed up and onto the platform.

'Hold up, Cass? Where's the fire?' Kyle ticked another item off his checklist. 'Right, if you're ready, turn to me.' He checked every part of her kit, double-checked the harness, and pulled at every pinch clip twice. 'Right, hard hat on.' He pushed the helmet into her hands. 'You happy?'

Cassie nodded. 'Of course.' She didn't want to say too much, she didn't want Kyle to realise how truly terrified she felt, and she held her breath as she spun around on the edge of the platform just as the winch took hold and she felt herself begin to float in mid-air and just like in her dream, she was flying without wings. The first foot was the slowest while all the time she felt herself looking down into the long, narrow, deep shaft. The smell got stronger; it hit her with force and once again she sniffed at the lavender oil. 'I guess that'll be the fungus,' she thought. She began breathing in through her mouth as she'd been taught. 'In through the mouth, out through the nose,' she whispered to the rough sand walls that peeped out between the wooden planks.

She opened and closed her eyes repeatedly as her eyes became accustomed to the lighting. Even though flood lighting had been erected, there were areas of the shaft that was still dark with gloomy unseen corners. Between the wooden supports, the walls were a mixture of dirt, gravel and sand and she could see the lines in the wall where the land would have been filled and she felt herself take a sharp intake of breath as she timed her descent. The drop wasn't that deep. Kyle had said it was just nine metres, but every millimetre felt like a mile and she gripped tightly to the rope until her feet finally touched down on the uneven sandstone floor.

Spinning around, she unhooked the harness. 'Noah?' she shouted as she crouched down and peered through the entrance, to see a small crawling tunnel of around two feet high that stood to one side of the shaft. 'Noah, where are you?'

With her hands above her head, she used them to help her navigate the small opening, and almost shuffled on her belly until the tunnel opened up before her. 'Oh, my God. It's so big in here.' She looked up. 'That's where you are.' Her eyes met Noah's. She smiled, blushed and stood up as he bent to give her a soft welcoming kiss.

'Good morning.' His fingers grazed her face, his eyes caught hers and she felt a rush of desire run through her as once again his lips came towards her.

She stepped back. 'I can see that this is going to be difficult.' She laughed but leaned in for another kiss.

Noah laughed too. 'I can't help it, now that I know I can, I want to kiss you over and over and... well, I guess you get the picture.'

Cassie did get the picture, what's more there was nothing she wanted more than to take Noah back to the house and make love to him for the whole day. But she couldn't. She had a job to do. And that job involved a promise to Aggie. She stepped out of his hold.

'We need to make a rule or two,' she began, but felt Noah's lips once again graze hers and she giggled as his arms caught her around the waist. 'We're probably going to have to try and act professional, at least while we're at work.' She prompted. 'At least for some of the time.'

'Okay. Professional it is. Let's see who breaks the rule first.' He looked back at her, winked and gave her a cheeky smile before turning and pointing at the wall. 'This is the carving of the Pope... beautiful, isn't it?' He picked up a camera with one hand and a compass and notebook in the other. 'This area of the tunnels is the fifth adit or entrance. Only this one chamber and the sixth adit are circular.' His hand pointed to the ceiling. 'Do you see the domed roof?' He smiled. 'And the floral bosses. Can you believe that all of this was filled in with concrete? Lost to the world, yet only a few feet beneath the pavement?'

Cassie stood, open-mouthed and stared up and into the void. 'It would have been even more beautiful back then... you know, when it was first carved.'

'Right.' He blew the air out of his lungs. 'We need to catalogue what we see while the team finish creating a path through the other catacombs.' He pointed to a small three-foot-wide tunnel. 'There are three more chambers through there and I'd say that the Elephant and Mahout is around twenty metres in that direction. We've reached the chamber, we just need to widen and shore up the tunnel before the intricate excavation begins.'

Cassie felt the excitement rise. 'How close? I mean, how long before we see him?'

Noah threw her a bottle of water. 'It won't be long.' He caught her eye and then allowed his gaze to glance down to her lips, he held the look for a moment too long and Cassie felt the air tighten in her chest, as a young man dressed in white overalls, hi-vis vest and hard hat suddenly appeared from within the narrow tunnel. 'Hi there, Cass,' he shouted, and stood upright. He pushed a crate along a ready-formed track, similar to a train line. The track made the movement of spoil effortless and Cassie approved.

'Oh hi, it's Johnny, right?' She recognised him as one of the men from the pub quiz. He held a hand out to Cassie.

'Good to see you.' He paused, and Cassie saw him look between her, Noah and the carving. 'The Pope, it's amazing, isn't it? Do you wanna see the next chamber? We've got another one through there, no carvings though. But it's big. Kind of gives you an idea of how immense these catacombs were.' He indicated to the tunnel beyond and Cassie couldn't help but follow him.

The next chamber was around two metres wide by three metres high. There were no carvings in this part of the catacombs, in fact apart from the arched roof this section held nothing of interest and Cassie looked over his shoulder. 'And the Elephant chamber, it's through there?' The words were more of a statement than a question. But Johnny nodded in response.

'What's coming out of the hole?' She hovered over a crate and looked inside.

'Apart from a few remains, we have sand, bricks, rubble and gravel. It was basically a rubbish dump.'

'Re... remains?'

'Yeah, we've found a cat or two, but nothing of great interest although we're pushing everything through the shaker boxes, just in case. It's really hard going, but we're almost there. Got to admit though, I'm dreading the final excavation around the Elephant and Mahout.' He paused, giving her a half smile. 'It's the whole reason we're here and I really don't want to be the one to get it wrong.'

She saw her chance, her only chance to get the Elephant to herself and went back into the first catacomb. Directing her question to Noah she spoke with confidence. 'Can I do the excavation myself. Of the Elephant.' Her eyes pleaded with his, desperation took over and she grabbed at his arm. 'Noah, it's important. It's the whole reason we're down here and it needs to be done correctly. With my experience and expertise...' She held her breath, waiting for him to answer. 'Please, Noah. Johnny really doesn't want to get too close, he's already nervous of spoiling it and, surely, it should be us that finishes the job.' She gave Johnny an apologetic look, knowing that what he'd just said might have been in confidence. But getting to the Elephant was too important. 'I can't allow it to become damaged. We...' she emphasised the word '...we can't let it become damaged.'

Noah tipped his head from side to side as though mulling over the answer. 'Okay, but it's your turn to cook tea tonight and, what's more, you need one of the labourers down here with you at all times.' His hands went affectionately to her cheek. 'It's dangerous. We've done everything we can to shore it up, but you know... and I couldn't bear it if something happened to you. Not now.' His face dropped towards hers, a long lingering kiss was placed on her lips until a cough was heard in the background.

'Okay, Johnny. We know you're there, but this is hardly a secret,' Noah said as he pushed the spoil crate towards him. 'Now, don't you need to get this to the surface?'

Cassie laughed. 'Don't be too hard on him.' She pressed her body close to his. 'It's only recently become news to us, hasn't it?' She glanced up at the ceiling, at the many powered roof supports that stood at intervals throughout the chamber. 'I think I'll be okay down here,' she said as she pointed to the supports. 'I think

Kyle has it all covered, don't you?' She needed to throw Noah off track, needed to gain his trust and ensure that she was the one to work on the Elephant first. What's more, even if it did put her in danger, she'd promised Aggie and she needed time to work on it alone.

26

Aggie turned onto her side. She was uncomfortable and needed to move. Today was not a good day. Today she was in pain, it had got gradually worse and worse and no matter what position she lay in, it simply didn't go away. She sighed, knowing that pain relief was a long way off as a breakfast of porridge and hot tea had only just been served. Her portion still stood there, on the overbed table, congealing. She wasn't hungry and already knew that the food would stay there until someone moved it.

She turned away and wished for sleep. She longed for her own food, for her own bed and for the familiarity of home and her own surroundings, she longed for almost anything apart from the endless monotony of the days spent in here. Every day in the hospital seemed so much longer than the one before and she wanted to scream or shout, do something, anything, just to break through the boredom. Her eyes rested on the chair that stood to her right. She wished she could get out of the bed, go for a walk or just sit in that chair, just for an hour or two.

The smell of the food seemed to constantly permeate the ward. It had drifted up and down the corridor long after the trolley had passed, and the smell made her feel nauseous. Her eyes grew heavy and she tried to sleep, but the noise coming from the nurses' station, from other patients, and from the hustle and bustle of the corridor made any idea of real rest seem impossible. The only saving grace was a breeze that came from the window behind her; the air was nice and refreshing.

Aggie felt herself drift in and out of a light sleep. Her eyes were closed, her breathing slowed, and her mind wandered to thoughts of going home. It was what she wanted more than anything in the world and the simple idea that she might once again sit in her very own living room made her mouth turn up into a soft half smile. But an unusual noise disturbed her thoughts. She heard a rattle, followed by a click. The noise was close, and she rolled her head to one side, opened an eye and gasped. Her bedside cupboard was open. The frame of a man dressed in a white tunic was knelt down beside her, her keys with their distinctive ladybird key ring clearly in his hand.

'What are you doing?' She moved in the bed, pushed herself up against the pillows far too quickly, felt the rush of blood and stared straight into the Todd's face.

'You alright there, Agatha.' He hesitated, looked over his shoulder and placed the keys in her handbag. 'I found your house keys, down there.' He pointed to the floor. 'Must have dropped out when you were last in your handbag.' He smiled nervously. 'I was just popping them back for you.'

But Aggie stared at him, knowing that the keys had not left her bag once, not by her hand. 'No... No... that's not right. They couldn't have been...' She didn't really know what she was saying. She was sure that both the bag and the keys had been in her bedside cabinet; they hadn't moved for days. After all, she was in a hospital, the days were boring, repetitive and there was nowhere to go, not in her state and certainly nothing to buy. So, how could her keys have ended up on the floor?

Todd moved to the side of her bed. 'You're all twisted, Agatha. Let's make you more comfortable.' He began pulling at the sheets, the pillows and manoeuvred her into a better position before placing his hands firmly on her shoulders. 'Lean back now, there's a good girl.' But Aggie didn't move, she didn't know what to make of his actions and simply continued to stare at him.

The moment was broken by a noise that came from the bed opposite. The bed was now occupied by a new lady who suddenly begun coughing and retching. Todd moved quickly to her side. A grey pulp bowl was grabbed from a shelf and he carefully held it under her chin. 'There you go, Mary.' He paused, and the sound of retching stopped as quickly as it had begun. 'Here you are, take the tissue.' He'd picked up a whole box and held it before her. 'You okay now?'

The sound of Patty's tea trolley could be heard rattling along the corridor. It had just been to Aggie and her tea was still too hot to drink, but the comforting sound of Patty's voice echoed from one ward to the next. 'Hello, my lovely. Tea, no sugar? No problem, my darling, I'll get that for you.' Her voice was refreshing, friendly, full of life and Aggie looked forward to her visits, as well as the hot drink, which was always welcome.

Todd continued to stand by the bed opposite. He looked fidgety, anxious, and had repeatedly picked up and checked Mary's chart, while watching Aggie just a little too closely. Then, after looking up and down the corridor and towards the nurses' station, he walked back to Aggie's side, gripped her wrist and made a pretence of taking her pulse. He leaned in as close and as low as he could, almost knelt by the bedside and glared into her eyes. But frail as she was, Aggie still had spirit. Dragging her hand away in temper, she caught her bedside cabinet and almost laughed as her hot tea flew up and into the air, the lid fell from the beaker, and its contents spilled all over Todd's clean white tunic.

'Damn,' Todd cursed as he jumped backwards. He quickly pulled the tunic off, screwed it up in a ball and threw it into the corner. Realising what he had done, he stepped away from the bed, turned his back on Aggie and tried to move out of her sight. But Aggie had already seen enough; her eyes were fixed on him as he stood before her in just a white vest. He was exposed, and she could clearly see a snake tattoo that curled its way around his upper arm and over his shoulder.

She shook her head in disbelief. Initially unsure of what she was seeing, she tried to think back to Cassie's words. 'It was a peculiar shape; similar to a snake, but then not like a snake at all, the scales were all wrong, they were far too long and only the ones down the middle lined up, the others went all over, in all directions.'

Could this be the same tattoo that her niece had described? The same snake? Last seen on the man who had murdered the girls' father? Aggie sat forward to look more closely. The shape of the head was quite strange, and all of the central scales were longer than they should be, not the round discs that you'd normally expect and as Cassie had said, the scales around the edge were all of odd and unequal shapes; they didn't line up or conform to the natural line of how they should have been.

'It was you... you killed him.' The words left her lips before she realised what she'd said. She swallowed hard, she knew he'd heard her and she looked around, hoping that Patty or a nurse would walk by, but they didn't. Aggie held her breath.

She began to panic. Todd was coming towards her. The curtain was suddenly pulled around the bed and she could feel her breathing accelerate out of control. 'Who the hell are you?'

she whispered, while all the time her eyes were fixed on the snake that spiralled around his arm, its bright yellow eyes glaring out from the artwork.

'Shush now, Aggie. Alright. Let's make you a little more comfortable,' he said a little too loudly. He grabbed at the pillow that propped her up and yanked it from under her. Her whole body dropped flat onto the mattress and for a moment she waited for the pillow to cover her face as the air dispelled itself from her lungs. 'Where is it? Where's the map?' His face was almost touching hers, his voice barely a whisper. 'I know you have it.'

Aggie shook her head. 'Wha—what... map?'

He punched the pillow. 'That brother-in-law of yours, he owed me.'

'So you killed him?' Her eyes shot all around, she prayed for the curtain to open and for someone to hear.

'It wasn't like that,' he whispered. 'It was an accident, just a terrible accident. It wasn't supposed to happen.' Terror crossed his face. 'I was just a kid.' His eyes pleaded with hers.

'So why did you stab him?' Venom spat from her mouth. He'd been the cause of so much anguish, of so much pain and without a doubt the shock and trauma could have brought on the cancer in Alice, her sister.

'He was a bad 'un, roped me into doing the heists with him. Promised me riches, he did, enough to keep my old mum in pearls, he said.'

'All of those robberies around the area, they were all you?' The words were more of a statement than a question, but she watched as Todd bowed his head.

Todd held a finger to his lips. 'He kept the gold, the diamonds and the jewellery. He hid them, said we had to wait. Said we had to sit on them, insisted on it.' He paused and once again looked over his shoulder. 'Kept saying that he'd tell me their whereabouts, then made out that he'd already told me, that I just didn't realise? Said I had to work it out. Like it was a bloody game.'

'So, why didn't you come looking for us before?' Aggie felt her courage grow, if Todd was going to hurt her, he'd have done it by now and she took the time to study the snake, to work out what it meant. The scales, the shape, there was something familiar. Something she'd seen before and on so many occasions.

He shook his head. Tears filled his eyes. 'Do I look like a killer? I was just a kid. A terrified kid. I reckoned that if I kept my head down, tried to do right by people, it'd all be okay and that one day, like he'd said, one day I'd work it out for myself. I'd realise where it all was.'

'What did you want with my keys?' Aggie felt the pressure leave her shoulders, the pillow was tossed to the bottom of the bed and Todd stood before her, his hands raking through his hair.

'Your niece. I know she saw me that day when Dave died. She was hiding, her and the other girl, her sister.' He paused and stepped from foot to foot. 'I thought they'd grass me up. But when the police didn't come for me, I decided to put it all behind me. Hoped I could turn a corner, become a good person. But, then, that day, when I saw her here and she said her name, I knew immediately who she was and it all came back, the nightmare I'd been trying to hide from for so many years, and...' His words were barely a whisper. He looked confused and sat down on the bed. 'I've got debts, bad gambling debts, I need the money... suddenly I could see a way out of it all. So, I took your keys, went to your house to look for a clue, anything that might show me the way.' He looked down at the floor. 'Sorry.'

Aggie suddenly felt a calmness she'd never known. Her whole body seemed to relax. Every ounce of her energy began to leave her. 'So you think the jewels will solve your problems, do you?' Again, she studied the snake, realised its significance and for some reason she had the urge to laugh. 'I'll tell you now, young man, they won't solve anything. They'll just make things worse.' She pointed to the snake. 'But my brother-in-law was right,' she nodded her head, 'he'd already shown you where they were. You've had the map all along, right there.' She pointed to his arm. The threatened laugh began, the tattoo, the snake, the odd shaped scales, they were a map of the tombstones in the cemetery that stood right by her house. A place she'd seen every day of her life and where she'd often stood and wondered why the tombstones didn't line up, why some faced east and others south or north. And there, on his arm in the style of a snake, was a map of the graveyard. 'At least I now know that the rumours were true,' she whispered. 'The robberies really were down to him. I knew he had an accomplice and I always wondered when you'd come, when you'd find us. But if you think he left the jewellery with us, you're wrong. It's been right there, on your arm the whole time.' Her mind began to drift, but then she thought of Cassie. 'You'd have never found us, would you? Not until you saw my niece, heard her name and realised who she was.' She, of course, had a different surname to Cassie and Lisa used her married name so it was only Cassie who provided the link with Dave Hunt. Aggie caught her breath; her hand gripped the bed sheets as a new and excruciating pain tore through her stomach. 'But, then, if only you'd studied your arm, you wouldn't have needed to find any of us, would you?'

He stared at the snake. The realisation registering on his face that he'd had the map all along. 'Agatha, please, tell me what it means... I'm begging you.'

'What are you begging for, my silence or for me to tell you where the jewels are?'

He nodded with tear-filled eyes. 'I... well... we had a deal, me and Dave. I've tried for so long to be a good person, to put the past behind me. I mean, look at me, I'm a nurse, I help people. But the debts, I owe bad people a lot of money and I have to pay them, and the jewels, they would do that.'

Aggie closed her eyes. A fog descended as she felt her hand being lifted from the bed. His fingers pressing on her wrist. 'Are you okay, Agatha?' Her hand was dropped, and he began shining a torch in her eyes, she didn't like the brightness, but couldn't move. 'Don't do this, Agatha, don't you dare do this, not now.'

Her breathing slowed. She knew that she should scream, shout out for help, but the sound wouldn't come. Her voice was suddenly caught within her. She felt confused. She didn't know where she was; her mind burned. A temperature ran through her and she looked around, tried to take in her surroundings. 'What's happening?' The words came into her mind but didn't leave her mouth.

'Agatha. Please.' His eyes were less than an inch from hers. His hands pressed down on her shoulders, but she couldn't move. All she could do was stare and a simple shake of her head felt impossible. A sudden wave of claustrophobia hit her, he was far too close, she didn't like it and she tried to lift her hand, tried to push him away and glared at her arm, willed it to move but it wouldn't. The strength had gone.

Terror filled her thoughts, she'd seen this before, she knew what was happening and had no power to stop it and then she closed her eyes as another burst of heat tore through her mind.

All she could do was stare at the man that hovered above her. She could see the anger, the frustration and the indecision in his eyes, but she no longer knew who he was or what he wanted.

But then she saw his hand reach out to bang at a wall.

'Can I get some help? CVA. We have a CVA in here!' She

heard him scream, a long-distressed scream and then, then there were footsteps, running, and commands being shouted out all around her. But she was tired. She had no wish to watch the commotion and, without any effort, she allowed her eyes to close and felt herself slip into a welcoming darkness.

27

Cassie watched the commotion. The chamber, along with the tunnels, had now turned into a continuous production line. A sense of excitement filled the air as more men had arrived, all went back and forth through the crawling tunnels, disappearing for a while and then reappearing sometime later with their boxes full of spoil. Shouting, cheers and whoops could be heard as boxes were pushed along the tracks and towards the shaft, where the hoist lifted them upwards to where more men would take the contents off to the tents, to be sifted and sorted.

Her stomach growled. She'd been in the first chamber for the whole morning, but the heat, the exertion and the continuous sexual tension that flew between her and Noah had made her hungry and she looked at her watch. Twelve thirty, not long now. She tried to think of what food she might have left in the fridge. But thoughts of old jam, bread and milk didn't quite hit the spot.

'You hungry?' She turned to Noah. 'I could pop to the garage for a meal deal, it's either that or the chippy for lunch, sorry.' She removed her hard hat, slid herself close to Noah, slotted herself into the curve of his body and then stood silently with her head on his shoulder as they both stared up at the carving of the Pope.

'Well, lunch might have to wait an hour, so it will.' He pulled her closer, his hand cupped her chin and he placed a soft kiss on her lips. 'We need to finish cataloguing all of this, make sure we have all of the detail, before the latex goes on.' His hand went to trace the shape of the floral carvings that ran in a line across the sandstone.

'Already done. I did the photographs when you popped into the other chamber. All are catalogued in the day book.' She pointed to a case that contained her camera, compass and notebooks. 'Shall I start cleaning it down?' Cassie questioned as her hand went up to flick away tiny sand particles that still spread themselves across the carving.

'That'd be great.' He pointed to the carved arch, to where the Pope's head rose up above it and the frieze of carved flowers that went along the sandstone around two feet below. 'I still can't believe they buried all of this and well... the concrete,' he tutted, 'it's spoiled him a little.' His fingers went across the face of the carving to where small lumps of sandstone were now obviously missing.

Cassie nodded in agreement, pulled herself out of his hold and stood on her tiptoes to examine the damage. 'I'll take the mould and then, when the exhibition goes up, we'll use the original photos to recreate him.'

A noise came thundering through the tunnel as a cheer went up and moments later an excited Johnny jumped out of the crawling tunnel. 'Here you go, Cass.' Johnny passed her a camera, then stood back, practically bouncing on the spot and smiled. 'I took a picture, we've cleared more of a space around the Mahout's foot... you can see the bottom half of his leg more clearly now.' A huge grin crossed his face. 'The tunnel, it's wide enough to get through safely, so you just have to come and see.'

Cassie felt the colour drain from her face. Her mouth went dry, her mind spun, and she simply stared at the picture. It was time to finish excavating the Elephant and Mahout and now she didn't know what to do. She felt as though her lungs had stopped working as she tried to push the air both in and out but couldn't. Reality seemed to stop, she could see both Johnny and Noah speaking, punching the air and laughing but couldn't hear a word. Her mind spiralled in every direction. She suddenly thought about every promise and every wish that she'd ever made. They were all remembered, all processed. And they all came down to this.

She looked up at the ceiling. This was what it had all been about, all the time spent at uni, all the training, and the research. It had all led to this one moment in time. So why did she feel as though she was staring into another world, and about to step through the wardrobe and into her very own Narnia.

Truth was, less than a week ago she lived in Italy and now, now she was here which gave her a feeling she couldn't quite comprehend. This place, this story had been a part of her life for as long as she could remember. She'd heard so much about it. She'd dreamed about it. My God, she'd become an archaeologist because of it, because of Aggie's obsession. She thought back to the days when they'd both stood on the pavement outside Aggie's house, looking down, wishing, hoping and praying for this moment, and now that it was here – now that she had the chance to finally see the Elephant and Mahout – she couldn't move.

'Cassie...' Gasping, she felt her whole body jump. Commotion and excitement suddenly surrounded her. Noah was laughing, he and Johnny were whooping and dancing. Others came out of the tunnel to join in the celebration. 'Cassie, we did it. It's time. We're ready to excavate.'

She smiled. Tried to look happy and reached up to hug Noah. 'I knew you could do it, I knew you'd find him.' She placed a kiss on his lips, lingered a little too long and then turned to see Johnny and the other men smirking.

'Come on you two, get a room,' Johnny yelled. 'We have work to do.'

She caught Noah's eye and winked. 'Yes, you, and I know the very room.' She laughed and began walking towards the crawling tunnel. 'Are you coming?'

Noah nodded. He followed her and knelt down by the tunnel's entrance. 'Go on then, ladies first.'

With hard hat back in place, Cassie moved on her hands and knees. The uneven surface made crawling uncomfortable and small stones dug into places that they shouldn't. 'Ouch,' she yelped as, inch by inch, she kept moving further along the tunnel. The hard hat made it impossible to look up, her neck began to ache and after a while she stopped briefly, removed her hat and checked the tunnel to see how far she had left to go.

'Noah, reverse, mate, you got an important phone call.' The words echoed down the tunnel. Noah responded, and she heard him start to move backwards and out of the tunnel.

'Cass, keep going, I'll be there in just a minute.' He sounded disappointed, she knew he'd wanted to see the Elephant as much as she did.

Cassie put the hard hat back on and continued. She made her way from one chamber to the other, but the closer to the Elephant she got, the smaller the crawling tunnels became, and even though her overalls were padded, her knees continued to be poked by every piece of stone she crawled over, making the going both difficult and claustrophobic. Which was senseless. She knew that the spoil box had fitted through, which meant that there was ample room for her to fit through too.

She lifted a hand to check the supports. They were all firmly in place. She was confident in Kyle's abilities and felt sure that he'd know exactly how many supports he should use. But as she well knew, history and time down here had a mind of its own and at any moment the tunnels could collapse, and with that knowledge her whole body shook with nerves.

She wiped her brow, tipped the hard hat and looked ahead. She was almost at the end of the tunnel; she could see how it would open up before her to show a new and bigger chamber. Cassie finally stepped out, rubbed her knees and stared up at a sheer wall of sandstone that stood before her. The Mahout's leg and foot poked out from beneath and, instinctively, she dropped to her knees. She took a moment to think of both John and Aggie's baby. She crossed herself as a tear dropped down her face. They'd both died close to this spot and, if nothing else, she felt the need to show them respect.

Standing up again, she stood, listened and waited for any noise. Nothing. She was alone, and right now even her breathing sounded loud. It echoed around the chamber, making Cassie more than aware that any noise she might make would echo too.

Moving around she took note of the area before her, the way that the labourers had dug around the central space where the Elephant would have been, a solid sandstone and concrete block now in its place. The tunnel arced around both sides where they had continued to dig a long and new crawling tunnel, which would take them to the final area, the area that led past Biddy and Pat, along with the route that had once led towards the graveyard. It was more than obvious that the men were still mining the tunnel. Galvanised metal mesh sheets were thrown on the floor, along with the supports that lay beside it. Both would be used to support the roof and were waiting to be erected. Without them in place, the roof could clearly be seen, and Cassie noted how the stratum changed, with the colour of the walls suggesting a much damper and much more dangerous environment than the one she currently stood in. She made a mental note to speak to Kyle to get more supports in place, but that would have to wait.

Turning, she looked back down the crawling tunnel. 'Noah, where are you?' She waited for a moment, realised that Noah was not there and that by some miracle she was actually alone. Her mind began to tick, like a clock adding up the seconds at speed, one by one. She spun around and began quickly trying to work out the size of the chamber. What was it that Aggie had said? She'd left the baby wrapped in the blanket under a ledge, right by the Elephant. She kicked at the sand. Where to start? Her hand went out to touch the Mahout's foot as she pictured the photographs and quickly worked out that the foot would have been to the right of his Elephant. So, that would mean that the Elephant would be here, and the ledge around about there. She pointed to the area near the floor.

Knowing that within seconds either Noah, Johnny, or one of the others would come hurtling into the chamber, she knew that time was limited. She had to act quickly and began to forage amongst the tools that Johnny and his men had left behind.

Picking up a small mattock, she began chipping at the sandstone. She had to clear an area beneath the Elephant's feet. Which shouldn't be too difficult. 'Once a void, always a void,' she whispered as she chipped away at the surface. If the ledge had been easy for Aggie to get to, then it should be easy to find. Every thrust of the mattock moved just a little more stone. Every scoop of her hand frantically moved the debris away and every inch cleared was another inch closer to where she needed to be.

Noise could be heard beyond the tunnel. 'Cassie, you there?'

Noah shouted, but her heart beat wildly, she couldn't stop, not yet. She chose to ignore him, pretend she hadn't heard, just for a moment, but she knew full well that if she didn't respond, he'd get worried and come through the tunnel. She looked over her shoulder and, once again, she swung the mattock. Another lump of stone was moved, another handful of debris. Her hands were grazed, her nails broken, she hadn't thought to wear gloves, but she didn't care. She could see a small hole, a space opening up before her, it was just a few inches wide but clearly showed a ledge that went right beneath the Elephant.

'This is it, it just has to be it.' Her words caught in her throat, her breathing accelerated, and her heartbeat continued to pound in her chest. 'Okay, here we go.' She cautiously pushed her hand through the rubble and beneath the stone. 'Ouch,' she stifled a yelp. The hole was small, her hand felt trapped and she had to keep turning it from left to right and back again. If only the hole was just a little wider. She thought about pulling her hand out, about using the mattock some more, but Noah's voice now bellowed.

'I'll be there in a minute,' she yelled back as she squeezed her hand further and further beneath the stone. But then, her fingers felt something quite rough, yet soft at the same time and an involuntary sob left her body.

Again, Noah shouted, 'Cassie are you there?' He sounded annoyed, upset. But she couldn't leave, not yet.

'Noah, give me two minutes.'

Again, she pushed her fingers forward. 'Oh my God, she's... she's there. I... I can... feel her.' She gulped and tried not to think of what she had to do. 'It's just a blanket.' She tried to lie to herself, but then stopped rigid as without warning, Noah appeared behind her.

He stood, mouth open, shaking. 'Cass, what the hell are you

doing?' He seemed to stand, motionless as she pulled her arm free and stood up before him.

'I... I found a hole. I just...' She looked back at the tiny opening she'd created. 'I got caught up in the moment, sorry. What... what's so urgent?'

Noah seemed to look everywhere but at her. 'We had a call... from the hospital. It's Aggie, I'm so sorry, but... she's had a stroke. A bad one.'

Cassie looked back at the Elephant, back at the ledge. 'A... a... stroke. But...' Again, she was rooted to the spot, she couldn't move. Her eyes went from Noah to the ledge and then back to Noah.

'We have to go.' His words were firm, but his eyes said it all. 'The hospital, they said you need to be there.'

28

The small private room was filled with the monotonous bleeping sound of machines, along with the smell of antiseptic. Night was drawing in and with darkness flooding through the windows, the room felt much smaller than it was, and Cassie found herself standing up to open the door. She needed the air to flow through the room, needed to make it feel bigger, in order that the walls might stop feeling as though they were closing in.

The whole ward bore a strange 'deathly' silence, as nurses whispered, glanced up and over their glasses and moved at speed, without making a noise, the moment they were needed.

Shaking her head, Cassie turned back to a sleeping Aggie who suddenly appeared to look very small. The bed was huge, and her tiny frame looked that of a frail and vulnerable child. What was left of Aggie's hair had been brushed away from her face, her mouth drooped to one side, her skin had taken on a grey, almost pallid tone, and although she was covered with a sheet and a blanket, her body looked all broken and defeated, even in sleep.

'Hey there, you okay?' Lisa whispered as she came into the

room and gave Cassie a quick hug. 'Sorry I took so long. I had to wait for Marcus to get home. Wh... what happened?' With tears streaming down her face she bent over the bed to kiss Aggie on the cheek, her fingertips reaching out to touch the old lady's face but stopped short as though afraid to touch her, just as a sob left her throat. 'She looks, she...'

Lisa turned away and her arms reached out to hug Cassie again, before she collapsed into the chair that stood in the furthest corner of the room. She looked drained and Cassie knew that right now she'd rather be anywhere in the world but here. It wasn't that Lisa didn't love Aggie, she did. It was hospitals that Lisa hated and had done ever since their mother had been sick. She'd avoided them so much that she'd even given birth to the twins at home, rather than deliver them in a hospital.

'I'll stay with her,' Cassie offered. 'You know, if you need to be with the kids.' Her words were a test and meant to give Lisa the chance to leave, to save her from what might come next and to allow her some dignity in not wanting to be there.

Lisa sank further into the chair and slowly shook her head. 'I... I need to stay. I owe... owe it to her.' Another sob was followed by a rustle of tissues and the loud blowing of Lisa's nose.

Cassie took a deep breath. For Aggie's sake, she needed to alter the mood.

'Aggie, it's Cassie, can you hear me?' she asked. 'Lisa's here. That's right, Lisa, in a hospital, she's come to see you. What do you think to that?' Cassie waited for a moment and sighed. She didn't know what to say, but knew that she had to talk, knew that it was possible that Aggie could hear. 'It's just the three of us again, just like you wanted.' She tipped her head to one side, waiting and hoping for some response. 'Do you remember, Aggie, what we used to do on the coldest of nights? Do you remember us dragging a mattress down the stairs?'

Cassie looked across at Lisa, caught her eye and saw the tears that fell down her face. 'Always took the three of us to get it down there, didn't it? And... we used to all snuggle up, and sleep there all together, for the whole of the night, didn't we?' She watched as Lisa once again blew into a tissue. 'What was it we used to sing?' Again, she paused. 'There were three in a bed and the little one said... roll over, roll over.' She began to sing the song of their teenage years and forced a smile, until Lisa joined in.

'Becky and the boys, they send kisses,' Lisa said. 'They've been playing at camping all week, we've had a tent up in the living room. Can you imagine the mess? I've left Marcus tidying up for me.' She paused, moved across the room and sat on the edge of the bed, taking hold of Aggie's hand in one hand and Cassie's in the other, she glanced between the two. 'Guess what, Aggie. I'm pregnant again. That's right, a fourth child.' She tried to smile, but sorrow took over as both girls knew that this baby would be the one that Aggie would never see. 'I told Marcus last night, he's so excited. You'd think I'd given him the best present ever.' She nodded and squeezed Cassie's hand. 'He's already talking of getting the cot down from the loft and painting it, so... so you need to get well, Aggie. We need you, this baby needs you.' A sob left her throat, 'No one rocks a baby like you, Aggie, do they?'

Cassie glanced from Aggie to the monitor, took note of how various lines, all different colours jumped up and down repeatedly and wondered what they all meant. To her, all they meant was that Aggie was still here, she was still with them. But Cassie knew that at some time soon, the screen would go blank and all of those lines would cease moving and Aggie, her Aggie would be gone. But a movement caught her eyes as she turned to see Aggie's hand begin to move. Slowly at first, just a finger and then two began stroking the sheet.

'Lisa, look.' Cassie held her breath, not daring to move. 'If she can move, she can hear me, right?' she asked, as Lisa jumped up.

'Shall I get the nurse?' She didn't wait for an answer and Cassie watched as she inched her way towards the door and into the corridor.

Cassie waited until Lisa had left the room. She wanted to speak to Aggie, wanted to tell her what she had found. She pulled herself as close to her aunt as she could and her hand touched Aggie's cheek in a soft, loving gesture and she took deep breaths. 'Aggie,' she whispered. 'The tunnels. I got there, I reached the Elephant. I even saw the Mahout's toes and... and I know where the blanket is. I found it, it was right there, I felt it.' The words fell from her mouth at speed and she closed her eyes as she took a breath and held back an involuntary sob. 'I'm going back for her, Aggie. I promise. I'll bury her, just like you wanted.' She glanced over her shoulder, saw Lisa talking to a nurse and then turned to watch the gentle rise and fall of Aggie's chest. She looked peaceful and, for a moment, Cassie wondered if Aggie had fallen back to sleep. 'I felt her, Aggie; my hand, it went under the ledge and I felt the blanket. She was still there, exactly where you said she'd be...'

There was another flick of Aggie's fingers. A noise suddenly left her mouth. Her eyes shot open and she tried to lift her head up from the pillow. 'S... na... a... ake.' The word was barely distinguishable, it was long, drawn out and so high-pitched that Cassie felt herself wince.

'Aggie. No... not snake, Elephant, I got to the Elephant.' Again, she looked over her shoulder. She prayed that Lisa would stay outside, but then gasped as Aggie's hand grabbed hers.

'Sna... a... ake. He... h... ere... dang... er.' Once again, her head was raised from the pillow, her eyes were as wide as saucers and fear crossed her face as deep furrows lined her brow. Then, she lifted a hand and pointed to the open door and the corridor beyond. 'Nu... r... se!'

Lisa ran back into the room. 'Jesus, Cass, is she okay? What the hell did you say to her?' she demanded as she ran to Aggie's side and picked up her hand. 'There, there, Aggie. It's okay. The nurse is coming... There you go, shush... That's it, you rest.'

Cassie felt frustration rise up inside her and walked across to the window. She looked outside and into the darkness. She was sure that Aggie had been trying to tell her something, but didn't know what. Something wasn't right. In fact, something was very wrong, and Cassie paced back and forth, as a nurse administered some pain relief to Aggie and Lisa sat beside the bed, holding onto her aunt's hand.

Turning, Cassie leaned against the window frame. Once again, she found herself standing, staring and waiting. Aggie looked as though she'd fallen back to sleep, her eyes were closed, and her hand was now very still. But every few seconds her eyes jumped open and then closed again, as though checking the room and confirming their presence.

Cassie turned to Lisa. 'So... is Marcus coming?' she queried.

Lisa nodded. 'Of course, his mum is on her way over to watch the kids... he shouldn't be too long now.' Her shoulders dropped.

Marcus had been coming in and out of Aggie's house for the past eleven or so years, since he and Lisa had begun going out. He'd seen her each Christmas, birthday, and every occasion in between. And from the age of sixteen had been as big a part of the family as the rest of them and Cassie knew that he'd want to be here. What's more, Lisa needed him.

Aggie had fallen back into a deep sleep and Lisa gripped her hands together in an attempt to hide the trembling. Cassie noted her bottom lip quivered each time she spoke.

'Hun, do you want to go and grab a coffee or something?'

Cassie walked across the room to her sister and put a comforting hand on her shoulder.

Lisa looked up with a wobbly smile. 'I won't leave her. I can't, not now. Not till...'

Cassie suddenly felt light-headed and tried to fill her lungs with air. She hadn't eaten all day, although now, she no longer felt hungry. She could feel her energy dissipate, feel every last ounce leave her body, but she couldn't allow it to win. She had to go back to the Elephant and she had to finish the job she'd started. Before it was too late.

'Look, there's something really important that I have to do.' She looked down as she spoke, knowing how heartless her words sounded.

'More important than Aggie?' Lisa's voice had turned back into a whisper. She looked defeated and Cassie knew that there should be nothing more important than being here, sitting with the woman who'd given you everything, during her last hours of life.

Cassie simply nodded. 'It's something for Aggie, something I promised, something I have to do before she...' She couldn't bring herself to say the word. 'Please don't ask me what it is, Lisa. Please, just trust me.'

Lisa's hanky was back in front of her face, another sob, followed by another rush of tears. 'So it was true, what Mum told me just before she died?'

Cassie grabbed hold of Lisa's hand and dragged her to the door and out of the room. They stood staring at one another in the corridor, both waiting for the other to speak.

'That's why Aggie insisted you came back, isn't it? Cause you're the archaeologist, she wanted to tell you her secret and you're the only one who could help her.'

Cassie threw her head back, glanced up and down the corridor. 'Her... her... secret?' she questioned. 'You know her secret?'

Lisa raised her eyebrows. 'So, it's true. What happened to her.' She paused. 'When Aggie was taken into hospital, when she said there was only you that could help her, I did think about mentioning it then. But I was never sure if it was true or not. Maybe I simply didn't want to believe it.' She spoke in a whisper from behind her tissue. 'You see, Mum, she was high on medication during her final days.' Lisa kept looking at Cassie as she tried to explain what she knew. 'She said she'd found an old diary of Aggie's. Our mum had been about ten years old at the time, had gone to play in the loft and had gone through a big old trunk that Aggie kept up there.' Lisa caught Cassie's hand in hers. 'It all seemed so bizarre, I didn't really believe it, and Mum, well, I didn't think she really knew what she was saying by then.' Lisa looked up and down the corridor and smiled as a nurse walked past. 'Mum kept repeating it, saying about poor Aggie having to have her baby, so young, so alone and in those deep, dark smelly tunnels and how sad it was that she had to leave her baby's body there all alone in the dark.'

'Why didn't you tell me?'

'Oh, Cass. It really didn't sound real. It didn't sound like something our Aggie would have done and I thought Mum was hallucinating. Besides, Aggie has always inspired you, she's always been your driving force. I didn't want to burst that bubble.' She looked back through the door of Aggie's room before continuing. 'Anyhow, her obsession with the tunnels kind of made sense once I'd heard the stories.' She turned back to Cassie and locked eyes with her sister. 'Is it safe? Do you think you can get down there and back up again without getting hurt?'

Cassie could feel the colour drain from her face. She took in two or three deep breaths, but then felt a sudden sense of relief.

Aggie's secret hadn't been much of a secret after all. But knowing now that Lisa knew, made her feel as though a weight had been lifted off her shoulders that had been so heavy it had been pressing down on her whole body since arriving home from Italy. 'I know exactly where the ledge is where Aggie left her baby wrapped in a blanket. My fingers... I felt... I felt it.'

Lisa gripped hold of her hand, lifted it to her lips and kissed her fingers. 'Don't be long, will you? Go and do what you have to do, Cass, bring her home to Aggie.'

Cass's eyes blurred with tears as she hugged her sister, suddenly noticing Aggie's male nurse hovering around, staring at them both. 'I'll be as fast as I can. I know exactly where I have to be. Exactly where it is. All I have to do is go down the shaft, through to the far tunnel, retrieve the... well... you know, and get the hell out of there. It really won't take me long. I promise. But I won't go until Marcus gets here.' She couldn't bear the thought of leaving Lisa alone.

Suddenly, her voice was sure and strong. 'We all have a role in life, Cass, and one of us became an archaeologist for a reason, and the other of us should be here, you know, when...' The words were typically Lisa. She'd grown up far too young and Cassie had always loved her for how calm she'd always seemed, even in the most difficult of situations.

Cassie walked back into the room and leaned over the bed. She gave Aggie a gentle kiss on the cheek. 'Aggie,' she whispered, 'I'm going to get her for you... wait for me.'

29

Cassie jumped into a taxi, threw her head back against the backrest and closed her eyes as they turned out of the infirmary and onto Thorne Road.

'I have to do the right thing. I just have to,' she told herself and to do that she knew she had to tell Noah everything. She had to tell him about the promise she'd made to Aggie and reveal the secret her aunt had kept locked in her heart for over fifty years. But, she reasoned with herself, it was no longer a secret that Aggie would take to her grave; a secret was no longer a secret when shared and now both Cassie and Lisa knew the truth of it – and it seemed so had their mother. All Cassie had to do was add Noah to that list. Besides, it was late and there was no way he'd allow her down the shaft, not without knowing why. And when he asked, she knew that she couldn't lie. Not to Noah. Not now. Not ever.

'So, now I know what I have to do, I just need to work out how to tell the man I love that I'm about to do something that goes against both our principles?' she whispered to herself. She sighed knowing that to remove human remains without calling in a coroner was not only illegal, but it also went against everything she believed in. It went against her professionalism, her respect for the human body and everything she'd been taught.

She jumped out of the taxi and walked along her alleyway, looking over at the site and at the shaft that now stood in darkness, knowing that whatever happened tonight, it was going to start and end in that tunnel.

Opening the back door of Aggie's house she found Noah standing by the sink. He was elbow deep in washing-up water, with far too many big white bubbles foaming up and over the edge of the bowl.

'I dropped the bottle in, as you can see, and I think they're multiplying.' He lifted a hand, flicking the bubbles towards her. A huge ball of white fluff floated through the air and without thinking she tried to catch it. The huge ball suddenly became a myriad of smaller ones, which landed all over her and the kitchen. She began to wipe them away only to find another handful being flicked towards her, making her give a genuine but stilted laugh, that quickly turned into a hysterical sob.

'Hey. Come here. I'm so sorry. I'm such an idiot, tell me what happened? Is it Aggie, did...?' Noah's arms were around her, she could feel herself being pulled into the warmth and security of his body. It was a body that smelled of lemons, of the shower gel she loved and for her, it was the smell of home. His hand went to cup her face, and she felt his lips rest on her forehead. She sank into his warmth. She wanted to stay there, in his arms forever. It was a feeling she never wanted to lose but knew that she was about to say something that could change things permanently.

'You know I love you, right?' She looked up and watched him nod. 'And... this... what we have, it's real, isn't it? And you don't get real without trust, do you?' Again, she waited and took deep breaths as the tears continued to flow.

Noah pulled her closer. His fingers wiped away her tears as he tipped her face to look up. 'Cass, you're frightening me. What have you done?'

'I... I haven't done anything,' she paused, 'not yet.' She chewed on her lower lip. 'But I do need to do something... It's the biggest secret of my life – yet not really my secret at all. It's something I've promised I'll do and I need your help.' The tears continued to roll down her face and she felt Noah's hold relax as he moved her away, to look into her eyes.

'Go on...' His eyes were full of concern, his lips formed a thin line between beard and moustache and his brow had more furrows than she'd ever seen before.

Grabbing at the kitchen roll, she pulled off a sheet and blew her nose. 'Oh, Noah. Aggie's dying, you know that. But now it's imminent and she has this "do not resuscitate" order on her notes and if she has another stroke, that'll probably be it.' Her chest heaved with the anticipation of what was to come. 'When I first got back from Italy, she asked me to do something, something I really don't want to do, but... well... I promised.' She wiped her eyes on the kitchen roll. 'I know it isn't right, it goes against all of our principles, but... but...' she rambled at speed '... I couldn't say no, not to Aggie... not after all she's done, but I love you so much and I can't lie to you either.' She grabbed at a breath and stared into his eyes. 'And Noah. I really need you to help me.'

30

The tunnels looked different at night. The darkness and shadows that surrounded the shaft not only made it feel eerie, but also made it look and feel much deeper than it had before.

'We can't use the floodlights, you know that, don't you?' Noah had said before he'd marched her to the site, strapped her into the harness and lowered her down the shaft. 'We'll draw all sorts of attention, and right now I'm really not sure how I'd explain what we're doing to Joe, or to the bloody authorities.'

Cassie had winced. To say that Noah had been annoyed had been an understatement. But, even though he hadn't been happy, he'd understood and without hesitation he'd helped her bypass security. He'd winched her down and, without drawing attention to what they were doing, he'd joined her at the bottom of the shaft, where with torches in hand, he'd led the way into the first chamber, to where the Pope carving now stood covered in latex that was drying out. They stood in the exact same place they'd been in that morning, revelling in the beauty of the catacomb as their torchlight revealed its shape, its architecture, the precision of every cut that was made.

'It really was beautiful, wasn't it?' she whispered before Noah slowly moved into the first of the crawling tunnels and then out again into the larger chamber beyond.

'Stay close to me, Cassie. It's dangerous and being down here in the dark, alone, really isn't the most sensible thing we've ever done, now, is it?' She could still hear the anger, the frustration in his voice. Noah didn't break rules, he never had, and she felt a surge of guilt that she'd asked him to help her at all but knew that coming down here alone would have been verging on crazy.

Cassie stayed close. She watched every movement he made, while all the time casting her torchlight up, around and ahead. Both fear and anticipation surrounded her, every corner was filled with shadows and she felt the history seep out of every part of the tunnel. She'd often wondered what it would be like to be down here, and now that she was it was suddenly the last place on earth she wanted to be.

'Careful.' Noah pointed to the supports, as Cassie carefully made her way through the maze, knowing that if they knocked into just one, the whole roof could come crashing down on top of them. She'd seen it happen once before and took note of her step, of every piece of sandstone that she walked over or crawled across.

Cassie practically held her breath as they encountered the final crawling tunnel. She could see Noah's torch as it shone right through, leading the way. The single beam of light forced her to concentrate on the job in hand and brought home the enormity of what they were about to do. Could she really do this? And once they had, what next? What would they do then? Her hand went to her chest and she felt for the bag that was pushed down her coat.

She felt a sudden urge to reach out, to touch Noah. Just because she could and simply to know that he was there, that she could reach him if need be. He turned, gave her a half smile, but Cassie noticed the worry in his eyes. He didn't like being down here any more than she did, not tonight, not to do this and she felt the need to apologise, to take him home, curl up with him and make love to him. She wanted to take away his stress but knew that the sooner they did what they'd come here to do, the sooner they could leave.

Noah's torchlight expanded, and the adrenaline began to build as she saw him step out of the crawling tunnel and into the Elephant chamber. Standing up, Cassie rubbed her knees and stared into the torchlight. Was this how Aggie had felt all those years ago, being down here, in this chamber, alone, with just a torch. Had she felt any comfort in being somewhere she knew so well, or had the darkness and solitude frightened her as she'd given birth to a baby that didn't cry? Cassie could feel her chest constricting at the thought.

The constant air that blew through the tunnel during the day was, like the floodlights, switched off, and she screwed up her nose as the smell of fungus seemed to grow stronger by the minute, making her gag, and she wished for her precious lavender oil, which was still at the house and, in her rush, she hadn't thought to bring with her.

'So, the ledge.' Noah pointed to where he'd seen Cassie with her arm pushed into the small hole earlier. 'This is it, is it?'

Cassie nodded, dropped to her knees and went to pick up the mattock she'd used that morning. 'The remains were just too big to drag through the hole without damaging them and my arm almost got stuck. Where are the digging tools?' She shone the beam of light around the floor. But only the bigger spades remained. The smaller ones that she needed had all been removed. Jumping up, she circumnavigated the chamber. 'They've gone. The men, they must have taken them out. Why...

why would they do that? I mean, it's not like just anyone could crawl around down here, is it?' She gave a smile at the irony of her question but then fell to her knees. She wanted to be strong, wanted to get the job done, but everything seemed against them and she grabbed at a piece of rough stone and threw it at the wall.

Noah knelt down beside her. Pulled her into his arms and rocked her like a baby. 'Hey. It's okay, we have more tools,' he whispered. 'All my stuff, it's all back there in the first chamber.' His lips grazed hers. 'Let me have a look and we'll work out what we need.' He shone his torch under the ledge, pulled a face and then sat back up and pulled her towards him. 'Cass, you know there isn't much left to retrieve, don't you?'

Cassie nodded. She'd been in the job long enough to know that it had been a long shot, that after fifty years the remains would have been subject to the cold, the damp, to animals. 'I know, but... I couldn't tell Aggie that, could I?'

Noah knuckle rubbed his eyes with his hands, before pushing them through his hair. 'Give me a few minutes, I'll bring a mattock, chisels and a hand brush.' He shone the torch towards the tunnel. 'You okay to wait here?'

Cassie nodded but felt a shiver travel through her as she watched him go back through the tunnel on his hands and knees, with his torch in hand. She remained sitting in front of the ledge where he had left her and looked up at the enormity of the sandstone that surrounded the Elephant, knowing that at that very moment she was in the same spot that Aggie would have been in over fifty years before. Her hand went out to touch the Mahout's foot and without warning the air left her lungs, making her grab for breath. She couldn't pull it in or push it out and the terror of choking went through her mind. But then, as though it had never happened, the foul-smelling air was dragged back through her, making her retch repeatedly. Her hands were pressed to the floor, she felt as though she were falling. Her mind began to spin violently and she felt the need to hold on. Taking small, short, sharp breaths she lay down on the floor while hugging the torch. She didn't like the floor, it was dirty, uncomfortable but at least she knew that while down there, there was nowhere left to fall.

The torch shone onto her watch; it was just before eleven. 'I've been gone an hour already,' she said to the Mahout's foot. She then shone the torch under the ledge, to where she could just make out what was left of the wool blanket. Its stripes had long since gone and all she could see were just small, ragged pieces of what had been. She'd realised long before, that this might be the case and that if the blanket was gone, then most of the remains would be gone too.

'I'm so stupid, I should have known,' she berated herself, but then looked back to the wooden tools that had been left behind. The spade was far too big, but a wooden Kennedy brush might just do the trick. 'This should help,' she said as she picked up the well-used brush and pushed its long broom like handle carefully under the ledge. Using it like a hook, she repeatedly moved it back and forth, until what was left of the blanket poked out from the hole.

Suddenly a loud bang echoed through the chamber, followed by shouting, screaming and a series of thuds that made Cassie jump up from the ground. With her back to the chamber wall, she shone the torch around, frantically looking for any sign that the tunnel was about to collapse.

'Do it... now.' A loud, angry voice came from the other chamber and she immediately shone her torch down the crawling tunnel to see Noah coming towards her, pushing his tool bag ahead of him, with anguish and blood all over his face.

'What the hell?' She tried to see past him, tried to see who was shouting, but the tunnel was small. 'Are you okay?' she screamed, but again the voice bellowed behind him.

'Ah, I thought she'd be here.' The voice paused. 'I heard her, at the hospital, said how she'd be coming down here, to retrieve it and be back within the hour.' The voice was laboured, but Cassie immediately knew who it was, and confusion and fear ran through her mind. What on earth was Aggie's nurse doing in the tunnels? Had something happened to Aggie? Was she okay? Why was Noah hurt and why wasn't the nurse helping him?

'What the hell did he do to you?' she asked Noah as she held out her hands to him, her fingers trying to wipe the blood from his face as she saw the concern and terror in his eyes.

'Why...?' was all she could say as Todd emerged from the tunnel, her very own mattock with the pink handle in his hand. 'How...?' She was going to ask how he'd got the mattock but immediately knew the answer before the question left her lips, what she didn't understand was why? The only way he could have her mattock was if he'd been in her house. He'd broken into her home and he'd been in her bedroom. He was Aggie's nurse not a burglar, so why would he do that...? She stood frozen to the spot like a shop window mannequin, her eyes suddenly fixed on his arm, on the snake tattoo that wound its way over his shoulder and a new and more terrifying scenario came into play. It was almost too much to take in. She literally couldn't move. It was the same snake that she'd stared at when she was eleven years old and, once again, she was sat in that gateway, behind the dustbin, feeling the same terror she'd felt that day when she'd heard her mother's scream. On that day she'd lost a man she'd loved, she'd lost her father and she began shaking her head violently from side to side. 'Not again,' she whispered. 'It can't all happen again.'

'Get over there.' He pushed Noah and kicked at the floor. A plume of dust flew up into the air making them cough and Cassie took a moment to check Noah as she shone her torch in his direction, highlighting his face. He looked disorientated; the left side of his face already swelling. And even with his beard, she could see that one eye and his cheekbone had fast become discoloured, making it obvious that he'd been hit with something much harder than a fist.

'You bastard, what the hell did you do to him?' Cassie suddenly found her voice. 'And why, why...?' Again, she saw the man who'd killed her father – but then the nurse, the carer. Her mind went from one to the other, it didn't add up. How could one man be both?

'You know what I want.' His words were stern, the mattock held up in the air and he waved it towards Noah. 'And you,' he pointed to Cassie, 'you're going to get it for me right now, or he gets it.'

'I'm sorry, but you're really going to have to fill me in because I've got no fucking idea what you're talking about.' Cassie stepped in front of Noah. 'And leave him out of this, it's obviously me and my family you want to hurt, not him.' She had no idea where her bravery came from; she was shaking inside, a trembling that began in her toes and vibrated its way throughout her body, but all she could think of was Noah.

'I... I don't want to hurt anyone. I'm not a murderer, your dad, it was an accident.' He then pointed to Noah. 'And him, he charged at me like a bull, so don't you blame me. All I want is what's rightfully mine, it's my damned jewellery. I played my part in the robberies, I worked for it... I earned it all. But, your dad, he hid them from me. Said he'd told me where it all was, but he hadn't.' He strode around, the mattock still swinging in his hand. 'And after I heard what you said, my guess is that he hid them down here. You told your sister you were coming to get it and I think you know exactly where it is.'

Again, Cassie felt her face contort with confusion. 'Don't be bloody stupid. My dad never came down here. The tunnels were filled in before he was born.' She stepped forward. 'Actually, he'd have been around a year old, so unless he'd turned into the world's most adventurous toddler before the tunnels were filled with concrete, I doubt he'd have even known they existed. So why don't you put the mattock down before you really hurt someone and then pretend for the rest of your life that it was just another bloody accident.'

Todd furrowed his brow as he realised what she'd said. 'But,' he shook his head, dropped the mattock to the floor and held out his arm. 'This snake, your dad he tattooed this. Seems he'd given me a map, but I didn't know that.' He stared at the snake. 'Your aunt, she recognised the pattern. But then, before she could tell me what it meant, she had a stroke and... and I tried to help her, honestly, I did.' He pushed his hand through his hair, but then held his arm back out and Cassie found herself staring too.

The pattern was familiar. The snake was coiled, with scales down the centre that all went one way, but the ones around the edge went in all directions. They were the wrong shape, far too long. But the pattern was one she'd seen before, one she'd seen quite recently, which felt quite strange, because as an eleven-year-old all she'd noticed had been a badly tattooed snake. The alarm bells should have rung back then. Her dad was an artist and she'd never known him create a bad tattoo. Not until she'd seen this one.

She pushed her tongue in her cheek as the penny dropped and now she saw exactly what it was. 'It's the graveyard, you have two scales that are different colours. Of course, as a child I thought they were bright yellow eyes.' She thought about it. 'And if I know my dad, that's where your gold and your riches would have been buried.' She looked towards Noah for affirmation. 'Do you see it? The one's that are all filled in, do you think... would that have been around the same area that Peter Booth was buried?' The words were obviously a lie. The graves had fallen in over fifty years ago, well before the jewellery disappeared. But, Cassie had a plan.

Noah grunted, caught her eye and stood up. 'I guess it would be, but why help the murdering bastard... he doesn't deserve riches,' he taunted as he moved around the chamber, in an attempt to steer Todd away from Cassie. But Todd was fast and, jumping forward, he grabbed Noah by the neck, and then ran him against the wall, his back connecting hard with the sandstone.

'You don't fool me,' his eyes were looking all around, all at once. 'I know they're down here. I know you were about to get them.' Again, he slammed Noah against the wall. 'I heard her say so.'

'I wouldn't do that if I were you,' Noah's Irish accent rang out with pain. 'One more sudden bang and the whole roof could come down and if it does it'll be the end of us all.' He glared at Todd. 'Now, if you think rather than act, let me tell you that the grave, the one coloured in on your arm, it fell into the tunnels many years ago, which means,' he lifted a hand and pointed down at the unfinished excavation, 'your treasure was probably buried in the place where they'd once been, x marks the spot on a map, only the original grave marked the spot and, if I'm right, the excavation could have allowed them to drop right down there.' Noah looked across at the tunnel. 'If you dig, you might just find them in the spoil.'

Todd looked from Noah to Cassie. And then, without thought he dropped Noah to the floor, picked the mattock back up and ran into the unfinished excavation. With one powerful scoop after the other, the mattock rose up and down as he used it to drag at the earth, a human earth excavator, hard at work.

Then, from nowhere, Declan burst out of the crawling tunnel. He rushed at Todd, knocking him to the ground.

'Get the mesh!' Noah shouted, as he and Cassie grabbed at the sheet of galvanised metal and thrust it over the tunnel entrance, making Todd turn and scream. Both he and Declan were trapped. Both circled the space, like wrestlers about to pounce.

'The police,' Declan shouted, 'they're coming!' He inched towards the mesh and Todd fell to his knees. He looked like a terrified animal, captured and confined with nowhere to go but he watched carefully as Noah and Cassie released the mesh just enough to let Declan escape.

'You can't hold me here!' Todd screamed, stood up and ran at the mesh, but his strength was no match for both Noah and Declan who now held it in place between them. Calculating a plan without speaking and, with Cassie's help, they placed the hydraulic supports between the mesh and the wall, trapping Todd safely inside. But Todd was not going to sit and wait, the mattock was raised. He swung it repeatedly at the walls, at the roof and finally at the only roof support that stood between him and safety. The roof suddenly gave way and began crashing down. The mesh prison was dropped. Todd was grabbed, the mattock tossed to one side and Noah held onto him as tightly as he could.

'You could have bloody killed yourself, you fool,' Declan shouted. 'And us... you could have killed us.'

Knowing that Todd was going nowhere, Cassie spun around to go face to face with Declan. 'And what the hell are you doing down here?' she screamed.

He continued to look down at his feet. 'Hey, don't shout at me,

I was following him. We could tell he was up to something.' He pointed to Todd who was now sat on the floor, a blank look of defeat on his face. 'Me and dad, we watched him lurking around, checking out the hoist and when he finally seemed to realise that he didn't know what the hell to do with it, he climbed down the scaffolding. Without a harness. Bloody fool. Dad said it's a wonder he didn't kill himself.'

Declan moved himself into place beside Todd, pulled Noah's tool bag to one side and after dragging a piece of rope from its depths, he tied Todd's hands tightly behind his back.

Noah had now sagged to the floor; the energy had dissipated, and protectively, Cassie knelt beside him. Pulling a tissue from her pocket, she wiped the blood that trickled down his face.

'Dad had already spotted you two on the cameras,' Declan said proudly. 'You should know he doesn't miss anything. And...' he shuffled his feet through the sandstone that lay underfoot '... well, we knew that you two were up to something too and well... you might want to know that he's phoned the police, and Kyle. Both are probably going to be here any minute, so... whatever it is you're doing down here,' he glared at the rucksack, 'I'd get it done. And quickly.' He bent down before turning to crawl through the tunnel. 'I'll send the police down the minute they arrive.' His words echoed around them, but Cassie was already on her knees, carefully placing what was left of the remains into the bag that she had brought down with her and whispered a prayer as she did so.

31

The front room had never looked so small or felt so cold. Aggie's coffin was placed by the wall, as mourners and neighbours all filtered past, kissed Aggie on the forehead and then turned to where Cassie and Lisa sat on dining chairs by a fire that had been laid, but hadn't been lit.

'I was too late,' Cassie whispered to Lisa. 'She never knew. I never got to tell her that I'd kept my promise.' Ironically, Aggie had died just before eleven, at the very same time that the breath had left Cassie's body and she'd found herself lying on the chamber floor, gasping for air. 'It was as though I knew she'd gone.'

Lisa squeezed her hand. 'Honey, she knew you'd keep your promise. That's why she asked you...' She paused, shook another man's hand and then sighed. 'Are you sick of all the people yet?' she whispered as another sobbing woman walked in, stroked Aggie's face and kissed her forehead. 'I mean, do you know any of these people? Are they friends, or neighbours?'

Cassie wanted to giggle. The situation had turned from sad to surreal and she gladly took the glass of whisky that Noah held out to them both and drank hers down in one.

The living room door opened. 'The cars, they're here,' Marcus announced. He stood in the doorway with a pale looking Becky, who was obviously keeping herself as close to her dad, but as far away from the coffin as she possibly could. 'I think, we should wait outside,' he said as he turned his daughter around and out of the room. 'It's not the place,' he said as he whisked her outside, 'not for a child.'

As if on cue, Noah coughed. 'If you don't mind. Could the family have a minute's privacy please?' His voice was commanding, as the last of the neighbours moved outside, leaving the three of them to stand alone with Aggie and for a few moments they all just stood, holding hands, staring at the woman they had lost.

'I can't believe she's gone,' Cassie whispered. 'I can't believe I didn't get to say goodbye.'

Lisa turned and pulled her into a hug. 'She knew you loved her, Cass and she loved you back, so much.' Lisa paused. 'The last thing she ever tried to do was warn us about the nurse, she could barely speak, but her last thoughts were of you, of that snake tattoo and of telling you about the danger. That has to mean something, right?'

Cassie nodded. She now understood what Aggie had been saying, how she'd tried to shout the words, 'snake' and 'danger'. How, unselfishly, she'd once again put them before herself and even in her final moments had tried to show them one last act of unconditional love.

Noah moved to stand between them both, an arm went around each of them and he bowed his head. 'Let us pray... Our Father, who art in heaven, hallowed be thy name...'

Cassie's heart filled with pride for him as he whispered the

Lord's prayer in a final act of kindness. It was just one more thing that he'd done for her over the past week. A week that had been difficult, but a week where Noah had taken control. He'd had to explain to his bosses and to the police why they'd been in the catacombs at such a late hour. That they'd both gone back down, just to admire the site, to make plans for the dig and to ensure the latex on The Pope had been setting correctly. Questions had had to be answered on how he'd ended up with a black eye, a fractured cheekbone and how his girlfriend's father's murderer had become holed up in a tunnel with them. The list of coincidences had been too many to believe but, somehow, he'd convinced the police that it had all happened just the way he'd said. Declan too had kept quiet about what Cassie had been doing in the tunnel and for that she would be forever grateful to him. The only person not convinced had been Kyle, he'd known that something had gotten past him, and he hadn't liked it. But Noah had stuck to the story, he'd protected Cassie when she'd most needed it and for that, and so much more, she loved him.

'It's... it's now... or never. You know that, right?' Cassie spoke quietly. Her eyes never leaving the coffin. 'If we do this, we do it together. We all have to agree that it's the right thing to do, don't we?' Her voice shook with emotion, her knees felt weak.

Lisa turned, pulled a tissue from her handbag and allowed a sob to leave her throat. 'It's the right thing,' she finally managed to say, her eyes locked with Cassie, both staring into the other's soul. Then together, they turned to Noah. 'It has to be unanimous.'

Noah blew out through his teeth and nodded. 'It's what she wanted, we can't let her down, not now.' Then from a bag at the side of the room he pulled out a small, specially prepared package. It was just a little bigger than a book. 'I took care of her, but I got rid of the blanket. I... I made the packet as small as I could.'

His hand shook as he held the package out to Cassie, who carefully took it to hold like a prayer book waiting to be opened.

For what seemed like forever, they all stood with their eyes closed in silent prayer, their hands carefully placed on the package in a final, unified act. No words were spoken. None were needed. Then, as though choreographed, Cassie stepped towards the coffin and, with a small pair of scissors, she cut a tiny hole in the satin along the seam by Aggie's feet. 'They'll be together again, won't they?' She looked at Lisa whose eyes sparkled with tears.

Placing the package under the satin and a hand on Aggie's, Cassie closed her eyes. 'I did it, Aggie. I found her for you. I did what you asked and now, just like you wanted, she'll be laid to rest, you'll both be laid to rest, with a proper service and with the people around who would have loved her, just as they loved you.' Her voice broke with the words and she stepped back, knowing what she'd just done was wrong, but somehow it seemed so very right and deep inside her conscience felt clear.

'It's time,' Lisa's voice shook with emotion. 'We have to... you know. Before...'

Noah's hand touched hers. 'Let me.' He reached up to touch the coffin lid and just for a moment he paused, said a final goodbye and then lowered the lid gently, just as the funeral director entered the room.

32

Cassie walked over the bridge and, for the first time in a month, she took in the sight of her precious Herculaneum.

So much had happened since she'd left. Aggie had been buried, the house had been emptied and both Cassie and Noah had exposed the Elephant and Mahout, together. The latex mouldings had been taken and preserved. The tattoo had led the police to the exact place where the jewellery had been buried and Todd now faced years of imprisonment for both grand theft and murder. She and Noah had no idea why the names Margaret Smithson and Peter Booth had been written on the torn-out page of her dad's sketchbook which depicted the snake tattoo but Cassie liked to believe that somehow, the fates had decreed that they would find love in the very spot where Aggie had lost hers.

And then, for the final time, Cassie had stood with Noah, both with tears in their eyes as they'd watched as tons of concrete had been poured and, for the final time, the tunnels had been filled. Never again would the catacombs be walked through. Never again would the Elephant and Mahout be seen, and never again would anyone become hurt or trapped in a place that had once been a Victorian marvel.

All they had was the future, along with the museum that would be built, and the exhibition that would be created within it. A lasting memorial to the man, Henry Senior, who'd first created the catacombs for all to see, but which once again lay buried deep beneath the pavement.

Smiling, Cassie stood on the bridge taking in the sights and smells of Herculaneum. It was a sight she'd never get bored of and now that Noah had permission to work here too, it was an archaeologist's dream that she had every intention of sharing.

Taking Noah by the hand she led him through the long tunnel that led under the bridge and brought them out near the old boathouses, by the area that had once been the sea.

'Oh, wow,' Noah gasped as he spotted the hundreds of skeletons, all huddled together, all in a heap in exactly the same position they'd fallen in when Vesuvius had erupted back in AD 79. 'I've studied this, I've seen the pictures before, so many times, but nothing prepares you for the reality of it,' he whispered while taking Cassie's hand in his.

'They were trying to escape, but couldn't.' She pointed to the sheds and they both stood for a moment, taking in the gravity of what lay before them and then, with sadness, they walked past and headed into the site, through the barriers and towards the dig.

'Oh my God, Cassie, you came back.' Sasha bounced with relief. 'I knew you would.' Her hands went up and waved around in the air, before pulling her friend into a long and overdue hug. 'Tabitha has missed you so much, she's grown so big and I have a new tomato plant called Ben. I've put him on the balcony to your room. I think you should look after him from now on, cause, well, I'm obviously not capable, not after what happened to Bill.' She suddenly stopped rambling, realised that Cassie was not alone and looked at Noah, 'Oh my gosh. I'm so sorry, you must be Noah.' She looked from Noah to Cassie and blushed. 'You must be here to see the skeletons.' She laughed and took both by the hand to walk them towards the tarpaulin before excusing herself and disappearing with soil samples.

'Now,' Cassie took Noah's hand, 'these are my skeletons.' She stepped into the tent, dropped to her knees and took in the sight. The skeletons were now fully exposed and not only did they have one hand from each skeleton holding that of the other above their heads, but their other two hands were protectively holding onto a much smaller skeleton. 'Oh my God. They had a child, a toddler?' Automatically, Cassie picked up the bristle brush and began sweeping at the dust. 'Look, Noah, they...' She couldn't speak and she just sat, open-mouthed. Her skeletons encapsulated life as it had been, and she couldn't begin to imagine their terror as the whole family had run through the streets, hoping to escape. 'That's why they couldn't run so fast, why they didn't get to the boats.' The brush skimmed the toddler's skull. 'They were trying to save him too.' She thought back to that day when she'd first uncovered them, when she'd first found her favourite bone and how she'd shrugged off the fact that two people could ever love each other that much. But now, now she had Noah, she understood. She knew exactly what Sasha had meant and knew, that given the choice, she'd now answer the question very differently. Noah had come back into her life at the very moment she'd needed him the most. He'd been there for her, helped her, protected her and had ensured that Aggie's wishes had been made possible.

Once again, she took Noah's hand in hers and as she looked down on the skeletons she remembered Aggie's words. 'Where love was lost, it can also be found,' she whispered, knowing that whatever happened and whatever site they uncovered, she'd always be reminded of those wise words.

'Noah,' she whispered, 'Sasha once asked me if I could imagine loving someone that much.' She paused, stood up, smiled and looked up and into the depths of his eyes. 'At the time I said that I couldn't.'

Noah nodded and pulled her close. 'And now?'

'And now...' she repeated, as she lifted her lips to his, knowing that finally, and without a doubt, she really could love Noah that much and that her kiss would give him all the answers he needed.

AUTHOR'S NOTE

If you loved the fiction, then maybe we could interest you in some facts about the real-life Sand House?

People are often astonished when they discover that the South Yorkshire city of Doncaster was once home to a unique mansion carved out of the ground from solid rock. It stood in what had once been a quarry, later converted into the Sand House's lush garden. As if the house were not amazing enough, there was also a network of carefully excavated tunnels extending from it, many of which were adorned with fine sculptures carved into the sandstone.

William Senior had bought a piece of land, about one kilometre south of the town centre, in 1832. With the help of his son, Henry, he developed a sandstone quarry on the land, to meet increasing demand as Doncaster expanded rapidly as a railway town. By the mid-1850s, Henry had an idea that he could create a unique house for himself, by leaving a massive block of sandstone in place within the quarry and then hollowing out rooms within. A traditionally built intermediate floor and roof completed a fine residence. When finished, the house was 36 metres long and had ten rooms, including a ballroom!

The gardens and tunnel network became local attractions in the latter part of the 19th century. Concerts were held there in the 1890s and visitors would explore the underground workings. One part of the tunnelling was known as the Catacombs, although it was never used for burials. Guests marvelled at the many sculptures, including kings, queens, Victorian 'celebrities' and, above all, a life-size elephant, with its mahout (Hindi for elephant-driver). Advertisements at the time referred to 1000 yards of tunnels, although barely a quarter of that length has been physically proven.

Henry Senior lived in the Sand House from 1857 until his death in 1900. Doncaster Corporation then bought it and installed various employees until it was finally vacated in 1934. Partial demolition took place a few years later and by the end of WWII, landfill operations had obliterated the house and filled the former quarry almost up to original ground level.

The tunnel network fared little better. Although there was no official access after the 1930s, local children found their way in. They became a wonderful unofficial playground from the 1940s to the 1960s. Changes to the road layout led to some tunnels being infilled, while the rest was finally grouted up in 1984, after a series of collapses had raised serious safety concerns.

After almost being forgotten, the Sand House is now being given a fitting legacy through The Sand House Charity. The charity's aim is to advance the education of the public in history, art, sculpture and other related subjects having a link to the Sand House. Its activities are bringing this Victorian marvel back from near oblivion.

You can find out more at www.thesandhouse.org.uk where

there are links to social media, too. You can also read the definitive story in *The Sand House – A Victorian Marvel Revisited* (2010) by Richard Bell and Peter Tuffrey, published by Amberley Publishing.

Photograph 1 – The Sand House circa 1900.

Photograph 2 – Sand House tunnel with carvings, looking south.

Author's Note 261

Photograph 3 – Sand House tunnel with carvings, looking north.

Photograph 4 – The Elephant and Mahout.

ABOUT THE AUTHOR

L. H. Stacey lives in a small rural hamlet in Yorkshire, with her 'hero at home husband' Haydn, and her puppy 'Barney'. In 2015 her debut novel won a prestigious publishing contract.

Sign up to L. H. Stacey's mailing list for news, competitions and updates on future books.

Visit Lynda's website: http://www.lyndastacey.co.uk/

Follow Lynda on social media:

- facebook.com/LHStaceyauthor
- x.com/Lyndastacey
- instagram.com/lynda.stacey
- bookbub.com/authors/lynda-stacey

ALSO BY L. H. STACEY

The Sisters Next Door

The Serial Killer's Girl

The Weekend

The Fake Date

The House Guest

The Safe House

The Accident

Buried Secrets

THE
Murder
LIST

THE MURDER LIST IS A NEWSLETTER DEDICATED TO SPINE-CHILLING FICTION AND GRIPPING PAGE-TURNERS!

SIGN UP TO MAKE SURE YOU'RE ON OUR HIT LIST FOR EXCLUSIVE DEALS, AUTHOR CONTENT, AND COMPETITIONS.

SIGN UP TO OUR NEWSLETTER

BIT.LY/THEMURDERLISTNEWS

Boldwood

Boldwood Books is an award-winning fiction publishing company seeking out the best stories from around the world.

Find out more at www.boldwoodbooks.com

Join our reader community for brilliant books, competitions and offers!

Follow us
@BoldwoodBooks
@TheBoldBookClub

Sign up to our weekly deals newsletter

https://bit.ly/BoldwoodBNewsletter